The Great Molinas

A Novel

Neil D. Isaacs

WID
Publishing
Group

Sport Literature Association

Also by Neil D. Isaacs

All the Moves: A History of College Basketball

Sports Illustrated Basketball (with Dick Motta)

Jock Culture, U.S.A.

Covering the Spread (with Gerald Strine)

The Sporting Spirit: Athletes in Literature and Life
(ed., with Robert J. Higgs)

Checking Back: A History of NHL Hockey

Grace Paley: A Study of the Short Fiction

Tolkien: New Critical Perspectives
(ed., with Rose A. Zimbardo)

Fiction into Film: A Walk in the Spring Rain
(with Rachel Maddux and Stirling Silliphant)

Eudora Welty

Tolkien and the Critics
(ed., with Rose A. Zimbardo)

Structural Principles in Old English Poetry

Approaches to the Short Story
(ed., with Louis H. Leiter)

To my brother Phil

(Uncle Phil, Sweet P)

who helped me see this through
all the way

just as he has been there for me
all my life

with love and appreciation

Note: This book is a work of fiction. Names, characters, places, and incidents are either the product of the author's imagination or are used fictitiously. Any resemblance to actual events or locales or persons, living or dead, is completely coincidental.

PUBLISHED BY
WID PUBLISHING GROUP, INC.
5450 WHITLEY PARK TERRACE, SUITE 507
BETHESDA, MARYLAND 20814
AND
SPORT LITERATURE ASSOCIATION
EAST TENNESSEE STATE UNIVERSITY
BOX 70683
JOHNSON CITY, TENNESSEE 37614
MANUFACTURED IN THE UNITED STATES OF AMERICA
LIBRARY OF CONGRESS CATALOG CARD NUMBER: 92-64147
ISAACS, NEIL D. 1931-
THE GREAT MOLINAS
I. MOLINAS, JACK, 1931-1975 – FICTION   I. TITLE

ISBN 0-9633834-0-X

FIRST EDITION

Acknowledgments

Over the years, many writers have walked these beats, and I am particularly grateful to the reporting of Phil Berger and Stu Black, Hugh Bradley, Jimmy Breslin, Ovid Demaris, Milton Gross, David Israel, Bruce Keidan, Bob Reed, Ben Tenny, and David Wolf.

Many others helped in various ways, with leads, research, memories, opinions, time, and—not the least of gifts—places to sleep and write during a decade of spring and summer odysseys. I am grateful to Rick and Lesley Abbott, Tony Bernhard, Mal and Betsy Brochin, Carolyn Coles, Charlie Eckman, Joe Goldstein, George and Lois Graboys, Steve Hershey, Jack and Reny Higgs, John and Robbi Howard, Anne Isaacs, Daniel Isaacs, Ian Isaacs, Jonathan Isaacs, Phil and Marilyn Isaacs, Rudy LaRusso, Ellen Levine, Bob Martin, Paul Neshamkin, Dee Neuhauser, Mort Olshan, Joe O'Malley III, Paula Phelps, Maurice Podoloff, Bernie Reiner, Nancy Richardson, Bob Sasson, Artie Selman, Paul Snyder, Barry Storick, Gerry Strine, Eric Swenson, Barbara Tanenhaus, Bill and Alma Ward, and Allen and Kathy Wells.

The CAPA Board of the University of Maryland, College Park, contributed support to this project with a summer grant in 1980, and the Department of English contributed some funding in 1991. I am grateful for both.

In addition to the debt honored in the dedication, I must also heartfully thank Jack Higgs for his unflagging belief in this enterprise, Lyle Olsen for his encouraging faith in it, Robert Walczy for tasteful and constructive attention to detail, Tom Dolan for contributions of substance and spirit, Jim Walczy for manifold gifts generously shared, and my wife, Ellen Isaacs, for all those little things that never show up in a box score but add up to a monumental contribution of support, energy, and collaboration.

NDI

Asheville, Athens, Barrington, Boone, Colesville, College Park, Jacksonville Beach, Johnson City, Lake City, New Haven, New London, New York, Potomac, Sarasota, Savannah, Severna Park, Swannanoa, Tampa, Winston-Salem, Woodbridge, Wytheville
1980-1991

PART I:
Commencement

Chapter 1:
Perfect Day for Top Banana

Molinas stood on his patio, gazing out on the lights of the city, smiling outside and in. He had a broad leer to greet the many things, great and small, that provoked his glee, ridicule, and irony, and he had a self-satisfied insmirk to acknowledge the winning results of a gamesman. It had been a perfect day, win after win after win in game within game within game.

Molinas looked at L.A. and felt that he owned it. From Thrush Drive in the Hollywood Hills, the view indulged the viewer in fantasy feelings of legendary opulence. This town was his, its tinsel phoniness and browned glitter providing the ideal, idyllic setting for what he was all about. The whole system was a goddamn game out here, a showbiz scam of show and talk but no tell, a gigantic shell game. The shell was what they called the Hollywood Bowl. Well, that was about the size of it, which would make the nut about the size of the Brown Derby—in shiny gold plate over solid lead.

Molinas had the kind of clout on the Coast he never had in New York, because he had the kind of big sticks they played ball with out here. He had front and effrontery; he had celebrity, no matter the tarnish on the shine, no matter the palpable grease on the slickness; he had the size and the looks; he had the gift of grab along with gab; he had the balls to move big numbers around; and he had no shame, no humility, no embarrassment. He never had to pay a bill

or a debt or a losing bet. He had full rationalizations for sus-
pending every ethical or moral sense he may once have
felt. He was, in short, a perfect winner because he wouldn't
allow himself to lose. He was a model L.A. hero. For a lot of
people back east he was still a kind of hero, too, but not in
the way he once had been. What he retained of that old
heroism resided in nostalgic, personal conceptions that
were as magical and papermoony as the scene he grinned
at tonight.

New York was never like this for Molinas. He thought
suddenly of the song he professed to believe when he first
went to Columbia but always inwardly mocked: "Oh who
owns New York...we own New York." Even when people
around him thought he owned New York, he knew better.
Oh, sure, he'd strut around the West Bronx as a kid with
hundreds of bucks in his pocket or in and out of his father's
place at Coney Island or around the halls at Manhattan's
Stuyvesant High School, the tall, handsome, bright, athletic
Mr. Everything, and look like he had triboroughs on a
string. But even playing in the Garden for the PSAL championship or taking Columbia through an unbeaten season
as a sophomore, he knew better. He knew something they
didn't know. He knew he was a winner only because he was
playing New York's game as well as New York allowed him
to play. He was yoyoing a ball on their string. And because
he knew it, without letting on, he was able to play other
games of his own.

They had taken a semester of eligibility away from him
at Columbia, and he had turned around and played with
college basketball as his own money-toy. They had kicked
him out of the NBA, made an example of him, but he used
what he knew, as no one else had, to dominate a kind of
antileague of his own devising. As a lawyer he had played
legal games until disbarred. Under investigation he played

the investigators like so many greedy puppets. Convicted, he played his own game of Prison like the dominant token on a Monopoly board, and he yoyoed for a Wall Street string at the same time.

He laughed whenever he told those bragging stories, but the loudness always echoed hollowly inside his head. Because in New York he always felt on the road, trying to stay ahead but knowing that They batted last. Here in L.A. he was the one who played with Them. There was no way they could hurt him. He used to say that in New York, but out here he believed it. They could touch him, yes, but with a price to pay for the temerity. And on a day like this he could not even be touched. He was the grand winner in the L.A. game of Game.

Sharon was inside the house now. He could afford to be patient—he *wanted* to be patient with her, as he never had to be with other women. He wanted to let her look around at her own pace, take it all in without him looking over her shoulder and pointing at objets d'art. She knew more about that than he did anyway. He just knew the prices, even though he hadn't yet paid for anything in the house, nor for the house itself. He'd wait before calling her out to join him for the view.

Molinas could hardly be said to be at peace. That was not a feeling he knew. But he was satisfied with the way the wheels were turning, rolling those little balls into slots with his numbers on them. And all those balls of his were being juggled in flawless suspension. Even those he was easing out of the act were going smoothly.

He was now out of the fur business and into even better deals. He had taken a loss on that investment, but the biggest debts were in the company's name and he had gotten out of the company just in time. But he had cleared half a million cash on the insurance policy he and his partner had

taken on each other's lives to secure a loan. Then Bernie
Gussoff had been murdered. They had dropped a dime on
poor old Bernie and it hadn't cost Molinas a nickel. Now
Gussoff's heirs could worry about the debts. He wouldn't.

He was out of porno movies, too, at least as a matter of
record. He could still call in some dollars from Jo Jo Productions if needed. But he didn't need, and again the big
debts were in the company's name, not his. The loan sharks
wanted their money, of course. He chose not to pay, instead
was shylocking on his own—with good returns. He knew
how to get paid.

Vegas wanted their money too, but Molinas had always
laughed at gambling losses. Lately he didn't even bother
trying to get even, just moved on to other action. The
action in the market was better. He was playing put and
call like a bowler working a 300 game. Strike after strike,
grooved on absolute confidence in his opinion.

Molinas turned to watch Sharon's shadowed movements
through the tastefully-lit house with its abundance of glass
doors, windows, mirrors, crystal fixtures. He felt a physical
well-being so powerful that he thought, at 43, he could still
hold his own in the NBA. His smile broadened as he
thought of how he had beaten Rudy LaRusso over and over
with inside moves and the deadly hook just last Saturday
morning in the gym at Hollywood High. He ate him up. He
used him.

Today everything had gone just that way, easy and right.
He had won every baseball bet. The suckers were betting
Detroit to snap their losing streak against Boston, and they
loved first-place Pittsburgh to snap the Mets' winning
streak. Jesus, he could retire if people kept betting to break
streaks instead of going with them. He had taken all the
action he could get on those two games, and then he
turned around and sent it all in on a three-team parlay for

himself. The Mets with Matlack against Kison, the Red Sox against the Tigers, and the Yankees now that Billy Martin had been announced to take over for Bill Virdon as manager. Winners all. It was as solid a lock as betting that Jimmy Hoffa was dead and buried deep.

He had been given a good table at Chasen's, not just because they had driven up in the silver Rolls but because they knew him. It certainly wasn't because of his date, the starlet with a phony southern accent he always thought of as Scarlett the Harlot. He had gotten the usual favors from Scarlett and sent her home in a cab. During much of that time he had been thinking about Lydia, with a mixture of longing for her and satisfaction that he had handled that situation so well. It was Lydia—with her histrionic, Latin youth, her marvelous body that she had learned to show off less obviously during their months together, and her wonderful mouth that she used so well—who had made him think for the first time of settling down with one woman. He had been engaged before, always expediently and without really contemplating marriage, but blue-eyed, golden-haired Lydia was the first woman he had lived with. And he missed her.

Yet, having considered marriage and even discussed it with Lydia, he had thought of how much more suitable, useful, and enriching a marriage with Sharon might be. Lydia could please him in many ways, but Sharon might be able to do that and more, raising his self-image to the level of his expectations with someone who shared more of his background and native abilities. It was as if Lydia had prepared the way for Sharon. Perhaps she had served his purposes and outlived her usefulness. If it was time to unload the investment, he could use the liquidity to play for the higher stakes that Sharon represented.

So he had arranged for Lydia to work a job in Ohio for

several months while Sharon would be here. If this worked
out he could deal smoothly with Lydia long distance, avoiding the kind of closeup scenes they might have exploded
together. But if Sharon didn't work out he still had the
option to get Lydia back, maybe marry her after all. He
couldn't help thinking of her now as his high took on an
erotic component. But he had thought, so long Lydia, while
heading for the airport to meet Sharon's late flight from
New York, taking the Mercedes so as not to overwhelm her,
saving the silver gem for effect later.

And now Sharon came to the sliding door and looked out
to the patio.

"Jacob?" she called softly.

The Molinas grin broadened again. He allowed no one
else to call him that, not even his mother. But coming from
Sharon, even as a child back in the old neighborhood, it had
sounded classy, elegant in her little mouth as she looked
way up at him with big eyes bright with awe. "Jacob," she
would say then, a ten-year-old package of precocity who
knew already that only Molinas in the whole generation
ahead of her had sprinted to such a start in life, "Will you
wait for me?" And he'd swing her up to eye level, already
6'5" at nineteen and soon to be a fraction too tall for the
draft, saying, "There's no one but you, Sharon-sweet-as-a-
rose, so I'll have to wait."

And in a sense it was true. Girls, then women, had meant
very little to him. So he waited till she said that "Jacob"
again, still awed at 35, though educated, sophisticated, and
cultured beyond him, but drawn to the power, the money,
and the dream long-cherished and nostalgia-nourished.

"Over here, Sharon." His voice sounded gentle, assured,
assuring, in his own ears, contrary to the tone he often used
deliberately to grate on people's nerves with his loudness,
parodying, caricaturing the common image he projected.

"It's just beautiful," she said, her gesture taking in the house and its treasures. Then as he waved her attention to the city he owned below, she gasped in augmented appreciation.

He reached, took her hand, gently drew her to his side. Just as gently, he dropped the hand, tiny—as they all were—inside his, so that they stood close but untouching, both facing the lights. If this was to be a part of his future, the one that justified the past, he would have to play it slowly. He could take his time, he should take his time, to build the hedge, improve the edge that would guarantee the class, the style, he wanted in her and from her. Slow was appropriate. Slowly he would appropriate those gifts she presented or represented.

"Why'd you write me, Sharon?"

"I thought it was time."

"Time...?"

"Time for us now, to get together, now that we've both finished doing those other times."

Again the smile, knowing that no one else could talk like that to him, talk without twisting a knife about prison and parole. For herself she meant her marriage and its twisted values as well as her meaningless career. He knew as much as he needed to know about all that.

"But why did you send me your picture, an eight by ten glossy at that, as if you were auditioning for a part?"

He could feel her smile now, in the dark of the patio, clear of illumination, lacking definition, but solid, substantial in his perception of her, the reality of her value. She was the kind of hard currency he could bank on to enrich his life.

"I wanted to make sure you recognized me, to see how the little girl had grown up."

"As if I hadn't kept up. Ma gave me regular reports, even when I didn't ask."

How detailed his information was—or how he got it—
he'd never let her know. But his latest reports had told how
her marriage had soured in the endless needs of her husband to dominate in every way; how she had sustained it for
several years by boozing up to her self-effacement—or
down to memory-blocks. And he also knew how her manner
and mind were too classy for the professional academicians
and she was repeatedly cut down or out as a malcontent—
or threat. She was, after all, the girl after his own heart.

And more: he knew the brightness of the blue eyes that
had never dulled, that were farseeing in their clarity and
yet retained their sense of wonder at the worlds they took
in; he knew the hair that had gone naturally from blonde to
gold to a tawny brown losing neither lustre nor body; he
knew the womanliness that had been there in the bright
child and knew too that she had never been treated as anything but the bright child, the bright young woman. If it
was time for them, it was time that she be treated as a
woman while the bright child be put away alongside his
own long-dead image of scholar-athlete in some collection
of neighborhood legends. If it worked, he knew, they would
have whipped a game on the world.

In the silence he seemed to feel her saying, "I know."

"And have you kept up with me, Sharon?"

"In every way, Jacob, every step of the way. From Jackie
and Jack through Jake the Snake and Counselor and Master Fixer, you've always somehow been my Jacob. And our
twice seven years have been served."

Pat answer, but right, he thought. She's playing it like a
champion.

"What do you see out there?"

"Make believe. What's real is us looking at it. Don't you
know that's the only reality? Don't you know me now?"

"Yes," he said, "I do know." And thought, and I know that

she knows.

It was all right now. He was sure. He could make a move, then let her lead. He began to turn slowly, easy, felt her doing the same. And it seemed that they had found the illumination to see each other's faces, the knowing eyes. Which was just when the world exploded and a .22 long bullet shattered his head.

He died instantly. Yet it seemed to Sharon in that mind-ravaged moment, even as the explosion filled and resounded in the amplified spaces all around her, that Molinas continued to turn slowly toward her and, with a calm half-smile of recognition, or knowingness, shrugged to death.

In the months that followed, she could only remember two thoughts, two questions that occurred to her before she went into shock: not "Why?" but "Why now?" and not "Who?" but "Which one?"

Chapter 2:
Green Lights

J esse Miller woke suddenly to a state of total disorientation. He didn't know where he was or what time it was. And how he came to be sitting bolt upright with a sensation of shock in his head was a complete mystery.

It was as if there had been a loud noise that had jolted him awake. Yet there was nothing of the after-vibrations that always follow a loud noise, especially to the ear just returning to a waking state, and there was nothing of a sound-memory that is always there when something loud enough penetrates a sleeping ear.

Nor was there anything to explain the feeling he had that there should be some pain from a blow. He touched his head gingerly, feeling all over with both hands, and then rather sheepishly looked at the hands in the dim light for signs of blood that weren't there.

Gradually a sense of place came into shape and the anxiety receded. The bed was familiar all right. The only thing rigid about it was the frightened fortyish body sitting in it. It had a tremendous sag in the middle (the bed, the body less so) and because it was a single bed, one of twins, there was no escaping the swale. It surrounded its victim with no subtlety—which is why Jesse used it instead of its twin, an insidious, sneaky bed that tricked you into believing it firm and sneakily sucked out your back during the night, like some perverse succubus.

The beds completed the claustrophobic ambience of the back bedroom of Arnold Burr's summer house on Cape

Cod. The ceiling sloped sharply down in two directions, and only the living sounds of ocean and beach around the clock relieved the kind of oppressiveness that would have made sleep very hard for Jesse. And he almost always slept well in that bed in that room.

There was no clock and he had no watch. For as long as he could remember, he hadn't needed one. He had the gift—or maybe curse—of always knowing the time, which some think is a sign of genius, others of strangeness, and a few, mistakenly, of affectation. But in any case that morning Jesse didn't know what time it was when something he couldn't figure out had jumped him awake. No dream, no noise, no blow. The house was quiet and dark. The light from the window told him little, because sometimes in Harwich Port the fog or even clouds can make noon look like dawn. But it had to be very early because he could hear no human sound from the beach, and in summer there's always someone there by first light in all but the worst weather.

It was chilly. Something like the cold sweat of fear was making his body feel clammy, so he put on a sweatshirt, then pulled on jeans and opened the door as quietly as possible. It is conventional for bedroom doors to be kept closed in Arnold's house, though it makes little sense to Jesse. The walls are like cardboard and there are knotholes anyway, so that you can easily converse from room to room. But the traditional latched doorhandles have a characteristic sound, so that a practiced ear can keep track of comings and goings.

Jesse thinks Arnold wanted to, though ironically his son Steven was in a removed room downstairs off the kitchen with a window that opened onto a side porch. He could have been slipping out at night anyway. Jesse doesn't know that he did, but all the natural conditions were right for it. Gwen, the youngest Burr, was in the tiny bedroom with

Jesse's daughter Susannah.

The friendship of Susannah and Gwen is the main reason Jesse is there. He and Burr teach in the same department and share some common interests, but Jesse has always sensed that real friendship is beyond the capacity of his colleague, who is known in certain academic circles as the Pope of Sleaze. Still, during the long period of Jesse's separation from Rachel, it had become an annual thing for him to take Susannah on a vacation trip to the Cape while Arnold, long divorced, had his kids up there.

Susannah and Gwen are of an age and think so much alike that they can talk with total mutual understanding for hours at a time. And though they live over a thousand miles apart most of the year they keep in touch—letters, phone calls, psychic communication that neither has yet been willing to acknowledge. Jesse opened their door a crack to see them sleeping, beautiful, innocent, Susannah, her tanned summer look setting off the highlighted fair traces in her brown hair, Gwen as dark as a half-breed Haitian and about to enter her teens as a deliciously tempting torment to the boys, the kind of sweet-limbed saucy-eyed pre-pubescent prettiness that makes male adolescence an agony—at any age.

The only open door on the second floor was to the one large bedroom, a spacious airy room with a clear open view of the water, cross-ventilation that fills it with the breeze and smell and sound of sea, and two decent beds along with two cots and a crib. It was empty, waiting for the arrival of favored guests in a couple of days. Of all his summer lusts Jesse sometimes thought that the greatest was to sleep in that room, but up to that time he never had satisfied that one.

Downstairs everything was quiet. He checked the clock in the kitchen. It was not quite 5:30 and he figured he had been up for just five or ten minutes. The dog didn't even stir as he got out the back door to continue his prowling. But then Lohengrin had never been very alert. All of Boulder Ness was still. It was the kind of leaden morning in which you can feel an atmospheric weight on your body, just overcast enough to block out any trace of stars. A slight trace of freshening breeze gave some promise that the day would quicken to bright beach weather—he wouldn't have to listen to Arnold grumble about it—but now it remained somewhat oppressive and chilly with the heaviness of dank air.

He walked around the front and over to the wooden steps leading down to the beach. The tide was halfway ebbed and gave no evidence of having run very high at all. Down on the beach the coolness of the sand on his feet felt good—it was the first appropriate impression he had had since waking up. And he turned left, walking only about a hundred yards toward Thompson's.

The vague malaise persisted, and though he was trying to breathe deeply and steadily he couldn't quite put away the anxiety. He thought about smoking a joint to help get back to sleep, but he wasn't sure he wanted to sleep. He thought about getting some work out of his bookbag, but he didn't think he could concentrate on anything. Back in the house, he drank a little orange juice straight from the carton and went to bed.

Even if he couldn't sleep at all, he was determined to rest so he kept his eyes closed. Relaxing and avoiding any attempt to reason, he lapsed into a kind of halfsleep stupor, allowing associations to move freely, shallowly, through his head. There were no dreams, no vivid images at all. He was dimly aware of the house stirring, the Ness waking, the beach coming alive on a clearing day, but he stayed immobile and stuporous until late morning.

Throughout the rest of the day he moved in a daze. He
didn't know what had hit him—it was as simple and elo-
quent as that cliché must have been before it became a
cliché. He sleep-walked through the day's familiarities—
beach, supper at Kreme 'n' Kone, a PG movie that Rachel,
more scrupulous in taste than in behavior, probably would-
n't have wanted Susannah to see. He couldn't get through
ten pages of the Updike he was reading. People moved
about around him, but he made no real contact with anyone. He was vaguely annoyed that no one said, "What's
wrong, Jesse?" but then decided to be pleased that no one
noticed the difference.

That night he had no trouble getting to sleep. And he
slept for a long time, fitfully, slipping in and out of a dazed
halfsleep and a shallow dreaming state. The dreams were a
varied selection of short subjects, all familiar, nothing jar-
ring, nothing retained.

And the whole next day was the same as the day before.
He played some desultory games with the kids after supper, and about eleven he excused himself to go for a solitary walk, waiting strategically until after Steve had taken
Lohengrin. Jesse believes there's a tacit understanding
among Susannah and the Burr kids that his solitary walks
provide relief from Arnold's prohibition against marijuana
being used in the house. It's a rule he respects, though he
knows it's just a joke to the kids.

He sat in the front seat of his car and rolled a funny little
cigarette with his funny little machine, having never mas-
tered the art of doing it by hand. But for some reason he
didn't light it before walking around and down to the
beach. Stoned, his associations are explosive, inversely
pyramidal, impossible to hold onto once the geometric pro-
gressions multiply past a couple of stages. Linear associa-
tive thought is impossible, and something must have told

him that he needed to hold onto a train of thought to get through the anxious lethargy he was mired in.

The Burr house is right at the point of Boulder Ness, its long side facing the water no more than twenty feet from the seawall—though that distance seems to shrink perceptibly from year to year. Yet it's not isolated at all because the steps down to the beach, which is private but serves all of the Ness community of thirty or forty houses, are ten yards from Arnold's front door. He likes it that way. It would be no fun for him to play lord of the manor in splendid isolation. He needs visibility that seems to put him at the center of things, knowing all that is going on around him and being known to all who pass in orbit about him.

If you stand at the seawall or on the landing for those steps, as Jesse has done many a night, and you direct your gaze to the right rather than the left to avoid the increasing lighting-up of commercially developing Harwich Port, that is, if you look down the coastline toward Dennis Port rather than up-Cape toward Chatham, your eye will naturally be drawn to the green light that shines at the end of the jetty in Allen's Harbor. He often thought of Gatsby when he saw that light, but that particular night his thoughts took a new associational twist.

It was a clear night, warm, with just a whisper of breeze. Both hands were stuck characteristically in his jeans pockets, the right one cupping the unlit joint. He stared out toward Allen's Harbor, let his focus go soft, and tried to let his mind go blank as he took in the familiar scene.

He thought of Gatsby.

He thought of Daisy.

He thought of Wilson.

He thought of Exley.

He thought of Gifford.

He thought, My God! Molinas is dead.

Chapter 3:
Jumping
the Gun

Two days passed before Jesse had confirmation of his knowledge. Reports were slow to come out of Los Angeles on the killing. It was not big copy with New England papers, and Jesse never once heard anything about it on the radio. Molinas was dead—not beastly dead, but extravagantly dead, appropriately enough—and no one seemed to care.

It was not a fond and wayward thought, as the poet says of his Lucy, that had brought Molinas to Jesse's mind. For four decades he had thought of Molinas as if he were the secret sharer of his life, holding him at different times to be hero, fellow-sufferer, incarnation of evil, and one of the singularly significant people of their time.

To Jesse, about to turn forty-four—a birthday Molinas wouldn't share—he was one of the best minds of their generation, even bent, and he had gone extravagantly bad. Even more to the point, Jesse had long projected a book about him.

Jesse doesn't consider himself any more clairvoyant than the next person, discounts any fantastic psychic display in his realization of Molinas's death. He had simply been very sharply focused on him, tuned in on his life, so when, in Arnold Burr's house by the sea, he was shocked awake at 5:20 one morning by a shot in the head more than three thousand miles away, it was natural to receive or perceive the experience of his death. And now he knew it was a story he had to tell.

*   *   *   *   *

The publisher was a man with whom Jesse enjoyed working. He thought of Leif as kind and canny, appreciative and tough-minded. He always took pleasure in their meetings, even if the only place he'd eat lunch was the New York Yacht Club—and that meant tie and jacket. But today, over shrimp salad that was worth its fancy price even without the shipboard decor, Leif was less than encouraging.

"What kind of material do you have access to?"

"Not much, I'm afraid. I was surprised that the Columbiana collection in the Low Memorial Library has only half a dozen clippings in its Jacob L. Molinas file."

"That should tell you something."

"What?"

"That the world is not holding its breath for a biography of Jack Molinas, a curious name in a forgotten scandal."

"But he's important, damn it."

"To you, Jesse, to you. But who else cares?"

"The right book will make them care. I'll be able to use newspaper files and of course the transcript of the trial. But most of all I'll rely on interviews from Columbia, from the NBA days, from people who knew him as a lawyer, in prison, in L.A., in Vegas. I have lots of great sources to draw on: I happen to know the man who was District Attorney Hogan's chief investigator on the case and I'm also in touch with one of Molinas's old girlfriends."

Leif paused for a moment, studying him. "There is something else you should know that makes it less likely: there already is a Molinas book."

"What?" A cry of pain, and yet with a note of vindication—of course it's a good book idea, and somebody's done it.

"It's his own, with Milton Gross. Bantam bought it for a twenty or twenty-five thousand advance. Didn't you wonder how he got his parole transferred from New York to California? Well, the reason was plausible—there were plans for a book and a movie based on his life."

"Movie too, huh?"

"No, that seems to have fallen through. But Bantam has the manuscript."

When Jesse assembled the details later, he discovered that the initial film project never got past the talking stage and the original book proposals not much further, primarily because Molinas always exaggerated the dramatics beyond any semblance of credibility. But when he turned to Gross, a sportswriter for the New York *Post* he'd always admired for his tough, knowing treatment of basketball, the scandals, and himself, he found a writer/collaborator who made the project commercially viable.

Molinas talked on tape, and Gross wrote it. How the hard news writer was able to separate fact from fantasy and put it into plausible form will never be known, because Molinas had a unique clause in his contract: he could stop publication at any time. And so he did, when the book was already on press. In his time, Molinas had given interviews to dozens of reporters, elaborating, fabricating, modifying, mollifying, compulsively inventing his life for columns, features, series. But to put it down between covers, even soft covers, once and for all, was apparently more than he could bear. For whatever reasons, he said stop the press, and that stopped Milton Gross's heart. He died with the book, if not because of it.

After the Gross family—understandably—proved unwilling to allow any of the notes or tapes to be seen or heard, Jesse would rationalize away his disappointment, deciding that the material might raise more problems than it would solve for anyone trying to write a cogent, comprehensible account of Molinas, despite its great psychological fascination.

But for now the discovery of this wrinkle in the saga only spurred Jesse's determination.

"Can Bantam bring out their book now?"

"No, that's as dead as your hero."

"Surely there will be new interest in the story as a murder mystery."

"Perhaps. Do you know who killed him?"

"Not by name, but the mob did it."

"No surprise, I suppose, but do you know why?"

"There are lots of reasons, and I know how to find out exactly which one was in effect."

"Those sources you've mentioned won't clam up now?"

"There's no reason for them to. What they know may be inside stuff but it's close to common knowledge in those circles and there's no way to trace it back to a source."

"Except through you."

Jesse shrugged. This was not a deterrent he could allow himself. He was aware of rumors that anyone who told this story would be killed. Molinas's own people, fiercely proud Sephardic Jews, in an agony of shame that his shamelessness tortured them with, were supposed to have promised death to anyone who brought his story to life again. And a larger family, or family of families, might carry out murderous revenge just because they said they would—or others said they wouldn't dare. A matter of *omertá* But in all *umilitá* Jesse didn't think it would happen to him.

Leif paused, wryly raising his eyebrows, then asked, "Have you noticed the kind of play the media have given the story?"

"Not much."

"Right."

"Wait. This will be more than a bio, more than straight reporting. I can get inside his head, his life, as no one can. It'll be like a memoir."

"Hold on, Jesse. The consensus is that no one cares about yesterday's scandals and no one cares about another Mafia murder."

Leif had a look on his face that said more. Jesse knew that the publisher respected the enthusiasm, the energy, even the compulsion that draws writers to certain projects, and his look—showing Jesse that he cared—had a calming effect. Jesse took a breath and tried a new tack.

"You read some poetry, don't you?"

"Not as much as I should, or that I'd like. You know our list."

"For an English professor I read practically none. But for my generation, Leif, there *was* a poetry to match Kerouac's prose rhythms of the road and of Cassaday and to match the shock and stink of Burroughs—there were Ferlinghetti and Corso and especially Ginsberg."

"Not Robert Lowell?"

"Lowell's the one who'll endure, I suppose—and Plath for the wrong reasons—but what catches me every time is Ginsberg's 'Kaddish' with its range of sound and sense, the way it rushes spiraling from trivial specific to universal and back again until it's all one in the embrace of the title word.

"And to catch a generation there's nothing like the first section of 'Howl'—a revolutionary credo that tears down institutions and norms and sacred cows of society while being so gloriously evocative of individuation at every level. He makes me want to howl my own 'Howl' about one of the best minds of *my* generation, not the one sitting cross-legged on a desk before the next generation of gentlemanly thugs at the Yale Law School, or the others coopted by the hollow icons of Wall Street and Hollywood and academe and Washington and Ted Turnerdom, but the one lying dead at forty-three with the back of his head shot away, who got high only on the myriad games he played and the kick of juggling the meaningless abstractions of numbers around until they took on meaning the way energy clusters move so fast they can solidify as matter, who believed in nothing but himself, having seen everything proved false except the one cliché he lived by, that what goes around comes around, who forgot even that and then died proving it.

"That's what Molinas is for me, Leif. He's my 'Howl.'"

Leif waited a minute, either to indicate he was impressed or appreciating Jesse's need to impress, then smiled as he said, "I have a suggestion for you. Write it as a novel."

"You mean, Molinas as fiction? And I could still use my memoir concept?"

"A fictional memoir."

"Of course!"

"It's a tricky thing to bring off. You'll have to invent yourself as narrator. And you'll have to be convincing about knowing all you know. The point of view has to be credible."

"But I *do* have that knowledge."

"A novel, Jesse—you can't plead life."

The concept took hold from the instant Jesse heard the suggestion, but it raised as many problems as it solved. Leif was a self-styled "point-of-view man" about fiction, and Jesse's idea was to come at the Molinas story from a variety of viewpoints, real and imagined, including Molinas's own. That was the way to convey his gut sense of their generation and his belief that it has a significance—like any other. To tell the life and times of the class of '53 is to say something about its little pivotal place in social and cultural history.

Jack Molinas's life was so melodramatic that it strained credulity, but one could look at it as life imitating art. If it's art, soap opera, sitcom, comic strip, still that derivative life could serve to provide the stuff of art. Imitation of an imitation of an imitation, melodrama in the first degree at a third remove.

Setting out to tell his story Jesse at times would fancy himself a loony greybeard Ancient Mariner, who might stoppeth one of three hundred thousand to tell him or her what he has to say. His glittering eye sees that Molinas's life has meaning, and his sad eye knows that he can only try to express it in fictive reflections.

And what about the threats? Would Jesse Miller be the Salman Rushdie of American sports? He would only set them aside, imagining himself as beating on with Molinas's life, though at times it may seem to run against the tide of his own. There is life against death here, and there is death in that life. But he believed this—and wished it to stand as the valedictory of this commencement, not its benediction—that not telling the story, Molinas's, his own, their generation's, is a death he could not live with.

He could not stop to worry whether he would literally be sacrificing himself. It is the story that's important, not any single teller of it. His own telling could be faulted either for not being true enough or for being too true, since he had chosen to do it as fiction. But neither of those charges ought to be a capital offense. If he were killed for it, he would have received Molinas's reward for Molinas's mistake of thinking he was beyond being hurt. "I'm Jesse Miller," he would, in effect, be saying, "and they can't get me."

PART II:
Preregistration

Chapter 4:
Jackie and Friends

At eight, Jackie Molinas is already the best-known character in his neighborhood—Creston Avenue in the Bronx. Everybody knows him, and he knows the names of almost everyone on the street. It is not clear exactly why such great recognition-value attaches to him, but he seems to think it's his due.

He is exceptionally bright, of course, and his family tends to broadcast every feat of brightness to the world at large: reading at three, in Spanish at four; prodigious memory of names, lists, catalogues; ability to do complex mathematical functions and solve algebraic problems in his head at seven. What's more, he's not reluctant to show off his skills at the drop of a hat, particularly if someone throws a quarter in the hat.

His athletic ability is already apparent. He is not unusually large for his age, except for his arms and hands and feet, but he is strong and well-coordinated far beyond his size and years, and fiercely competitive far beyond his peers.

And good-looking. "Oh, Jackie," they all tell him, stroking his shiny black hair or reflecting his already brilliant smile, "the girls will never be able to keep their eyes off you, or their hands." He is always well-dressed. His father's successful business in Coney and his mother's devotion are evident. He wears the signs of both as simple givens of his place and thinks nothing of it, absolutely nothing.

His father's presence—Louis Molinas, a tall man whose

erect bearing suggests that he wants to be regarded as distinguished, is very visible in the neighborhood from Labor Day until Decoration Day—and his mother's attentive adulation are more or less acceptable burdens for Jackie. The birth of his little brother he regards as a godsend because the kid is getting the attention now. He likes the way the kid bears up almost stoically under constant scrutiny, but he has little to do with him. Jackie prizes his own independence and doesn't think of anything he does as rebellious.

As broad as his acquaintance is, he has few friends. He is contemptuous of most kids but without showing it, and they all constantly seek his company. To himself he thinks that, for now, he has only three friends—and it might as well count as just two because two of them are identical twins.

Stanley and Richard Miller, from Mt. Hope Place around the corner, have just turned twelve. They're not much taller than Jackie, but they are reading and figuring at about his level so he appreciates hanging out with them. They seem to share his gifts for memory (especially baseball stats) and street smarts, and, like him, they are well-known (simply as "the twins") and comfortable showing off their special talent of apparent telepathy.

They complete each other's sentences and voice each other's thoughts. They often speak, spontaneously, in unison, and it is uncanny the way their pre-adolescent voices break at the same time. The only way most people can tell them apart is the way their hair whorls on the back of their heads: Stanley's clockwise and Richard's counter. But Jackie seems to know instinctively which is which, perhaps from the way they habitually flank him in the same position, Stanley to the right and Richard left.

The twins' family is a mixture of English- and German-Jewish stock, but their dark coloring seems compatible with the Molinas Sephardic identity. Jackie was pleased to discover that Yiddish is as foreign in the Miller apartment as in his own, and the twins' parents are also appreciative of that degree of compatibility. It sets them off from most of the neighborhood.

Jackie's other friend is Joe Hacken, and he too shares a high recognition-value. Operating a small hand-book out of the corner candy-store, Hacken is always around. At nineteen he is just getting started on a career that he loves—living by his wits and integrity in a world of sports and numbers—and he has made the Molinas kid a kind of protégé. The agility of the boy's mind and body has made the young bookie a most indulgent mentor.

On a fair spring evening in 1940, the Millers are being entertained at table by the twins' stereo account of the highlight of their afternoon with Jackie Molinas. This is a regular feature of their dinner, usually initiated by their sister June's bemused question: "And what did the great prodigy do today?"

Almost without fail they are ready with another unrehearsed anecdote, a pair of Boswells basking in the heady ambience of their charismatic subject.

"Everybody in the neighborhood knows what a good athlete Jackie is..."

"Even though he hasn't really started to grow yet."

"And they're always talking about what he can do and what he can't do."

"So we're walking home from school..."

"And Mr. Godnick and Mr. Friedman are standing in front of their building."

"As soon as they see us, Mr. Godnick says..."

"'I bet Jackie can throw a rock over the house.'"

"Mr. Friedman says, 'What? This size kid and this big a house? No way.'"

"'What'll you bet?' Mr. Godnick says."

"And Mr. Friedman says…"

"'A hundred.'"

"'You're on,' Mr. Godnick says and whips out two fifties."

"Mr. Friedman counts five twenties from his wallet…"

"And they hand the money to us."

The twins pause for synchronized breath-taking, prompting June to say, "What happened?"

"So Jackie takes a rock and hefts it…"

"And smiles…"

"And looks at the wiseguys…"

"And throws it over the roof."

"But he makes it look good…"

"By huffing…"

"And puffing…"

"And clearing the top by just a couple of feet."

Now they pause to look at each other before continuing.

"So Mr. Godnick is happy…"

"And pockets the two hundred bucks."

"But before we leave…"

"He gives Jackie a ten dollar bill."

They have slowed down the delivery in such a way as to indicate that there is more to come. June is affable and obliging: "What then?"

"Jackie says, 'Come on.'"

"And we go with him to the candy store…"

"Not to buy anything…"

"But to tell Joe Hacken what happened…"

"And to see if there's still time…"

(in unison) "To bet a baseball parlay."

But this is still not the punchline. The narration proceeds.

"Joey says, 'Instead of taking your money…'"

"'I'll teach you a little lesson.'"

"'What lesson?' Jackie says."

"And you could tell he's mad."

"So Joey says…"

"'Listen, Moe Godnick tipped you ten bucks…"

"'Because you won a bet for him. Right?'"

"Jackie says, 'Yeah, right.'"

"Then Joey says, 'Let me ask you a question…"

"'What do you suppose Babe Friedman would have given you…"

(in unison) "'If you promised him you wouldn't do it?'"

They take another dramatic breath before the final curtain.

"So we're on our way home…"

"And Jackie's muttering to himself…"

"And we say to him…"

(in unison) "'What's wrong?'" Both voices crack on the diphthong of the second word; everyone at the table can visualize the stereophonic effect of the twins on either side of their young friend.

"So he says…"

"'Joey's right…"

"'I should have thought of it myself."

"'I could have gotten at least twenty…"

"'If I had made a deal…"

"'And hit the building with the rock."

"'But now he'll never bet against me again…"

"'And what's worse…"

"'When will I get another chance…"

(they finish, as usual, together) "'For such easy money?'"

Chapter 5:
Down by the
Schoolyard

A group of boys are gathered on the corner of Mermaid Avenue and West 27th Street in Coney Island, in front of the Manufacturers' Bank. In the light rain of a summer afternoon they are playing "under the feet" for quarters, calling out odds or evens to guess whether the coins will match heads or tails.

Willy, at 17 the oldest of the bunch, is standing apart, looking up into the spotty gray sky. "I hope it stops by three," he says.

The boys all know what he means. That's the time Cozzi shows up for basketball, and that's when the serious play begins. Every player who counts in the area is supposed to be there today.

Jackie looks up quickly and takes in both the cloud formation and the look on Willy's face. He realizes how much Willy *wants* the rain to stop in the next half hour. "Bet it doesn't," he says.

He has said the magic word. "Five says it does," says Willy.

"Make it ten."

They don't shake hands on it. They reach into their pockets and pull out rolls of bills, equally thick. Jackie's roll has twenties on the outside, so that the boys can only guess how much he's carrying. Willy has his ones at the outside, in the manner of a professional bookmaker—which he is. It's the only way he can support his own betting habit. He is already one of the most active accounts for Shlombo over on West 29th. Cozzi works for Shlombo too, and that's why he's not available till three o'clock—after he's made his rounds and brought in the afternoon baseball action.

Willy and Jackie each hand a ten dollar bill to the nearest boy, who happens to be Murry. It is a solemn duty to hold the bet; gambling is almost sacred to them—as important as basketball. To the other boys ten dollars is serious money, and their appreciation of these two—the only ones around with that kind of ready cash—is profoundly respectful. They have attained the status of living legend among the rest for their willingness to bet on anything, but it is usually Jackie who wins.

A couple of bobby-soxers walk quickly by, their ponytails close together under an umbrella. They ignore the remarks directed at them from most of the boys, glancing only, with shy smiles, at Jackie, who ignores them.

"He's taken," Murry calls after them, "faithful to his Sharon," and the others all laugh.

Jackie has told them about a seven-year-old girl back home in his Bronx neighborhood, who's "already smarter than all these broads" and is "gonna be a knock-out." He doesn't mind being teased about Sharon; he's proud of her in an unembarrassed way. It's as if he's glad he's given them one thing to tease him about.

They don't mention the fact that at this time, rather than heading for the park to play basketball, he's supposed to be working the counter at his father's place at Surf and West 12th. Louis Molinas's Eagle Bar and Grille is what brings Jackie to Coney for the summer with more money and a much higher standard of living than any of these other boys have.

By three, the half dozen of them have sauntered up to West 28th and over to Neptune Avenue where the courts are. It's still drizzling, but some younger boys are already shooting around. It's easy to spot Louie from a distance; he's the only black kid in the park. And they can recognize Mark and Stick, too, by the apparent skill and grace that allow them to hold their own with the older boys.

Just as they get there, Bobby and a couple of others are coming along Neptune from the other side. Jackie holds his hand out to Murry, who passes him the twenty dollars without a word, Willy pretending not to notice. It is still perceptibly raining.

Within fifteen minutes, though, after a very brief last gasp of a downpour, it stops suddenly and the sun breaks through. The hard-top courts are almost instantly dry, though the boys' high-top sneakers slop heavily as they run and jump. And now Cozzi makes his appearance.

It is as if he owns not only the playground but the players as well. He is a young man among boys and he never lets them forget it. His whole manner is intimidating, but especially so in a game, where his reputation precedes him and his performance constantly reinforces his image.

The style of play here emphasizes fundamentals of a particular variety. Because winners continue to play, the boys have learned to play defense and to look for high-percentage shots on offense. Because the games are relatively short (fourteen baskets wins), each possession is vital, and so the rebounding is aggressive. And because the play is rugged the boys have learned to use their bodies, especially elbows, as tools of their trade and also to use feints and clever moves to avoid contact. Strength, determination, and deception are much in demand; they are learned behavior, acquired properties. Accuracy and quickness are natural; they seem to be in the general gene-pool here.

Cozzi has played with pros, semi-pros anyway. When he passes and cuts for the basket, he expects a prompt return pass. If he doesn't get it, you won't play on his side very long. This is elementary, and so is the extent to which you may hold your ground when he is muscling his way into inside position against you. You must resist, but only up to a point, and then yield.

All summer it has been clear that Jackie's skills are at least equal to Cozzi's. For that matter, so are Bobby's and maybe even Gooch's. But Cozzi has continued to dominate by the force of his inside power-game. He owns the unmarked area within eight or ten feet of the metal baskets. Jackie, taller now, can score consistently over him, his long arms arcing hook shots from either side, his overlarge hands controlling the ball out of reach.

But the challenge here is not a matter of skill. It is a question of who is the man. The threat of fights is a constant in these games, but Cozzi is the enforcer—whenever he chooses to be. You can square off all you want, but if Cozzi raises his arm between you, or his fist against you, all bets are off and there is no fight.

Until today. Murry, playing on Cozzi's side, has been exchanging elbows with Jackie, with escalating aggression. And now it goes too far. Jackie fakes Murry out and drives left toward the basket. Murry, badly beaten on the play, cracks back with a flailing right elbow. But Jackie avoids it, grazing Murry's side with his knee as he goes up for the shot (good). Cozzi has dropped off to help out, goes up to block the shot, but catches only Jackie's elbow on the way down.

Murry pushes Jackie and they square off. Cozzi steps in. "This one is mine," he says.

"Not this time, Irving," Jackie says with a broad grin. There is a collective catch of breath among the boys crowding around. No one ever dares use Cozzi's given name to his face.

Cozzi freezes, confused, flustered.

"You're not gonna touch me," Jackie says, "and you're smart enough to know why not." Then he calmly steps around Cozzi and throws a perfunctory punch into Murry's unprotected belly. Murry shrugs it off and halfheartedly jabs his left hand into Jackie's chest.

Cozzi shrugs, too, starting to walk off the court. Then he stops and turns back, saying, "Any of you suckers want anything for tonight?" There are no takers and he leaves.

Jackie, instantly in command of the turf, says, "OK, me, Bobby and Louie. The rest of you can shoot for sides."

It is a very small shifting of balance, a minor adjustment of equilibrium, but the boys play on with the confident knowledge, buried at some secure level of unverbalized knowing, that a significant change has come to the life of the park. Jackie Molinas, however, is consciously aware that the order of his world has inched closer to anarchy, that for some time to come he will have to battle Cozzi in the unforgetting aftermath of this day, and that sometimes the smallest wins require the greatest risk.

Chapter 6:
Near Things

Saul Benjamin never had a nickname until he knew Jackie Molinas, and the one Jack gave him was the only one he would ever have. From the middle-class upper-Bronx (he grew up within walking distance of Baker Field), Saul had an incredibly long commute every day for three years to Stuyvesant High School in Manhattan, and it was on the subway that he got to know Molinas.

He had known about him long before that, and the truth was that he had chosen Stuyvesant just because Molinas was there, two years ahead of him. Saul was a bright boy, not exceptionally bright but exceptionally quick with numbers, and he could have had his choice of high schools. Bronx Science was the logical one, Clinton was the most convenient, and his parents wondered why their only child had to travel all the way to Fourteenth Street.

In their eyes, his future was assured: business, accountancy, statistics, insurance—anything directly to do with numbers, except math, because Saul faltered when it came to abstract concepts—and he was happy to share his family's expectations for him. Give him the concreteness of numbers, especially applied to realities like batting averages and stock-market quotations, and he was comfortably sharp. Years later he would laugh to himself in Biblical parody over his dealings with Molinas: "Saul has his thousands, Jacob his tens of thousands."

He was not an unhappy boy, though he rarely made friends, was totally uncoordinated in any athletic activity, and with his nondescript features and dumpy build could never attract any girls. He took pride in his schoolwork, putting extra effort into bringing other subjects up to his arithmetical level, and read voraciously on sports, especially baseball with its particular appeal for the numerically-minded.

Yet it was a young basketball player who excited his adulation, a Jewish boy from the Bronx just two years his senior, and that hero-worship profoundly affected his life. He took measurable vicarious pleasure in every point Jackie scored even in a playground game. No wonder he determined that if Molinas could commute to Stuyvesant so could he.

Such decisions are mysterious anyway. When Saul read somewhere that F. Scott Fitzgerald had chosen Princeton because of a football game, a heroic performance by Buzz Law in losing to a much stronger Harvard team, he not only believed it but understood it. He didn't tell his parents about it, though, because he knew they wouldn't understand.

At first he would look for Molinas throughout the train once they had passed his stop, sitting or standing nearby if possible. In a matter of weeks he worked out his hero's schedule and even knew in advance which car he'd be most likely to enter. And then it was easy to start up a conversation because they were in such a tiny minority taking that long ride.

Jackie made it easy for him. He accepted the younger boy's idolization as if it were his natural due, and so they both were comfortable with the relationship. Saul could talk knowledgeably about sports, and Jack never made fun of his clumsiness or pudginess. In time, Molinas would come on the train and look for Benjamin, until one day he greeted him with a new name.

"Hi, Red."

"Hi, Jackie," he said, his rising blush being the only red about him. His hair was not sandy but mousy brown, and not even his pubices gave a hint of prophecy that thirty years later when he let his beard grow it would come in with a variety of colors featuring a rich golden red.

"I've got an idea for you."

"What?"

"Since you love sports so much, why don't you be student manager for the basketball team? We need someone right away, and if I say so you're in."

"What would I have to do?" he asked, worrying whether it would interfere with his schoolwork.

"Keep track of uniforms and equipment and like that. Of course you'd have to be at all practices and sit on the bench for games."

That was all he needed to hear. And so Red Benjamin, as he was introduced to coach and players who never questioned the nickname, became student manager of the Stuyvesant basketball team for the 1949 season.

And what a season it was. Saul couldn't have been happier. He not only kept careful count of everything in his charge, he also kept stats for the coach during games. Best of all he spent twenty hours a week with Molinas (even though Jack spent many evenings in Coney, staying with friends, instead of riding back and forth to the Bronx everyday) and saw him dominate play through the PSAL.

The tournament that climaxed the season had Benjamin in a frenzy of anticipation. He knew Molinas would take them all the way. On St. Patrick's Day in Madison Square Garden he was ecstatic watching a record-breaking performance by his hero in the semifinals. Taft, led by center Neil Dambrot, stayed close in the first half, but in the second Jackie turned it into a romp. He controlled the boards, stifled Dambrot, handled the ball and, scoring virtually at will, himself outscored the whole Taft team.

It was basketball week in New York. Molinas rewarded his faithful manager by taking him to an NIT doubleheader. They saw four good college teams—Bowling Green, Bradley, San Francisco, and Loyola of Chicago—with such fine players as Charlie Share, Don Otten, Paul Unruh, Gus Chianakis, Gene Melchiorre, and Don Lofgran, but in Saul's eyes there was no question that the best player on the Garden floor that week was Jack Molinas.

The PSAL championship game on Saturday promised to be a good one, a worthy challenge for Jack. Lincoln had the big reputation as the basketball powerhouse of the five boroughs, unbeaten in four years of regular league play. Saul read the analyses in all the papers. They talked about Lincoln wanting to make up for being upset the last two seasons in the finals. They talked about the size, strength, defense, depth, and balance of Venty Leib's team. Despite Stuyvesant's "quickness and the inspired play of their center, Jack Molinas," the sportswriters leaned toward Lincoln.

Saul Benjamin knew better. He knew that Jack had played with and against these Lincoln kids all his life and that no two of them could stop him. "They couldn't carry his jock" was the popular phrase, and whenever Saul heard it about Molinas now he had enough confidence to say, "No, but I do, every day." Despite what the papers said, he wasn't surprised to hear that the game was rated a toss-up by bettors, or even that Stuyvesant was a one- or two-point favorite.

The first quarter supported the smart money. With Saul leading the cheers from the bench, Molinas made several big-time plays. He went up for a power rebound and before both feet came down released an outlet pass for an easy breakaway layup. He took a long rebound in traffic and went downcourt with the ball past two defenders for a basket. He stood at the free-throw line, cool and concentrat-

ing, and swished two. At the end of the period Stuyvesant
led 14-9.

Throughout the rest of the game Saul could hardly
believe what he was seeing. Molinas played small: Lincoln
players went up over him. Molinas played weak: Lincoln
players took the ball from him. Molinas played slow:
Lincoln players went by and around him.

Through the second and third quarters the teams played
evenly as Stuyvesant's coach, Doc Ellner, prowled the sideline in an agony of frustration, shouting at Jackie, "Low
post, low post" and at the others to get the ball to him
there. Saul went hoarse screaming echoes of those instructions and exhorting Jackie to come on.

But Molinas was not in the game. He didn't want the ball.
When he got it inside he'd pass it back outside. Stuyvesant
tried to stall, but Lincoln came back in the fourth quarter
and took the lead with less than a minute to play. At thirty
seconds, Jack went to the foul line for a shot that could tie
the game. He missed badly, and Lincoln ran out the clock.

Saul wept without shame on the bench. He looked at
Jack coming off the court to see if there was a sign of why,
but Molinas never looked at him until later in the dressing
room. By then the whole shrugging attitude was fixed in
place, and with a slight touch of sadness in his smile he
could say, "Sorry, Red. Hope you didn't bet on the game."

There was a new sense of awe in Saul's feelings about his
idol from that day on, a new mystery. He felt almost at the
mercy of what he came to call "greatness refusing." He
knew, too, that there were limits to how far he could follow
Jackie.

Two years later he tried to follow him to Columbia, but
didn't get in. Ironically, the commute to NYU (Uptown) was
much easier than the daily pilgrimage to Stuyvesant. His

grades had suffered even after he quit being manager of the basketball team—it all seemed pointless after Jack graduated. It pleased his parents, too, that he could spend more time at home. Best of all, his academic success was astonishing after the disappointments in high school.

The numbers were finally adding up for their boy. His eventual success in the stock market was the triumph of their life, but they continued to shake their heads over the way he kept the connection with and the faith in Jack Molinas.

Chapter 7:
Witnesses

"**J**ackie threw that game."

"Are you sure?"

"I knew about the dump at least a day before we played them." The speaker is Bernie Reiner, who calls himself the "fourteenth man on the thirteen-man Lincoln team." More than thirty years after the event, he remembers it clearly.

"It was well known among our group. Murry knew it. Bob Licker knew it. Jackie told us. He said, 'I'm betting the game and we'll lose.' I don't know how many of us bet on that game. Fifty to seventy-five people had knowledge of it. We were betting on Lincoln but we knew we couldn't beat Stuyvesant if Jackie played an honest game. Even though we had that long winning streak during the regular season, Stuyvesant was a slight favorite—and should have been, because we had no player of Molinas's ability."

Reiner is sitting in a conference room of a small frame building that houses Social Sciences offices at Fairleigh Dickinson University, where he is a history professor. He is tracing, with the careful expansiveness of his discipline, the history of his friendship with Jack Molinas.

Jesse has sought him out here, in the wake of new basketball scandals involving point-shaving at Boston College and Tulane and an aborted investigation of widespread fixing in the Big Eight and the Southwest Conference. Jesse's idea is that the name of Jack Molinas is synonymous with point-shaving in most people's memory, and Reiner agrees openly and even enthusiastically, giving him just the kind of material he wants.

"I met him in the summer of '42. I was ten, he was eleven. My friend Bob Licker introduced us. All the rest of us lived year round at Coney, lower-class Jewish children of immigrant parents. We moved frequently, but stayed in the neighborhood. A family would rent a flat for a year or so, the landlord wouldn't paint for Passover, and you'd move to another place.

"But Jackie was just there for the summer. His father had a place called the Eagle Bar and Grille, a few hundred feet west of Luna Park and diagonally across from Feltmann's, a turn-of-the-century posh eatery-cum-amusement center. If you wanted a ten cent frank you went to Feltmann's, with its faded past, but for a nickel you went to the Eagle or two blocks down to Nathan's. The Molinas place catered to transient street trade from Luna Park, and it was open only from Memorial Day to Labor Day.

"About a yard up from the street a counter ran along the building, the long side on Surf Avenue, the short side on West 12th. There was an open space above the counter, enclosed with glass at night, and then another yard or so of walled facing. Through that open space, Jackie dispensed hamburgers and beer. I can see him vividly, the bright smile and the jet-black wavy wiry hair, and the white apron tied around his waist and hanging down to his ankles."

"Wasn't there a batting range next door?"

"Much further down the street, but that came later, after Luna Park burned down after the war. They would get some of the Brooklyn Dodgers to take some swings and advertise their appearances to attract customers. But the Molinas place was there before the outbreak of the war.

"Of course Jackie didn't work all that much. He'd plead with his father for a couple of hours off to play some ball, and then he'd stay all day. So in the summer of '42 we started playing basketball in Leon Kaiser Park, named for a former principal of Mark Twain Junior High School, that's JHS 239, where all of us went, except Jackie. At that time Jackie was shorter than I was. I must have been five feet tall, and he was about four-ten.

"The park was built during the Depression with WPA funds, the only park in South Brooklyn which had a baseball stadium with a poured concrete sculptured grandstand that seated probably three thousand. Sandy Koufax pitched there later for the Nathan's team—I remember Molinas betting on the game. There were tennis courts, a quarter-mile cinder track—unheard-of in Brooklyn in those days, and six or eight full-length basketball courts with metal baskets. No nets of course; we had chains occasionally."

The historian is warming to his task. He has set the scene and now he's going to people it.

"Most of the characters in the park were never known by Christian names—in fact, none of our parents knew we had Christian names. There was an occasional Shloime, and Jackie was Jackie; but I was Bones; Raymond was Razzie..."

"Is that Ray Miller who played at LIU?"

"Yes, a crybaby, always complaining he was getting hacked on the wrist, called Razzie because of his raspberry-colored hair, had a great one-handed set shot like Freddy Scolari. Murry was Shoulders, who became a cab driver in New York, a Runyonesque character who used to fight with Jackie over elbows to the mouth—at which Jackie was adept, especially after he suddenly grew past us while we were still five-eight or five-nine.

"The king of the court was Cozzi, surely the best until Jackie came along."

"Italian?"

"No," Reiner laughs. "His real name was Irving, but he

was called Cozzi because he resembled Quasimodo—and was proud of it. He had gone to Lincoln but never graduated, and he played with a couple of barnstorming teams, the Brooklyn Visitations and the Jewels. But by the time he was nineteen or twenty he had become a bookmaker. He took bets, mostly baseball—no numbers, there was no policy bank there at that time—for Shlombo the bookmaker who sat at a table in a storefront on West 29th Street. It was wide open. Shlombo, who could have passed for Sydney Greenstreet from the shoulders down, operated as a bookmaking lieutenant for Mickey Goldstein, whose professional name was Micky Doyle, part of the Joe Bananas family."

"So the mob was in the neighborhood?"

"Of course. Everyone knew it."

"Weren't there some handball courts behind a parking lot where...?" Jesse has routinely researched places as well as people and events.

"That was down at the end of Surf Avenue at Brighton Beach where the New York Aquarium has the property now. There are still handball courts adjacent to the Aquarium."

"The lot was Mafia-owned?"

"Oh, that was a different parking lot, on West 12th about two hundred yards north of Surf. Yes, that was known to be a Mafia place, and the people who ran it and Joe Bonanno himself used to take their meals at a restaurant called Giuliano's at Mermaid Avenue and 15th Street. They had money in that place, and there was some suspicion that they had some money in the Eagle Bar. But I couldn't say that with certainty. It was just talk.

"The park was our living arena—we just went home for food. All year round, after school we'd play. Jackie would come almost every day, take the subway out after school. When he went to Stuyvesant, he'd often stay over at friends' homes in Coney rather than go back to his family after school. His friends were the Lincoln crowd, not his Stuyvesant teammates and classmates. At night, in the winter, by the light of an incandescent street lamp, even in the snow, we'd play.

"Mostly we played three-on-three halfcourt games, officiating by choosing. Jackie quickly became skilled at choosing. He had extremely long hands, could palm a basketball by the age of fourteen, and he was the most proficient in the park at manipulating fingers at choosing, so that his team would always get the ball out after every call. This often infuriated Cozzi and occasioned a number of fistfights between them. Cozzi was several years older and had everyone else intimidated, but Jackie would say, 'He can't do anything to me.'

"Jackie had other memorable battles on that court. He duelled in basketball with Bobby Sassone, probably the only Catholic in the park, who went on to a fine career at St. Bonaventure. Then there were some younger players coming up, particularly Stick, who eventually changed his name, Morton Stourazumnick or something, to Barry Storick and captained the Washington and Lee basketball team. Then there were two kids I coached on a Recreation League team: Mark Reiner, a distant cousin who now coaches the Brooklyn College team, and Louie Gossett, the only resident black on our courts, who went from the park to NYU but is better known now as an actor."

"When did the gambling start?"

"I'm not sure exactly, but I know we were betting on the Yankee-Cardinal World Series in '43. By the time we were fourteen we were gambling on every conceivable sporting event. At the end of the war we were playing those punch cards on college football and we were selling them too. We played the horses some—Bob Licker started sneaking into Jamaica race track and became our champion horseplayer.

"Listen: at that time there was a new bookie on the street, Willy the Q, who was maybe a year older than Jackie. He ended up a few years later on the floor of the Barracini's Candy Store in Columbus Circle. The police had staked it out because it had been held up so many times. He tried to hold it up and they ordered him to stop and throw down his gun, but he ran and they shot and killed him. Turned out he was carrying a wooden pistol. Well, if Willy the Q was number one in addiction to gambling, Jackie was one-A in an entry."

"Weren't there crap games on the handball courts?"

"Yes, but not that big with us. We'd bet on baseball games and then stand around on street corners listening to static on KMOX to get the scores. And of course basketball."

"That was the center of your life?"

"Basketball and betting. We played some softball, called 'indoor,' at a park on West 33rd Street where there was no right field. Jackie was quite adept at hitting to left. But we played basketball seven days a week, winter and summer. That was our world. No women—women just didn't exist in that world—and no drinking. We were a Jewish group, mostly poor, except for Jackie. And most of us were motivated to do well in school, though Jackie was by far the brightest. Some of us went on to college and professional schools and academe, but on any measured intelligence test Jackie easily outscored us. He took the test and was admitted to Stuyvesant while the rest of us went to Abraham Lincoln."

"Molinas wasn't involved with girls?"

"Not till Columbia. It wasn't important. Don't forget Stuyvesant was all boys. There were some groupies around, even then, but who cared? We were almost asexual—sports and gambling were our love affair."

"That's a part of it I find hard to imagine, Bernie. I mean, sports and gambling were important to most boys in the forties, but dating and dances and parties and making out were central to their lives too."

Reiner smiles at Jesse as if kindly indulging an understandable innocence. "That *was* our social life. We had no country clubs, just the park where we played ball and gave Cozzi our bets."

"Was pro basketball always in the back of Jack's mind?"

"I can tell you just when it started. It was November 11, 1946, the first professional game Jackie ever saw. He sat in section 325 of the old Garden to see a BAA game, the Chicago Stags beating the Knicks. I know because I sat next to him. Murry was there, and Gooch, and Bob Licker, the five of us. Max Zaslofsky was high scorer for Chicago, Sonny Hertzberg for New York. And I can remember Jackie saying, 'I'm ready, that's for me.'"

This is Bernie Reiner's element, not just as a contemporary historian, but as a man who has lived at the center of Sportsworld, USA for years. Before he had finished high school he was doing statistics for hockey and basketball broadcasts at the Garden, and continued to work in the sports media for four years before he was drafted.

His personal history sounds like a who's who narration, as he recounts intimate associations with Win Elliott, Curt Gowdy, Marty Glickman, Red Auerbach, Johnny Most, Red Barber, Vin Scully, Bill Stern, Joe Lapchick, Bud Palmer, et al. Then, as a GI-bill undergraduate at Kent State, he was sports publicity director, assistant basketball coach, and recruiter. In other words, he speaks authoritatively about the inner workings of the American sports scene.

"Were you betting point spreads on pro basketball?"

"No, just college. But we also bet regularly on high school games."

"Was there a line?"

"Initially it was just crude betting—no spread. If we were playing Erasmus, we'd show up at their gym on Flatbush Avenue on Friday night, and there'd be twenty guys in front of the gym saying, 'Wanna make a bet? Wanna make a bet? I'm taking Erasmus.' By '48 it was more sophisticated. There was now an officially circulated point spread in Brooklyn on high school basketball games. No Bronx games, but the betting was widespread in Brooklyn. I must have bet several hundred dollars on Lincoln games over the years. When Lincoln played Madison, our archrival, several thousand would be bet on the game, mostly by students, not professional gamblers.

"Jackie was still part of our group. We knew that he had been betting on Stuyvesant games from his freshman year on. And in the last two years he was betting the point spreads against his team. If you look back over the scores of his junior year, you'll see that Stuyvesant seldom covered. He wasn't throwing games, not deliberately dumping, but he'd think nothing of blowing a layup or throwing the ball away to stay under the spread.

"Now it happened that those were the glory years in Lincoln's basketball history. Everyone of Venty Leib's players went on to play varsity college ball, like Morgan Wootten at DeMatha now. And for that championship game in Jackie's senior year, I think he started Sassone, Seymour Sedacca, Sid Youngelman, Mark Solomon, and Joe Massa. I don't think Archie Lipton started or our friend Gooch. That was a fine team, but Mark Solomon at center couldn't handle Molinas. Jackie could have taken Mark any way he wanted; he could have had a thirty-point game. If Jackie had been at Lincoln, we'd have dominated everybody the way Alcindor's teams did at Power Memorial. But Jackie was betting on Lincoln, so Stuyvesant had to lose. He dumped."

"For how much?"

"Probably under a thousand dollars, maybe eight or nine hundred dollars."

"Why? He didn't need the money."

"No. He was the wealthiest guy in the park. But he had to gamble and he had to win. Besides, in his psychological hardware he had a need to do things in the devious way.

"You know, the next year, his freshman year at Columbia, he kept coming back to the park to play. That was when he had a famous spitting duel with Cozzi. Cozzi was driving for a layup, Jackie blocked it, and Cozzi took offense. Here were the deposed old king of the hill and the visiting absentee reigning king spitting at each other.

"But Jackie told us then that he was doing business and bragged that next year when he moved up to the varsity we'd be in great shape and we would all make a lot of money. He couldn't keep his mouth shut. Jackie's thing was this: I can con the world; I can bullshit the world; I can connive the world; I'm brighter than you guys; I can steal; I can manipulate; I'll always get another chance. If I get caught, I'll get out of it—my father deals with the cops all the time.

"In psychological retrospective, that could be important. He had learned that he could always get away with things. He certainly got away with things with his father. And his father apparently got away with things himself."

"So nothing that happened later surprised you."

"Up to a point, no. But then I lost touch. The last time I saw Jackie, I had taken my bride to the Garden for a game in the winter of 1960, and there he was in the lobby of the main entrance standing next to a young man I had tried desperately to recruit for Kent—Connie Hawkins. I hadn't seen Jackie for about seven years. I introduced my wife and asked him how he was doing. 'Great. I'm doing very well,' he said. 'I'm making a lot of money.'"

*   *   *   *   *

"There's absolutely no truth to that."

This is Bob Sassone, speaking on the phone to Jesse from his home in Olean, New York, where he'd settled after a fine college career with the Bonnies. He is a teacher and guidance counselor as well as part-time assistant basketball coach. He, too, remembers the game very well.

"It was a good, close game, but we were a slightly better team that day, on all-around balance and depth."

Sassone is modest about his own play, but acknowledges the great pride he took in being named to an all-city first team that year, along with Mickey Hannon, Johnny Rucker, Ray Felix, and Jack Molinas.

"Didn't you know he was a gambler?"

"No—and I knew him too well not to know if he was."

Sassone was never a gambler himself. He spent his life around amateur athletics. He could accurately be called a sportsman.

"Remember Cozzi?"

"Sure. When we started up, he was *the* player in the playground."

"But you didn't know Jack was betting with him?"

"I thought his father's place, the Eagle Bar, was a gambling place—but *never* Jack. Oh, once in a while we'd stop into the pool hall on 29th Street where we knew there was betting. And we were all aware of betting on basketball games during the summer in the Catskills. Then there was nickel-and-dime gambling at the so-called social athletic clubs. There was a lot of it around—but never Jack that I knew."

"Then what happened later must have shocked you?"

"Yes. You know, I almost went to visit him when he was at Attica. It's not that far. But then I worried about a school teacher's reputation, and I didn't."

"Do you have any idea why he did it?"

"Well, he always had the moxie to do anything. But the key was that he was bored with anything that didn't challenge his mind."

*   *   *   *   *

Barry Storick is an attorney practicing in Charlotte, North Carolina. He stayed on at Washington and Lee for law school after his undergraduate basketball days were over. And he never came back north for more than short visits. In conversation from his office, he generously suggests to Jesse a number of people who might talk about Molinas. He obviously enjoys talking about basketball, is quite expansive with his memories, but when it comes to matters of impropriety or illegality he is briefly dismissive, sounding like, well, a lawyer.

"Do you remember the basketball games in Leon Kaiser Park?"

"Very well."

"How about the gambling?"

"I was never aware of any of it."

"Did you know that Molinas and some of his friends were betting on games?"

"No. I was a few years behind them, never really a part of that crowd."

"The scandals must have shocked you then?"

"I never could understand how they could have done what they did."

"And Jack Molinas?"

"He was brilliant. He could have made a great success. I never could understand why he turned out that way."

PART III:
Matriculation

Chapter 8:
Roar Lion Cubs

L ivingston Hall at Columbia is part of a row of dormitories along Amsterdam Avenue between West 114th and West 116th Streets. For Molinas it's a short walk across the quad, past the Low Memorial Library to where the bus is leaving from West 120th Street to take the freshman basketball team to Princeton. After winning their first six games, Columbia lost one, just three days ago, to Manhattan, and most people can't understand it.

What Molinas can't understand is what freshman coach Dave Furman is up to, or for that matter what varsity coach Gordon Ridings has in mind for him. He knows what is obvious to all, that he is the best player on the team, whether he plays center or forward, but about a dozen kids are getting equal playing time. Even two of his classmates at Stuyvesant are playing as much as he is, and he's the one that carried them to the PSAL finals.

Molinas has started only one of the seven games, but he is still the highest scorer. In the last win he came off the bench to score 25, making a last-second lefthand hook shot to send the game into overtime. The Columbia *Spectator* has begun to call him "Big Mo" and they praise his rebounding and passing. The report of the Fordham game, which Molinas did not start but led with 22 points, says, "Mo ...didn't seem to work up a sweat," while against Rutgers he "amused the crowd with a keen exhibition of passing." In the loss to Manhattan, he had had his first bad game, picking up four fouls and a lot of bench time, but he smiled to himself in satisfaction that no one got on him for it.

On this dank mid-February day, Molinas is making an effort not to dwell on these matters. As usual he is looking forward to the game, to playing, but there is the nagging thought that the coaches are playing with him. Still, this is Princeton, and he relishes the idea of beating those preppies. Somewhere in his consciousness, too, is the knowledge that Princeton's anti-Semitism is the most overt in the league, though Columbia's quota system is just as restrictive percentage-wise.

On College Walk, as 116th Street is called as it crosses the campus with only pedestrian traffic, another thought slides naturally into Molinas's head. He is hungry and they're not going to get any more to eat until after the game. Aware that he's got a few minutes to spare, he turns abruptly toward Broadway, passes through the gate, and lopes across the street toward the Barnard dorms—already a familiar path. At Louie's he is given immediate service— corned beef not too fat on light rye and coke to go. The sandwich is extra thick; Jack's a good customer, well- known, a pleasure to take care of.

Even though he exchanges loud greetings with half a dozen people, Molinas manages to wolf down the sandwich in five minutes as he walks up Broadway to 120th. At the corner, he is draining the paper container of coke when he sees the bus receding, its exhaust making its earnest, fractional contribution to the Upper West Side pollution.

Molinas is not shocked, hardly even surprised. He thinks, How can they do this to me? But it is an automatic thought, without emotional content, and it is instantly succeeded by a mental shrug: They need me more than I need them.

He checks his watch and confirms the time in a store clock. He is no more than two minutes late now. The bus has left on the dot. Then he laughs to himself at his own joke—Eisenhower's been president of Columbia for a year and a half and already the buses are running like Mussolini's trains.

He shrugs, this time visibly, and heads for the subway, knowing that by the time he gets to Coney there will be a better basketball game in the park than anything he could possibly find at Princeton. It's just a little over a week since he was there last, but he is welcomed as a long-lost prodigal. And there is some challenging play, with Gossett and Storick in action. When word is passed that Molinas is in the schoolyard, half the old Lincoln crowd gathers.

Nobody asks him why he's there, until Cozzi shows up. The bookie knows the freshman schedule, though he doesn't make a line on it. "Been benched for Princeton, Mr. Ivy League?"

"Had something better to do and missed the bus." His leer is meant to suggest a nooner at Barnard, and so it is assumed by most of the players, though some of them are contemptuous of such a choice.

"They don't need you anyway, today."

"I don't need them, but they'll probably lose without me."

"Bet?"

"Sure. Half a buck, pick 'em, but there's no vig on this, Coz, it's man to man."

"You're on."

"You bet I am," says Molinas, and he proceeds to muscle Cozzi down low in the post and flip an easy hook over the frustrated bookie.

*   *   *   *   *

The extra fifty in his pocket next day is just a little icing for Molinas's gloating, but no one on campus sees any change in his attitude. Nor can they tell how annoyed he is when the *Spectator*, no longer calling him Big Mo, turns to pious moralizing: "We certainly would like to see Jack Molinas play against the Army plebes tomorrow, but if he can't make the bus he might as well quit playing ball, regardless of how capable a player he is. ... He had better show some hustle tomorrow on the court as well as in making the bus."

There are four games left on the freshman schedule, and Molinas wishes it were over. Furman doesn't start him against Army, but when Columbia falls behind he turns to him. Jack responds with 27 points, but it is too late—and he gloats about that too. In an easy win against Regis he plays little as a reserve, but he starts the last two games and is high scorer against both Choate and Carteret.

The day after the season's end Molinas reads the *Spectator* only because of a headline that catches his eye: "Gambling Ring Attempts Smashed." It seems that a group of enterprising Columbia students, mostly graduate but including a few undergraduates, had been pooling money to bet on horse races and other sporting events through a bookie in Nevada, only to be warned off by the authority of the Dean.

Molinas enjoys a laugh at this, not only at the naiveté of the report but especially at its emphasis on the fact that the students were not violating any law.

"What do you think of that?" a classmate asks him.

And he says, "What's the matter with our Dean? Doesn't he know that's why they call them 'sporting' events?"

Chapter 9:
Fraternity Brother

Molinas looks out his dorm window and sees Bernice's Chrysler doubleparked in Amsterdam Avenue. "These Japs think they can get away with anything," he says to himself with more sympathy than contempt. Then he gives her another two or three minutes to cool her heels before going down to the lobby.

The heels she's wearing are three-inch jobs and she's dressed to the nines. He looks her up and down with appreciation and approval and walks slowly over to her. She's about to say something, about him being late or not dressed, but his disarming smile makes her pause just long enough for him to speak first.

"I'm sorry, Baby, but something's come up and I can't go with you tonight. Maybe some other time."

Her face clouds over and her eyes threaten rain. This pleases him somehow, perhaps because he expected a temper tantrum. But the whine in her voice is annoying when she does speak.

"It wasn't easy getting these *Kiss Me Kate* tickets, and we have reservations later at the Byline Room."

"Like I said, something's come up. You can go ahead to the show or sell the tickets at the door and make a profit. Either way, I can catch it some other time."

"But I wanted to do it with you, and..."

"And Mabel Mercer will be there forever. We'll do it some other time." He smiles again, knowing that what they'll do another time is something else, and that she knows the same. This thought comes to her, too, and she is mollified, then embarrassed, then angry.

Her face goes into a coy pout that he associates with Japdom and that he detests, so when she starts to say, "Well, promise me that..." he interrupts.

"Listen, I've got to go. Call me day after tomorrow, OK?" As he walks out he can hear the anger in her high-heeled stomp and thinks, "I hope she has a ticket—no, she'd just get it fixed—I hope she's been towed."

So far so good. She didn't even ask what came up, but what it is is a poker game. For months the kids at his fraternity house have been after him to play. They nagged, cajoled, wheedled, and baited, and he's decided that tonight's the night. At first they told him they played nickel-dime and he just laughed at them. Now they've graduated to quarter-half.

The stakes are not attractive to Molinas at all—they're not yet in his league, but he thinks he can teach his TEP brothers a lesson. In effect he intends to punish them for their adulation of him, for the obvious pride they derive from their association with him, for their foolish pleasure in the mere fact of his acceptance of a membership in Tau Epsilon Phi.

He is the seventh hand in the game and it looks all right. They're playing with money, not chips, so it's better for what he has in mind and he can get a good figure on the available take around the table. There are two weak links, Ernie over there and Herb next to him, both with little more than twenty bucks to play with. He concentrates on them. For almost two hours he goes only against them, and only when he's got them locked. They are easy. By 9:30 they're both gone, and no one at the table is aware of what he's been doing.

Stanley comes in to take an empty chair, and he flashes a good-sized roll, maybe two hundred. Everyone else has at least fifty to play with. Molinas has fifty on the table and another eight hundred in his pocket.

He plays his cards automatically. He makes a lot of noise but is quiet in terms of action. It's primarily a seven-card stud high-low game, and he only plays with two or three low cards or a high pair with matching third card. Then he folds if he doesn't improve on the fourth. If he is still in after five cards he pushes to maximum raises. He allows himself to be bluffed out, conspicuously. He gets caught bluffing, conspicuously. All this is an automatic routine. He doesn't care about this game. Without trying he's better than them all, especially Stanley, a chaser who never gets bluffed. But Molinas is setting up another game.

At about eleven he deliberately starts losing. He misplays his cards and calls his hands wrong, complaining loudly about his luck. He carefully loses to whoever has been losing. He wants them all feeling lucky. He loses the forty dollars he's ahead and his fifty-dollar stake, then another fifty. At the same time he begins yawning and slowing down the game. By one o'clock there are four guys up about fifty each, and Stanley's the other loser, out about sixty.

The timing is perfect, Molinas thinks. He says, "Let's gamble a little bit," and pulls out a pair of dice. There are four players feeling it's their lucky night and a sucker who thinks his luck's about to turn to get him even. They go for it. He knew they would.

They set up a rolling area on the floor with a sofa cushion for a backstop, and the crap game is on. Again Molinas is slow and careful. He's in perfect command of this terrain but he is not ready to let anyone know it yet. They're shooting two or five dollars at a time. Sometimes he fades, sometimes bets with the shooter. When the dice are his he shoots just five and doesn't let anything ride. He lays or takes the odds but only on a five buck base.

A few other players drift in from around the house as the news spreads about a dice game and Molinas playing. Everyone wants to see the big man in action. He doesn't mind the audience at all, but he makes it clear that people without money involved should shut up. Occasionally he grins around the room, acknowledging with pleasure the awe and affection he sees directed toward him, and at the same time he is contemptuous of them all.

It's Seymour, one of the late arrivals, who gets the hot hand. Molinas is betting with him at first, not against him. Seymour starts doubling and taking odds on any point he comes out on. He makes five passes and the faders are discouraged. He's got sixty dollars to shoot and no one wants to fade.

Now Molinas throws down the money and says, "Shoot."

Seymour doesn't hesitate. He doesn't care whose money it is. He's hot. His eyes are bugging out of his head, transfixed in a gambler's high. He rolls the transparent red cubes. Molinas reaches out a huge hand and catches them before they hit the cushion.

"No dice," he says.

"What's wrong?" Seymour gasps. He's pissed but confused. Everyone else falls silent.

"I just want to know whether anyone will fade me when I shoot that much. If not, I guess the game is over."

This is the moment of truth for Molinas, not the actual play of the game. The cast has been made. And very quickly the hook is in. A chorus of voices gives assurances. He'll be faded whatever he wants to shoot. Stanley's voice is even louder than Seymour's. His face is glowing a bright red with excitement and he can't stop sucking his teeth. He's holding his roll tightly in his fist—almost back to two hundred now as a result of careful betting—but he's clearly ready to be carried away with the action.

Now it's just a matter of time. Molinas has the bankroll in his pocket. This game is his. Seymour rolls a natural, shoots a hundred. Molinas, testing, covers only thirty. Sure enough, the other players get back in action and the bet is covered. Seymour rolls a four, puts up another fifty for the odds. Molinas lets everyone else take that action, and Seymour craps out.

Less than an hour later the dice heat up in Molinas's own hand. And in fifteen minutes he breaks the game. He's six hundred ahead and offers any part of it, but there's no money left in the room. Stanley has stormed out, and Seymour, looking punchy, has spilled a beer on the sofa. Smitty is the only player left. He'd been winning all night until his own last roll, and then he went broke laying the odds when Molinas made two nines and a five. Now he reaches into his pocket and tosses his car keys on the rug.

"One wheel of the car for three-fifty," he says.

Molinas likes his spirit—and the action. Smitty's Chevy convertible is almost new. He nods, throws, and crows, "E-yo-leven" as the cubes come up six-five.

"Another wheel against the first," says Smitty.

And Molinas comes out eight—six and two, comes right back five and three after chanting, "I eight all night and I eight all day." He's now half owner of a Chevy coupe.

"One more wheel."

He rolls a natural.

There's not a sound in the room. He looks up at Smitty who has lost all the color in his face. Smitty gulps, twice, and nods.

Molinas throws craps, ace-deuce.

Smitty grimaces in a tight half-grin and offers, "Both wheels now."

And Molinas craps out after rolling a six.

The game is over. Everybody is relieved. They wonder whether Molinas would really have taken a fraternity brother's car. He just smiles when they ask him. But they never invite him to play in their poker games again, and they never kid him about not gambling with them.

Chapter 10:
As in a Dream

For many years, in many ways, Jesse was asked the question, "What happened to you in college?" And the best answer he could give, in one form or another, was, "I don't really know."

What was clear was that for four years at Dartmouth he studiously avoided the academic distinction that had marked him as unusual before college and then again in graduate school. But there was no pinpointing a clarity in the pattern of activity and experience that filled the time. It flew by; he drifted with it. To form a narrative of it, he would have to invent transitions—between drunks, between games, between girls, between gambling escapades.

He took profound delight in gambling and had elaborate rationalizations for it. Here was a game of transcendent competition, in which smartness could make you a winner. You invested a part of yourself, your stake, paying for the privilege of using your wits (or testing your luck—in either case part of your human essence) against the odds. If you were right (or lucky) you multiplied your stake and experienced an exaltation of ego. You were potent, stronger than fate in wisdom, above inexorable forces of nature and therefore—in a sense, for a moment—immortal. If you lost, you still had the excitement of the action, never mind the nifty ways of externalizing any sense of inadequacy or insecurity. There were things much worse than losing, like not playing. In a nutshell, to gamble was to feel alive.

So there was a seemingly endless round of poker games,

not only in Hanover but in Boston, Providence, New Haven, Storrs, and Philadelphia, punctuated by sudden outbursts of crap games and spontaneous jaunts to race tracks. In steady counterpoint there was also an inexhaustible supply of sporting events to bet on, and Jesse took great pride in—to use a favorite phrase of Jack Molinas—his "good opinion."

Among the transient images that flash on his memory-screen, making Jesse's collegiate career a dream-like phantasm, is one of him ending a Winter Carnival weekend by directing traffic at the Inn Corner late Sunday afternoon, conducting like an Italian maestro, not at all helping the tangled traffic jam but at least making some of the jammed laugh. Another has him in the dorm shower, sitting sprawled out, too drunk to stand, grinning up at the nozzle and thankful for the hot water supply that is a major blessing of Ivy League education.

In that same shower room, Jesse and his friend Jim conceived a fronton, inventing a game of jai alai, with rolled-up magazines as cestas (*Life* had the best size and flexibility, but *Fortune* had the most clout) and a squash ball as a pelota. They climbed the side wall for scoop shots, went to the floor for the *rebote*, and made so much noise that they were threatened with a quiniela of eviction and expulsion.

Jim along with Wayne and Mitch also invented hallwall-ball, a better game, actually, but more annoying and even noisier because it was played more often for longer periods. With a tennis ball that had to hit both walls on every shot and unlimited width on the court, that is, with the whole corridor in play, hallwallball was public nuisance number one in the dorm.

Inside their own room, Jesse and Mitch worked up the best game of all. With rare absence of invention they just called it the room game. On top of a small bookcase sat the familiar maroon portable Webcor phonograph. A small inverted lamp shade was centered on the closed cover of the phonograph, but back almost against the wall, maybe a half inch out, forming a target to shoot at with a ping-pong ball batted or stroked or guided with a rubber-surface ping-pong paddle. You got only one bounce on the floor but every other surface in the room was in play. The beauty of the room game was that only two could play; indeed Jesse and Mitch are the only two who did. It was uniquely suited to their matchup. They could go for hours, nearly silent, without completing a game.

Anything would suffice, it seemed, as long as it passed the time and kept him from any serious or sustained thinking, reading, studying, learning. Little if any coherence emerges from these fragments, but there are two episodes that may demonstrate what Jesse thought of as "the way we were."

* * * * *

On a brilliant late-October Saturday in Ithaca, Jesse made his television debut. The drive from Hanover had been, as it always was whenever he traveled from anywhere to Ithaca, longer than it looked on the map. There was not much hope that Dartmouth would beat Cornell, but by game time that didn't seem to matter much. Associations of autumn and dying elude him in the mingling pageantries of foliage and football. It would be decades before he started singing "September Song" or understood the symbolic slaughter of this sport.

For the moment the color and brightness of the day exhilarated him beyond normal breath. He was sharpening the day, obliterating the prospect of defeat, and bracing himself with another indirect lift from his mother. Her going-away-

to-college present for him was a smartly initialed pint flask
from Mark Cross. Now every weekend he ritually filled it
with martinis, eight to one and chilled, but with no ice getting into the flask. By Sunday afternoon what was left
would be potently warm, but he was usually past caring
after mid-Saturday, and small sips sustained the smart
oblivion of his not-caring.

Dartmouth was losing. Clayton was having a bad day, but
this large elegant man nevertheless exemplified T-forma-
tion quarterbacking at its best. More than a field general he
was a field hero, deft and demanding, clever and quick and
strong. To the skills of the game he brought a larger-than-
life artfulness. So even in crushing defeat he inspired Jesse's exultant refrain of cheering: "Time for one more pass,
Johnny." He'd been known to reprise this cry hours after a
game was over, down the bricks of Back Bay or across the
motley stones around Nassau Hall.

Cornell won 28-13, but the score failed to register the
total domination. As the undersized Big Green moved
toward a final, meaningless score, Jesse was moving with
equal determination toward the field. As his team went for
the goal line he made his decision to go for a piece of the
goalpost.

Dartmouth scored. Jesse edged toward the sideline.
Maybe a hundred others had the same idea. Cornell ran out
the clock. At the gun the small mob sprinted in a massed
post pattern. Dozens of hands grabbed each upright and
started rocking. Jesse had a stratagem to dupe his enemy
hosts. "For Russell Sage," he cried disingenuously, invoking
the name of his dorm in Hanover, which also happened to
be the name of a girls' school in Troy, familiar to most
Cornellians.

The goal resisted stubbornly. A couple of leapers went
for the crossbar and missed, but he saw that as the way to

bring the quarry to earth. A loutish face full of Big Red acne leered toward him and shouted, "Let's lift this little guy up." Up he went, locking arms around the bar, while the crowd tugged at his legs to topple the trophy. It was a wonderful feeling. He was at what they call the point of attack. He was the focus, the fulcrum, the cynosure. He was not the weakest link: the goalposts began to give. But before anything else came down, his pants did. And it was at this instant that he realized that the game was on regional television, that if the director was no nitwit he'd have a camera on this scene, and just as the whole thing fell Jesse caught sight of the sideline camera with its acknowledging red light beaconing toward him, and as he fell into the crowd, still clutching the crossbar, he grinned directly in closeup into the astonished faces of his parents back home in the den of their New Haven apartment. It was the first recorded occasion of the "Hi, Mom" greeting on TV, and you could look it up.

*   *   *   *   *

Running a streak of bad luck, Jesse has drawn low card for the blind dates at Skidmore. He had promised to fix his old friend Sissy up with a Dartmouth man (turns out to be George), while she finds a date for him. It got complicated when Jim and Wayne wanted to come along, but Sissy, ever a good sport, lined up two other girls. Jim and Wayne were both lucky, ending up with attractive, pleasant, appealingly sharp girls. Jesse drew Sissy's Hawaiian roommate.

He has nothing against Hawaiians, supports statehood and all that, but this one's no hula dancer. She's short, squat, built like a grass shack rather than for a grass skirt. Her name has been playfully shortened to Mitzi-Pitzi, but to him she's Muttsy-Puttsy. Sissy confides that she's a wonderful roommate, outgoing, easygoing, thorough-goingly kind. But with Jesse she's defensive, belligerent, playing oriental Beatrice to his smartass Benedick or slant-eyed Martha to his big-nosed George.

Skidmore made a virtue of necessity by having private homes near the campus converted into minidorms, saving a fortune in capital outlay and providing a healthy environ-ment for the girls. But the greatest advantage of being in Saratoga Springs was the largest density of saloons per capita this side of the Continental Divide. The idea on a Skidmore date was to hit as many bars as possible before curfew, 1 A.M. on Saturday night for underclass girls.

Barely five in the afternoon, the four couples have crowd-ed into Jim's Plymouth. Jesse knows it's going to be a long, long night, so he makes a deliberate, prudent decision not to be a rocket man as far as the drinking's concerned. What he'll do is drink beer. He never gets drunk on beer. His small stomach fills up too fast for his head to be affected, and his bladder capacity is disproportionately great. But he has never given it a Saratoga Springs test with a dog of a date and a bad luck streak to wallow in.

They make the rounds of cafes and bistros, getting a meal somewhere along the way, hearing some music, danc-ing a little, and Jesse is straining both capacity and creduli-ty with the beer he's putting away. Conscious of the rest of his party trying to enjoy themselves, he does a lot of table-hopping wherever they go. Some of it is obnoxious, some comic, some absurd, some just pathetic.

In one place he gets nasty with a guy at the bar who is ready to take a swing at him. He backs up and squares off James Cagney style, and there materializes around him a whole company of dark green blazers. Dartmouth men stick together, at least in places like Saratoga Springs. There is no fight.

In the lounge of a restaurant he comes upon Roger Pierce, a journeyman player on a mediocre Dartmouth basketball team. "Hey, Rodge, how's the Dodge?" Jesse says. They've never talked before, but they are both wearing the big green so Pierce acts friendly.

"Who's the toughest player in the league, I just want to ask you that one question, Roger. Who's the best you've had to face?" Jesse is drunk enough to sound like a stupid sportscaster.

"Jack Molinas" is the answer, right on cue.

From that moment Pierce becomes one of the cleverest of players in Jesse's eyes, a genuine basketball maven, making up in sharpness what he lacks in physical skills. Before this revelation makes him maudlin, he feels Jim tapping his shoulder.

"Come on, Jesse. It's time to go."

"Already? I was just getting to like it here."

"We've got to get the girls back by one, and it's a quarter of."

"Time sure does fly when..."

"Yeah. C'mon."

"Speaking of fly, I've got to go before we go."

"We don't have time. Curfew, you know, curfew. We've got to leave right now."

Jesse grits his teeth, which feel like they're about to float away, and piles into the car with the rest. He is in the back, pressed up close to Muttsy-Puttsy, and feeling fresh out of hostility for her now that it's over. He grins at her. She looks glumly back, then laughs a little. But as the car rolls toward the campus the bladder pressure builds past the danger point.

"Jim, you've got to stop. I can't hold it."

The whole group roars back at him a jumbled chorus of encouragement and refusal and anxiety.

"Can't stop," Jim says. "We'll barely make curfew as it is."

Jesse works up his most desperate voice and earnest look as he says to his date, "If you don't get him to stop, Mitzi, I'll have to pitzi in your pocket."

"You do," she says, mimicking his own mock-oriental dialect, "and I give you such a judo chop you wish you never survive Pearl Harbor."

He knows that if he laughs, as everyone else is doing, he'll never hold it in. He bites his lip and hangs on, seeking some suspension of time. Jim hurries, running a couple of red lights, but pulls up in front of the girls' house with a minute to spare. Jesse's three friends and the four girls pour out of the car and join the crowd at the door.

He is immobile, curled up, knees tight, whole body aching for release. He knows he can't move. And then he knows that he can't *not* move. He unwinds out the door, stumbles onto the front lawn, assumes the wide stance, unzips, fishes out, and casts his water in a delicious, steaming, interminable high arc. The pleasure is extreme. He looks up in his ecstasy and girls are crowded into all the front windows watching the spectacle. Some are applauding, others holding hands over faces, but whether in horror or mirth he'll never know.

What he does know is that the whole scene will be instantly fixed in his memorybook, like an emblem of that whole time. The light from the front door gives almost a spotlight effect on his face. The girls' heads are lovely, backlit by the lights in their rooms, shining hair framing soft-focused faces. The other boys are an unseen or unidentifiable presence, grouped in the walk in front of the door or dispersing to their cars. All the light is picked up in sparkling points along that gleaming arc as, gloriously, eternally, he pisses his youth away on the Skidmore lawn, and the only sound is an endless a cappella "aah."

*   *   *   *   *

The attitudes revealed in these fragments, welling up
like unconscious drives from a dreamer's id, would in time
be acknowledged, adjusted, and rejected. But Jesse was
oblivious at the time, stumbling unfocusedly through the
wasted collegiate years. And at the end, still unconcerned
about the future or about a larger context in which it would
be lived, he had found a false focus in his pursuit of the elusive Rachel.

Chapter 11:
Good Clean Fun

I t is exam week at Columbia, the end of May in New York. The spring has been cold and damp. Now, suddenly, two days before Memorial Day, it is summer. Everything comes off—clothes, wraps, the lids on tension, whatever it is that inhibits irrational behavior in the face of frustration and repression and demands for mature behavior in the emotionally immature.

The seventh floor of Livingston is bedlam. Everything is going out the windows into Amsterdam Avenue—pillows, cushions, even mattresses. All the good clean fun of a riot.

Molinas sits in an oasis of calm in his room. He has refused to take part in the horseplay, calling it horseshit. His door is locked against the insistent attempts of his neighbors to draw him in. Exams have nothing to do with his attitude. All he's studying is his scorn.

As he thinks back over the whole academic year he begins to realize the extent of his contempt. Here he is at one of the world's most respected universities, and in the fall everyone is occupied for weeks with the freshman-sophomore rush, complete with queens and abductions. What horseshit.

Here's the university's president saying no to Tom Dewey's request that he run for President on the Republican ticket. Ike says that service to Columbia "offers such an individual as myself rich opportunities for serving America." More horseshit. Two months later Ike was on leave to head NATO and would never resign from Columbia until after being elected President of the United States.

The basketball season itself, with all its triumphs, was a mixed blessing. Columbia went undefeated through 22 games but lost to Illinois in the NCAA tournament, was ranked either third or fifth in the country, depending on which poll you read. Molinas himself was the star of the team, its leading scorer and rebounder, frequently mentioned on All-America lists. Yet he played in the shadow of senior John Azary, a lesser player, but consistent, reliable, and not smart enough to know when to make a bet. Molinas didn't even start in seven of their games, while Azary, Bob Reiss, and Al Stein started them all.

Before the season began, Coach Ridings was saying, "Jack Molinas can be a great ballplayer, but he has a lot to learn." Molinas thought he could teach the coach a few things. Ridings, however, spent most of the season in the hospital, and it was Rossini who made Molinas a regular starter at center and told *Newsweek*, "He's the one who makes our fast break work." Molinas liked what the man said, and he believed old Lou knew more than he said.

Back at his desk in March, Ridings said, "Molinas is potentially one of the greatest players here ever, offensively." The "potentially" gave Molinas a laugh: he knew he already was. No first-year player ever scored so much (never mind the average per minutes played), and the team had the best record ever in the history of Columbia sports. And his rebounds exceeded his points. So why did they begrudge him? Why didn't he get his due? The only break he ever got was permission for a girlfriend from Barnard or his little friend Sharon from home to watch practice sessions at University Hall. He was doing more for them than they were doing for him, he was sure of that, and he believed he was entitled to do something for himself.

Of course the scandal had clouded over the whole basketball season. But what horseshit was coming out of Columbia while most of the other New York schools were being investigated if not implicated. He heard that Cardinal Spellman was intervening on behalf of the Catholic schools, and he chalked that up to business-as-usual in New York.

Poor Sherman White, maybe the only kid in the area who could play on his level (except for a seven-foot freak like Walter Dukes), was out of basketball, and they were issuing pious crap like: "We consider the NIT a commercial enterprise which invites the scandals we try to avoid."

But the NCAA is OK? What a joke. They think the Ivy League is above it all. Even when he was a freshman he knew he could do business with the gamblers any time he wanted. Now Ralph Furey is saying, "Our policy of playing games in college gyms was set for the purpose of avoiding just what has come to light in the last few weeks." Don't Athletic Directors know that it's not where you play the game that matters but how much action you can get on the point spread?

The only one he's heard without horseshit all year was J. Edgar Hoover just last month, fingering all the "hypocrisy and sham." He blamed the colleges for violating their own athletic codes in handing out workless jobs, outright gifts, and summer jobs to kids for the express purpose of getting them to play football and basketball. The colleges are not creating the proper atmosphere for rejecting bids from gamblers, Hoover said, while Molinas thought, No, and they're not re-creating a just world either, so people will keep on taking what they want if they think they can get away with it.

The rioting subsides but the weather stays warm and Molinas's contempt thrives. The next night several dorm-mates barge into his room, taunting him as the big basketball star, too big for his friends, afraid to have fun, too good to take part in whatever's happening. "How come, Big Jack, how come?" Their ragging becomes a chant.

"How come, Big Jack, how come?"

"I'll tell you why. Because it's stupid, that's why. You think it's smart to throw things out the window? I'll show you how much smarts it takes." He picks up a glass of water from his desk and throws it out the open window, saying, "Big deal."

Two sounds come up from the street, a light splintering crash and a slight gasping cry. He looks out the window as the other boys scatter. The glass has hit a parked car and done no apparent damage, but an old man is looking up toward the window, his hand feeling the top of his head where the water must have splashed him, his other arm comforting the old woman who is huddled against him in fear.

In the Dean's office the next day Molinas is surprised that he has been found out. His victims were Professor Mark Van Doren and his wife. He is more than surprised that the almost innocent prank is going to cost him a six-month suspension. He can't understand it. Why are they zeroing in on him? Aren't there more important things than making an example of Jack Molinas? Why aren't they out mourning the death of Fanny Brice or something?

His so-called friends in the dorm must have ratted on him, the same guys who love to bask in his popularity. All their intellectual and cultural pretensions go out the window, like their mattresses, when they can be seen in public with the athletic hero all New York knows and loves. And now he alone has to bear the burden of offense for the whole seventh floor of Livingston. This is an injustice he'll neither forget nor forgive, and he smiles in spite of himself at thoughts of how he'll get even with them all. Later, the suspicion grows, planted and nourished by his Coney cronies (and tacitly supported by Joe Hacken's noncommittal silence on the matter), that Columbia was really out to get him because they believed he was shaving points. Some paranoia here? Surely no guilt. But Molinas knows he can be phony with the best of them.

He puts on a good front, and the press and public eat it up. He says he will work in the defense effort at Grumman Aircraft, but what he does is odd jobs at resort hotels in Florida, through connections of his father, and he takes very good care of himself. When he comes back for the spring semester, tan and healthy, he's ready to play basketball for Columbia while making it pay for Jack Molinas.

And he's inordinately proud of the humble statement he makes: "I am eager to make up for my pointless action. I am deeply sorry for what I've done and am looking forward to returning to the team and all my friends at Columbia." He alone is aware of all the irony in that; he especially admires his choice of the words "pointless" and "action." Molinas has learned. He has jumped in up to his neck in the horseshit, and he's murmuring with the rest of the world, "Don't make waves."

Chapter 12:
Crusader
Games

Molinas was back, primed to play basketball and primed to play other games as well. During his suspension Columbia had struggled to a record of eight wins and five losses, with the hard part of the schedule ahead of them. What a comedown for a team that had gone undefeated the previous season. Without Azary, who had graduated, and Molinas, they lacked rebounding, scoring, and most of all coherence or cohesion. In "Dunkel's Cage Ratings" published daily in the *Journal-American* (Molinas loved the irony in the daily disclaimer that "the ratings are not helpful as, nor to be construed as, nor used as, gambling information") Columbia was listed at 63.6, not even in the top ten in the region—after being third in the nation last year.

But on the night of February 6th, the Lions were a different team. They blew Brown out of their own gym in Providence 95-75. Molinas scored 27, but more important, with his rebounding, ballhandling and speed, he got the team's fast break into high gear for the first time all season. They could have broken a hundred easily if Lou Rossini had kept his starters in.

After the team had gone back to the Biltmore in the center of town, just down the hill from the Brown campus, and been given their post-game food money, most of them went to stuff themselves with burgers. They only had a short time before curfew—they had an early rise and bus trip to

Worcester next morning. But Molinas called room service for his meal and then placed a collect call to the Bronx at precisely 11:01. He was not calling his parents at home. The number was a pay phone and the call was to "anyone" from "Mr. Lyons." Joey Hacken was on the other end to accept it.

"Congratulations."

"Thanks."

"How do you feel?"

"Great. It's exactly as I thought. The whole thing is different with me in there; it all revolves around me—I have complete control."

"Calm down, will you?"

"I've never been so up. We went to the Hummocks this afternoon for dinner and I could hardly eat. When have you ever seen that?" The Molinas laugh was raucous but so open sometimes as to be infectious.

Hacken joined in, then said, "You might be interested in an item from Milton Gross's column in the Post today: 'Basketball betting is reviving. There is considerable action now on NBA games.' "

Molinas's laugh turned to a sneering snicker and he said, "Now isn't that a disgrace?"

"Here's another laugh. Howie Dallmar says Ernie Beck could start for any team in the pros."

"Beck couldn't carry my jock in the pros."

"Well, before you get too carried away, he only scored 45 against Harvard tonight, new league record."

"Probably got 'em all on fouls."

"Well, he did tie Lavelli's 17 for 19 free throws."

"See."

"But that's still fourteen field goals."

"Against Harvard."

"They're better than Brown."

"What about Holy Cross?"

Hacken paused. Fun-and-games time was over. This was business.

"OK, here's the story. The early line is 4 or 4-1/2. After what you did tonight, it'll go to 5 or more."

"Wait a minute. They're 13 and 2 and they'll be playing at home. Why are we favored?"

"You think everyone's so dumb? They got no size. Quickness but no size. You've got both. They haven't played anybody, just patsies. And they just got knocked off by Canisius, for Chrissake."

"Yeah, everybody is dumb. We rubbed it in on Brown tonight because we were sky high. The whole team was bloodthirsty. We knew we'd win. We were smelling it all week. But Holy Cross is a good team, and we'll get tired tomorrow."

"All the better for us. You get five big ones to make sure you don't win by more than five, OK? If the line is anything but five points, I'll let you know."

"You gonna be there?"

"No, but if you want half up front I can arrange it."

Molinas laughed again. "I don't want anything up front. Just bet it for me."

"What?"

"You're a bookmaker, aren't you? Give me five dimes on Holy Cross plus five."

"You got it."

Molinas went out on the court in Worcester with Hacken's last line playing like music in his head, and his whole spirit was singing a response—"and if you got it, flaunt it." He easily won the opening tap, controlling the ball into Bob Reiss's hands, then broke for the basket, getting a return pass from Reiss and driving past Earle Markey for a layup. On the Crusaders' first possession they worked the ball into young

Togo Palazzi at the baseline. Molinas went up to intimidate
the shooter, then wheeled to rebound the short shot and
dribbled the length of the court. Bob McLaren cut him off in
the lane, so he planted his right foot, pivoted away on the
left, and swished a hook shot.

That's the way it went throughout the first half. Molinas
was all over the court, playing in a kind of controlled frenzy,
as if he could do no wrong, and apparently without thinking
about what he was doing. It's what a ballplayer means when
he says "unconscious" without an insulting inflection, or
what a tennis player means by being "in the zone." It is like
the application of Zen to athletic activity. Only in this case,
all *this* was just the appearance. The reality was that
Molinas was thinking about everything.

He was playing three games at once. There was the game
of basketball, which he loved with as much intensity and
depth as anything in his life. There was the betting game, a
game of wits in which he was matching his opinion against
the public's and moving numbers around in the confident
belief that his opinion was best and in which he was always
looking for an edge. And there was the game of control, in
which he juggled appearance and reality according to his
own vision, playing to the hilt the conflicting roles of star for
one team and mastermind of the other team's victory. He
saw himself as a kind of creative artist, composer and performer, taking all the risks and fearing no punishment.

He genuinely felt he could do anything that night and not
only get away with it but get praised for it, with the ultimate
pleasure of being the only one who knew just what he was
doing. There wasn't the slightest twinge about selling out
his team, because he felt he owed Columbia nothing after
what they'd done to him. And yet he was doing all he could
to help them and redeem himself in the eyes of the world.

Playing the game this way—fast and clean and smart—

was what made basketball so appealing to Molinas. Strength mattered, but not roughness, and quickness of mind most of all. Columbia was maintaining its lead throughout the half, but Molinas, piling up points and pride in his performance, could see Holy Cross beginning to make adjustments that would turn the game around in time. That was perfect for him. He could go on doing his best for Columbia and for Molinas and still win the bet he had made on the other team.

At halftime Holy Cross trailed 40-34, and Molinas had 23 points. In the locker room he couldn't help beaming. His teammates and Coach Rossini were exhilarated, thinking they shared the star's good feelings. They couldn't have known that what was giving him the greatest satisfaction was his certainty that the Crusaders would come back and win the game, no matter what he did. As he saw it, their superiority in the backcourt would be decisive in the second half.

Their coach, Doggy Julian's successor, Buster Sheary, made a good adjustment for the second half. He wasn't going to allow one man to beat his team. First he shut off the fast break by attacking the offensive boards with at least two players, so that even when Molinas rebounded he could not bring the ball upcourt himself. Then in the half-court defense he double-teamed Molinas inside by fronting him with McDonough or O'Neill while Palazzi or Markey dropped in behind.

Columbia's answer to this strategy was vintage basketball. If anyone is double-teamed, someone is open. As Dave Bing says, you take something away and you have to give something up. Molinas and Al Stein started hitting the open man, usually Reiss, and Reiss responded with five straight baskets. Columbia's lead after three periods was 58-53, and they ran it to 68-60 with four and a half minutes to play.

Still Molinas was unshaken in his confidence about his

opinion, his bet, his deal with Hacken. He could see his teammates tiring badly and feel his own strength fading. And then the Crusaders' brilliant young guard Ron Perry took over the game. He stole the ball twice and set up Palazzi for fast-break baskets, hit an open jumper himself, and worked the ball patiently to hit Markey on a back-door play. Holy Cross had the lead with thirty seconds to play, 72-71, but Columbia had the ball and called time out.

Molinas wanted the ball. With the five-point spot, his bet was safe, so he wanted to go ahead and try to win the game with a basket. But Rossini, figuring Holy Cross would be looking for Molinas to take the shot, called a play for Reiss. Molinas would pop out to the high post. If he were open for a pass he would get it and then give it off to Reiss who would be cutting behind him. Otherwise, assuming Molinas would be double-teamed so that he couldn't get a pass, Stein would go directly to Reiss on the wing for a drive or set shot.

The play never got going. At ten seconds, when Molinas made his move from low to high post, he was fouled without the ball, at that time strictly a one-shot foul. So Molinas went to the line, but Sheary called a time out to let him think about it. Molinas had something else on his mind. He had an image of Joey Hacken sitting by a radio, probably with some of his business associates, listening to the game, and sweating more than the players. The only way he could lose his sure thing now was an overtime period in which Columbia could cover the spread. But Molinas was in his pocket so he would miss the free throw. And yet Molinas had personally made the game as close as it was.

Joe Hacken had been his mentor back in the Bronx and had first told him about a fixed basketball game way back in 1938, when Jackie at seven hadn't even started to play. He had watched Hacken begin to move on the fringe of the

Frankie Carbo fight mob, where he was known as Joe Jalop and appreciated as a stand-up guy with savvy. Jack had learned a lot of what he knew about odds and angles in gambling from Joe, and had turned around and made it pay off for him in Coney. But sometimes Hacken had chosen to trick him and tease him as an object lesson. He'd learned his lessons well—as Cozzi and Shlombo could testify—but it was the occasional indirection of the teacher that he thought of now.

So now Molinas had yet a fourth game to play, jerking Hacken around in a delicious torment. And he knew he could enjoy playing it to the hilt without fear of losing the other games. Hacken was going to clean up, but Molinas was going to make him sweat for the profits. With perfect aplomb and utter arrogance he went to the line and swished the shot.

The Columbia bench and their few fans let out a great cheer, and Molinas laughed to himself at his picture of Hacken's apoplectic rage. If he could write the scenario himself he would have Columbia win now, by just exactly four points in overtime. But he knew that the game was really out of reach for the exhausted Lions. He had prolonged the agony and covered himself with glory. He was a quadruple winner, as he saw it, but his team would lose.

And so they did. Molinas controlled the tap but Perry stepped in front of Reiss to steal the ball. In two and a half minutes Perry had three assists and a basket, while Columbia managed just one point, for an 80-73 Holy Cross lead. The final score was 85-80.

It was 11:30 before Molinas reached Hacken at a different pay phone. This time the call was collect from Mr. Hitchcock, and Hacken accepted it, though Molinas knew the name meant nothing to him. In honor of his 39 points, Molinas had made an allusion to one of his favorite movies,

The 39 Steps. But Hacken was in no mood for playing any kind of trivial pursuits.

"You son of a bitch. Are you a wise guy or what? Were you trying to cross me?"

"What's the matter, Buddy?"

"What's the matter? I bet my lungs on this game, on your word, and you tried to beat my brains in."

"I had to make it look good, didn't I?"

"Not that good. You could have missed that foul shot."

"No, Joe, I couldn't. I just couldn't miss. But I also knew we couldn't win."

"You really are a wise guy. Well, let me tell you something, wise guy, you're too wise for your own good. If you think I'm gonna pay you for what you did up there tonight, forget it."

"Wait a minute, Mister. I never said I wouldn't play well. I just guaranteed you we wouldn't win by five. And we didn't. You won, didn't you?" The silence was punctuated by some agitated breathing and then a couple of snorts. Molinas cherished the moment; he had never heard of Hacken getting this mad before. And then he added, "Well, so did I."

"That's right, you won. But it's not worth it if you make me lose my credibility—and yours too—while you're at it."

"But it's my credibility on the court that really matters, see. It's results that count as far as you and your credibility are concerned. How I bring them about is my business. So why get pissed? It's like we found the money tree. We're in business, man. You can have my cash ready tomorrow and we'll talk about another game, because you can be sure of one thing. I can do anything out there, and I can get away with everything. This is perfect, because no one can know."

Molinas was a hero in the press the next day. They talked about his "tremendous 39-point scoring spree" and his "one-man scoring show." Molinas loved what the *Post* said: "Columbia has a tremendous basketball player in Jack Molinas, but even Coach Lou Rossini today was willing to admit that the recently returned star can't carry the entire load." He also loved the feel of ten big ones in the envelope that Hacken handed him as they ate their corned beef sandwiches at Louie's.

"Did you read Dan Parker in the *Mirror* today?" the bookie asked. "Claims there's still considerable worry about fixing basketball games. He drummed up something from that pompous old windbag from Kansas, Phog Allen, who says that if things go on the way they're going, there's likely to be fixes on high school basketball games."

"Now who would ever believe something like that?" said Molinas. "What public would accept the proposition that there's enough action at that level to justify a fix?"

Hacken missed the irony in that, maybe because there was so much food in Molinas's mouth he couldn't see the tongue in his cheek. He answered with a sincerity that was almost an innocent scolding.

"The trouble with you, Jack, is you think too big. There's kids today who'd throw a game for ten bucks and a piece of ass."

Molinas laughed and shouted for another sandwich. He was on top of the world, at the top of his games. It was true that he thought at a higher level than other people. He was getting what he deserved, whether he earned it or not. He had neither a fear of punishment nor a qualm of scruple. And he never had to do anything to get laid, not even ask.

"Hate to eat and run, Joe, but someone's been waiting for me."

Hacken watched him go, a smile of satisfaction on his face that said something like "That's my boy." And in his eyes a wistful look expressed the kind of phony nostalgia that serves as cosmetic for those who only live vicariously in the size, the skill, and the beauty of others. For those to whom the trophies, the pleasure-winnings, never come easy if they come at all, the cosmetic of nostalgia is the only way to cover or color their envy.

Chapter 13:
The Draft and the Artful Dodger

Sleeping with Patsy Flynn moved Molinas way up in class as a gamesman, if not a cocksman. He had noticed her first on the bright winter day when he held a news conference outside the draft board office. His picture made the back pages of the *Mirror* and the *Post* that day—the basketball star, eager to postpone his career in order to serve his country in the armed forces, ironically had been declared ineligible because, at 6' 6 1/4", he was too tall.

Molinas made a big point of talking with the press about his ambition to be a fighter pilot in Korea. His vision was equal to Ted Williams', he said, and his reflexes and judgment were equal to anyone's. It was perfectly safe to go on about this, because there was no chance that any of the services would take him. The truth was that he had no intention of putting on any uniform but a basketball one, but he had an instinct for image and loved any media attention—especially from an elegant young blonde in a rich fur jacket who took no notes and asked no questions, just stared at him with a half-smile.

Then she had started showing up at the press table at Columbia games. By the time she asked for an interview, near the end of the season, Molinas had checked around about her. Pat Flynn was just three years out of college. She had finessed journalism school and gone straight to a job at the Wall Street *Journal* with no credentials but her dazzling ability to interview. But the routine of daily assign-

ments had been tedious, though her byline appeared far
more often than recent Columbia J-School graduates, so
after a year she had quit to go freelance.

She was formidably ambitious and had already acquired
a reputation not only for a startling streak of successful
magazine features but also for her willingness to do anything to get assignments and stories—including sleeping
with editors and subjects alike. But her copy was clean, her
style distinctive, and her respect for space limitations and
deadlines thoroughly professional.

She now had a contract to do several features for *Look,*
and she had an idea that one of them would be on Jack
Molinas.

"May I call you Jack?"

"Sure, Patsy."

"No one's called me that since I was a freshman. The
contract and byline say 'Pat'."

"Good, then Patsy will be my special name for you."

He grinned into her grimace, which she managed to turn
into a smile. She already figured she was going to have to
take this big jock home to bed, and she was going to try to
enjoy it.

They were both sipping scotch in a bar not far down
Broadway from the Columbia campus, close enough for
most of the people there to recognize him. But Flynn appeared just as comfortable as if she were on her own turf.

"Does it bother you, Jack, that sub-par games like tonight will cost you all-America and all-star-team status?"

"Why should it?" He laughed in a quick burst. "Those
who count know how good I am, and so do I."

"I do too." His smile turned cynical in a flash, as she saw.
"I'm not trying to flatter you, and I don't think I have to
demonstrate how well I know basketball. What I'm after,
frankly, is a portrait of you as the model of the new athlete.

No more dumb jock. A man who has choices and makes them intelligently. You're the prototype of the players who are going to change the place and image of athletes in this country."

"Is that a prepared speech or a first 'graph?"

"Neither. I don't work that way. I'm a quick read and I travel light. Always have."

"How'd you learn? You look like you've spent your life in Scarsdale and Bryn Mawr, Palm Beach and Westhampton."

"Wrong. I'm an Army brat. Dad had high enough rank to move in good circles, but not high enough to avoid frequent transfer. I went to fourteen different schools in five countries. But who's doing the interview here?"

"We both are. We both have a proposition to consider."

"Fair enough. I want an exclusive on your plans for the future and complete openness for an in-depth portrait. I'm willing to pay for it, if we can work out an arrangement."

He hesitated. The pause was brief, but it was strange for him to pause at all, and it had the eerie effect of taking her breath away.

"I don't need the money. I'd like to do it with you," he said finally, and there was no mistaking the double meaning in his words and smile, "but there are two conditions."

"I already know one of them, and I'll think about it."

"That's not a condition, it's a fact of life. So what's to think?"

Smiling in acknowledgment of his self-confidence, she said, "What are the conditions, then?"

"One is that everything I say to you is on the record for your use but off the record until I say so. In other words, I'll give you everything you want for your story, but you have to clear the story with me before you print it."

"You're on," she said, almost too quickly. "What's the other?"

"That you put this agreement in writing. That way, if you go ahead without my approval, I'll not only sue you but also guarantee you'll never have anyone's confidence for another exclusive again."

Later, in her apartment on East 78th Street, the interview continued right up until they had their clothes off. She had done her homework.

"You've always been listed as a pre-dental student, Jack, with a chemistry major. Was that your family's choice?"

"Yeah. My son, the dentist. Can you see these hands spending years inside other people's mouths?"

They both regarded the huge but well-shaped hands for a minute and then he self-consciously began to caress her with them.

"You never had any intention of going to dental school."

"Never."

"Why stick in the program with that major, then?"

"What difference does it make? It's all the same. I had no particular interest in anything else."

"Being a student was just a game for you? You can't have spent much time studying."

"It was too easy to be much of a game. I missed a whole semester and I'll be away most of this one, but I'm graduating on time and with good grades, too."

"There's a rumor that you're considering Harvard Business School."

Molinas laughed, the fabulous full laugh that characterized his moments of great delight in himself and his relation to the world.

"You want to know what that was all about? A lot of guys at school heard me on the phone talking about 'business.' They were all preoccupied with graduate school so they assumed I was too. But I was *in* business. I was doing business on basketball games, and I'm a partner in a bookmaking business."

"Joe Hacken's?"

He was genuinely impressed at that, and again, minutes later, with the beauty of her body and the casual way she presented it to him. Molinas had been to bed with many girls and a few women—he thought of them all as broads—but he had very little experience. In fact, he cared very little about the whole business of sex. He did it to have done it, and he had no ego-investment in his performance.

The only female he could be said to have an intimate relationship with was a precocious twelve-year-old in the Bronx. Sharon he could talk to with the confidence that she understood and accepted him totally. With that little girl he could be "himself"—whatever that was.

Flynn was the first broad he'd known who was more attractive without her clothes on. She was good and she knew it. He appreciated that. She had a side-to-side motion that he'd not known before, and even while he was thinking that she was perfunctory with it, almost mechanical, she was getting him off quickly. It was rare for him to enjoy his climax so much, and he didn't even wonder whether she climaxed at all.

They had been completely silent during the act, but almost as soon as he rolled off she was back at work again.

"You're a natural for business, Jack. Look at your assets: unlimited nerve and skill and self-confidence."

"Just like you, Patsy. You're not in business, either."

"And you don't have traditional liabilities to business careers, like a sense of morality and a notion of limits to what you can get away with."

"Business isn't the only field to play in with all that, as you know. There's the media and entertainment and law. And you forgot the most important quality—the ability to fool people."

"So there'll be no business school for Jack Molinas."

"No. I'm not headed for an MBA, I'm headed for the NBA."

"I thought so, but I'm not sure I understand why."

"They play the game at my level."

"Some do, but so what? A lot of the best college players go on to service teams or industrial ball or the AAU. For every Mikan there's a Kurland."

"But there's no betting line in those other leagues. The future's with the NBA. Pretty soon all the best players will be there, and there's big money to be made despite the salary scale for players now."

"It's still a small-time, small-town operation, run by a hockey man from New Haven."

"Hah! Eddie Gottlieb calls him 'Pants Podoloff' but Marty Glickman has a better one—'Putz Podoloff'."

"You know, I happened to be at the one basketball game he'd ever seen before he took over the league, at Payne-Whitney Gym, a Yale game with Tony Lavelli as the star."

"The accordion player."

"Right. But you've got to hand it to Podoloff. He raided the other league and brought all the strong franchises together."

"Remember what he said after the '49 season? 'Our dreams of grandeur turned to nightmare.' No crowds, too many fouls."

"Why do you think it'll change? I mean besides providing better betting propositions."

"First, better players, especially the blacks. Then changes in rules and styles. The college draft idea will help, too."

"Haskell Cohen's brainchild." She continued to impress him. On into the night they talked basketball. To Molinas it came naturally, and he gained confidence in her level of understanding of the game. For Flynn, it was a matter of getting this stuff out of the way.

"I know the Celtics best," she said. "I know that Auerbach's running style is fun but it doesn't win. They were better off with Doggie and especially with Honey Russell."

"A great Brooklyn basketball man."

"I can tell you a story about Russell's first Celtics team, with Chuck Connors. Remember he was also under contract to the Dodgers as a first baseman? Well, when Branch Rickey announced they were bringing Jackie Robinson up from Montreal as a first baseman, Connors came running out for a practice where the Celtics were all gathered around Russell, went into a long hook slide ending at their feet, looked up at them and said, 'the great white hope.'"

"Good story, but you're wrong about Auerbach."

"He's abrasive and obnoxious. I don't like the way he pushes men, antagonizes opponents, and baits officials."

"But he'll win, because he's getting away from the bullying style, beating on everyone. In time, running and gunning will not only draw crowds but win. Besides, he'll win because he doesn't give a shit about anyone as person, only as player."

"But he's such a bad judge of talent. Didn't even want Cousy. Sits Bill Sharman on the bench and starts Bob Donham."

"You'll see," he said.

"And what about the scandals?" she said. "How will they get over that and the residual suspicions?"

"Podoloff handled that right by banning Beard and Groza for life, though they're great players. Sherman White and Floyd Lane would have been just as good. Remember Sol Levy, the official? He was indicted for controlling a college game, but he was stricken from the NBA rolls."

"Does Podoloff know about the gambling?"

"He's an innocent babe in the woods. But he's on solid

merchandising ground, legal too."

"Well, he has a Yale Law degree."

"But here's the paradox. Gambling is an essential part of sports, inevitable really. Pro sports, especially, exist for betting. How can you take the gambling action away from the entertainment, the excitement? The people who run sports have to pretend they're independent of gambling in order to convince the public of their integrity. But on the other hand they have to keep a vigil over the integrity of their games in order to insure the fair shake required for gambling."

"The NBA knows?"

"They have to. But their hypocrisy is great, it's cool, they carry it off with such aplomb. The whole league must be in on the action."

"Nobody's ever brought charges against a player in an NBA game."

"That's what's so great. I can hardly wait."

"What about the college players who got caught?"

"I don't pity them. They weren't very bright, that's all."

"What if there were accusations against you?"

"I deny everything. I admit nothing. They'll never touch me—I always get another chance."

Chapter 14:
Stop the
Press

All spring they met, usually after basketball games, and repeated the same pattern. They talked, they stopped talking for quick sex, and they talked some more. She never took notes. One night she amazed him by dictating her copy on the phone, without reference to anything on paper, to the *Herald Tribune*. She had covered the social gathering occasioned by a charity screening of a new film, and the next day the story read exactly as he had heard it.

She saw most of his games but drew the line when he wanted her to travel along on the annual spring tour of college all-stars against the Globetrotters. She was in the Garden, of course, for the first game of that series, when he scored 18 points including 6 in the last two minutes to beat the pros. He went on to be named outstanding collegian in the whole series.

All spring he played in all-star games with an eagerness, a manic energy, bred of his confidence in his prospects. Flynn teased him about it.

"You trying to prove something?" He hadn't made any all-America teams, usually getting honorable mention after three full fives had been named. His Ivy arch-rival Ernie Beck was a unanimous first-team choice along with Walter Dukes of Seton Hall at center. Tom Gola of LaSalle, Johnny O'Brien of Seattle, and Bob Houbregs of Washington usually filled out the first team.

"I don't have to prove anything. I'm just having fun."

"Aw, I thought you were just showing off for me." They both laughed at that.

Molinas took great satisfaction in being named metropolitan-area player of the year by the New York basketball writers, over all-America Dukes and his teammate Richie Regan. "You see, Patsy? *They* know that stats don't tell the whole story. They've seen me when I was trying to win. The pros know it too."

The weekend before the college draft they spent at a beach house in New Rochelle, the secluded weekend place of an economist Flynn had interviewed sympathetically for the *Journal*. Molinas was tense, but they both pretended he wasn't. They turned to the subject of his future.

"I'll give basketball maybe ten years."

"And then?"

"I've been thinking about the law. Think of all the games involved. Legal proceedings are played out in competitive formats, and the way the system works there are no limits to the way a clever guy can juggle dozens of balls at once."

"Conflict of interest?"

"Hell, the way they have the rules set up, that's a very difficult case to prove. Practicing law can be like playing games within games, balancing one set of Chinese boxes against another. And the lawyer himself is in charge because he's the only one who knows all that's going on."

"In ten years you think you'll want to go back to law school?"

"Hell, no. I'll just do it in my spare time—while I'm playing ball."

"Jack's so quick and nimble he can jump over any candlestick."

"Even while it's burning at both ends."

"You're not sorry to be leaving college, are you?"

"I can take it or leave it, always could. I always knew it

was empty, chaos in the void," he said, laughing. "I'm cynical, too, and hostile, but that just makes me optimistic,
maybe even mellow."

"That's what I admire most about you, Jack. You take
charge of your life, you make things happen. You accept
the void and work out your own place in it. You make chaos
work to your advantage. I think that's what charisma is."

"Charisma is a word made up by people like you. To me
it's horseshit," he said, but they both knew he believed he
had it and wanted to credit her with the same quality. "I
just know exactly what I'm gonna do, play basketball in
the NBA."

"OK, so you're going into the NBA. Tell me how the draft
will go?"

"I figure only three teams will take territorial picks."

"New York and Philadelphia, for sure."

"Right. Dukes to the Knicks, and the Warriors will take
themselves right out of the draft with Beck and some other
Big Five players who'll never be worth a damn. The Lakers
will take Jim Fritsche from Hamline, but they don't need
him."

"So the draft proper will go Baltimore, Milwaukee, Fort
Wayne, Rochester."

"The Bullets will take Felix. These big guys, Dukes and
Felix, will make out all right. Neither one is a Mikan, but
they can play. I should be next."

"But you won't be."

"Right again. Kerner will look at the size and the press
clippings and take Houbregs. He's a bright guy, too, but he's
got very limited ability."

"Then you go to Fort Wayne?"

"Unless they go for Regan; then I'll go to Rochester.
What a joke. Richie's as good as Beck, but that's not saying
much. Gola's the only college player in my class and he's

still in college."

"Where do you want to be?"

"Wherever I can play more and control play best. I'd get more minutes in Rochester, but Fort Wayne's a better team so there'll be more business possibilities."

"But what about the location?"

"Hell, what's the difference. It's all Jersey or the Midwest out there. Home is still the Garden."

*   *   *   *   *

The NBA draft went just as smoothly for Molinas as the draft board action had, but the summer was rocky for him and Patsy. Her quick, sharp, cynical observations—which made her such a good writer—made her more exciting to him. But he would aggravate her by outdoing her with a nihilistic attitude that may have been genuinely absurdist but struck her as absurd.

They argued about everything, except that they both shrugged at the apparent end of the "police action" in Korea. The Rosenbergs were put to death: Flynn was cynical about a system that had sliding scales of justice; Molinas laughed bitterly about an America that could win a war and take over the right to scapegoat Jews. Ford Frick worried publicly about gambling in baseball: Flynn was cynical about the owners protecting their economic free ride; Molinas laughed at the hypocrisy that couldn't acknowledge the main reason for baseball's popularity—for decades it was the game with the biggest handle in illegal betting, but was now losing ground to football.

A University of Maryland student was convicted of trying to bribe the Terrapin center to keep the football team from beating LSU by 21 last fall (34-6 had been the score, apparently an honest count): Flynn was cynical about football players' intelligence; Molinas laughed at the fixer's stupidity—he hadn't set the right guys up. Don Lofgran, who'd been a great college basketball player and first-round NBA choice, disappeared and then was found over two weeks later wandering aimlessly in Salt Lake City: Flynn commented acidly about pro-basketball life style; Molinas laughed at others losing their way, knowing he never would.

When Molinas heard that Hogan was going to play for the first time in the British Open, he made a substantial bet that Bantam Ben would win. He told Patsy that he appreciated the "arrogance and meanness" in the great golfer. She was persuaded and promptly flew over to cover the tournament in her inimitable way. She dogged Hogan's trail on and off the course, cursing the lack of satisfactory facilities all the while, and had the best coverage anywhere when Hogan won.

Wimbledon was a different story. Molinas argued that only a sentimental chauvinist could believe in an American double, and Flynn was persuaded not to go. Maureen Connelly won, and then Vic Seixas. Patsy was furious. Molinas laughed.

They used each other, openly and aggressively, and by Labor Day she was tiring of it and wanted to close out her story with his signature on his Zollner-Piston contract. But he refused to sign. He belatedly took the Law School Aptitude Test and bragged to Patsy that he had scored in the 99th percentile. Then he told her about the deal he had cut with Brooklyn Law School: he could take courses at his own speed and if he passed final exams in others he would earn those credits without paying for them; until he passed the bar, neither he nor the school would publicize his matriculation or the arrangement.

"Who are you trying to kid, Jack? You know you're going to play for Fort Wayne."

They had come back to the house in New Rochelle for a last weekend before the solstice. They wouldn't be seeing each other very much once he reported to training camp and anyway her story was finished.

"You and I know that, but Fred Zollner doesn't. The big-time Aryan industrial magnate needs a lesson from Jack Molinas."

"What have you got against Zollner? They picked you because they want to win. His softball team is a national champion and he wants the same for basketball. Nine thousand is way over scale for a rookie—what do you need a five hundred dollar signing bonus for?"

"For playing in the sticks. Besides, I want a little more money than any other rookie, and I'll earn it by being rookie of the year."

"Listen, Jack, the Pistons have already signed fifteen players, including the last three NBA rookies of the year. Aren't you a little concerned they might not need you on a twelve-man squad?"

"They need me, and they want me, too."

"Podoloff and company are already talking about your greed."

"Let them talk," he said and held out a telegram to her. "You didn't think I'd get it, did you?" He savored her surprise. "Now we can celebrate."

When they got out of bed a half hour later, Molinas having been impotent for the first time with her, she said, "I have a surprise for you, too."

She handed him the 5,000-word typescript. It began, "When Jack Molinas of Columbia signed his contract with the Fort Wayne Zollner-Pistons, the $500 signing bonus on top of the $9,000 salary made him the highest-paid rookie in the NBA. He is the new prototype of the professional athlete in America today—intelligent, articulate, opportunistic, and versatile."

He read the piece straight through while she walked on the beach. He was waiting for her, smiling broadly, when she came back. But her feeling of relief was short-lived.

"No way," he said. "If you ever try to use any of this, I'll have an injunction in five minutes. And if you sneak it into print, your publishers will find out just how expensive a writer you are."

On the day the NBA season opened she sent him a telegram with a single rhymed couplet: GOOD LUCK—I HOPE YOU'RE UP FOR THE GAME/I THOUGHT YOU SHOULD KNOW—I NEVER CAME.

In times to come he was happy for her every success, because he bragged about sleeping with her, and she in turn rejoiced whenever he took a fall.

PART IV: Postgraduate

Chapter 15:
On the Road

Molinas regarded the visitors' dressing room in Syracuse with amused contempt. Along with the Boston Garden, with its ancient, honored aura of palpable rot, this was the pits of the NBA. But he didn't care; he was eager to play. It wasn't the fact that he was getting his first start tonight that excited him, but as soon as he had heard about it he had called Hacken to bet a couple of dimes for him. They had beaten the Nats without him and he knew that he would more than make up for their home-court advantage this time. It was a golden opportunity, with the Pistons a five-point dog.

The Fort Wayne Zollner-Pistons had completed the previous season as the second best team in basketball. They had extended the champion Lakers to the full five games in the Western Division finals, and Minneapolis had gone on to beat the Knickerbockers, four games to one, for the title. Zollner, his manager Carl Bennett, and coach Paul Birch all figured that the way to clear that final hurdle was to strengthen the team in the front line to match up with Mikan, Pollard, and Mikkelson of the Lakers.

At center, Larry Foust was a proven all-star, very nearly Mikan's equal now, and playmaker Andy Phillip was consistently among the league leaders in assists. With Fat Freddy Scolari and Frank Brian their backcourt was better than the Lakers' already, but they strengthened it even more by trading reserve center Charlie Share to the Hawks for Max Zaslofsky, an eight-year veteran, third leading all-time scorer in the league, and high scorer in the first pro game Molinas had ever seen.

Now, for the first time, they had assembled such talented forwards that they could afford to sell veteran Fred Schaus to the Knicks. There were last year's rookie of the year, Don Meineke, and Mel Hutchins, who had won that honor the year before at Milwaukee and been bought from the Hawks in August. And then there were the two sensational rookies, Jack Molinas and George Yardley, who had led his team to the service championship, beating teams led by Dick Groat and Paul Arizin along the way.

This was surely enough talent to go all the way, if it was used properly. Molinas thought Birch was an idiot, however, and the coach seemed to prove it by starting Meineke and Hutchins ahead of him and Yardley. Despite that, they had won all seven exhibition games and beaten the Lakers in their first meeting of the season. But they were only 5-4 when they arrived in Syracuse for this November 19 game.

Now they were about to start moving, Molinas thought, as he moved ahead of Meineke into the starting line-up opposite Hutchins, with whom he shared a house in Fort Wayne. He was shocked to see that Joe Hacken was there when the team went on the floor for warm-ups. The bookie rarely went to any games at all and never out of town. They had a brief conversation at courtside.

"Come to see history made, Joe? First start of the all-star rookie, or couldn't you believe it unless you saw it?"

"Thought I'd better bring you some news, Jack."

"Am I down?"

"For two dimes, spread around at plus five. But after, I got wind of something you should know. It's three against two tonight."

Molinas loped onto the floor for the pre-game drills but his mind was racing. If three guys on his team were giving the points, he was about to blow twenty-two hundred bucks. And it had to be the guards and the center, who had the ball almost all the time in the Fort Wayne offense. Birch had no idea how to use his abundance of talent at the forward positions. Molinas would bet anything that Hutchins was OK, a clean-cut straight arrow if he'd ever seen one. He called him Jack Armstrong. Now he'd have to depend on him to play an outstanding game and, of course, on himself.

Just before the tap he went over to shake his roommate's hand and said, "It's me and you tonight, Baby, just me and you."

Mel grinned back, but didn't get the message. As play started, Molinas hustled for every rebound, every loose ball, and so did Hutchins. But Jack would pass only to Mel if he didn't have a shot himself, while Mel would usually give the ball to the guard or pass into the pivot in the Pistons' regular patterns.

Birch saw Molinas as disrupting the offense and benched him for most of the second quarter. The team went through their usual motions but fell further and further behind. At half-time they trailed 39-20. Molinas was furious, more so when Yardley started in his place in the second half, but he didn't show it.

Yardley had a hot hand, but the Pistons were not taking advantage of it, trailing by 20 or more most of the third quarter. Then, in desperation, Birch sent Molinas back in while Meineke and Hutchins sat out the fourth quarter.

For twelve solid minutes, Yardley and Molinas played two against eight. They played as if they knew each other perfectly, though they had rarely been on the floor together before and barely spoke off it. They rebounded, blocked shots, intercepted passes, ran two-man fast breaks, and never passed the ball except to each other. When Molinas scored a driving lay-up at the buzzer off a Yardley feed, it

was his 20th point of the period, and it made the final score
79-76. Fort Wayne had lost but covered the spread.

In the locker room, Hutchins threw an arm around him
in congratulations. Yardley remained aloof after they nodded in acknowledgment to each other, and everyone else
was sullen and silent. Hutchins said, "They're taking it hard
because they lost."

Molinas said, "You don't know how right you are."

*   *   *   *   *

Joe Hacken shut down his book on the afternoon of
December 15th. Any bettors who dialed his numbers heard
an operator say that the phone was temporarily out of
order. He was making one of the biggest plays of his life
that day and he didn't want any additional action or aggra-
vation. Besides, he didn't want to tip anyone off, however
indirectly, that something special was going on.

Hacken was as pleased and proud as Punch. Starting
with that day in Syracuse, Molinas had demonstrated that
he could control pro games as well as he had college, and in
Joe's head, like a broken record, rang the phrase, "That's
my boy."

He talked with Molinas every day, not that Jack demand-
ed a running count on the profits of their partnership, but
because both liked to keep in touch. Hacken also got regular reports from others around the league and kept Molinas
informed. He knew, for example, that even though the
Pistons had won eight of their last eleven games, it was not
all strawberries and cream on the team. Molinas played
with these guys every day but never got close to most of
them, so that Hacken's contacts were useful.

Meineke was sulking about losing his starting position.
Yardley had hurt his elbow and couldn't play, withdrawing

further into his shell. Foust had started shouting at Molinas whenever Jack moved into the post, and a couple of times had tried to elbow him out of his turf.

Even Andy Phillip, who had the reputation around the league of being a good-natured, even-tempered team player, had been grumbling. He complained to Birch that he couldn't adjust to Molinas's unpredictability, that the cohesive patterns were breaking down, and that he was losing control of the offense. But Molinas seemed to like it that way, free-lancing, playing in sensational spurts, but at others' expense. "That's my boy," went Hacken's mental refrain.

Now Fort Wayne was coming into the Garden to play the Celtics in the first game of a double-header. It was a homecoming for Molinas, and Hacken knew he was determined to make it a personal triumph in every way possible, to let all of New York know that Jack Molinas was back in town. Jack had spent more time on the phone lining up broads for his teammates than he had checking on business with his partner.

All day Joe had been betting on Boston, using as many contacts as he could, spreading the money around, trying to disguise the source—but betting with both lungs. The game had opened with the Celtics a 2-point favorite, but the size and persistence of Hacken's action had moved it up to 5 or 6 with local bookmakers until—about an hour before game time—they had smelled something rotten and taken the game off the board. The usual lay-off books in other states had taken all the action they wanted, the locals were left holding a lot of Boston money themselves, and Hacken was incommunicado.

When Jack Molinas was introduced as a starter, Hacken joined the sell-out Garden crowd in a warm greeting for one of their own who'd made it. Molinas responded in the first half with a bravura performance. He outdazzled the

great Cousy, stealing Celtic passes, running past Easy Ed
Macauley on fast breaks, and rebounding vigorously at both
ends. At half-time he had 18 points and the Pistons led by
5. Hacken beamed down at what he beheld. It was less than
two years since his anguish over the Columbia-Holy Cross
game, but now he had complete confidence in Molinas's
genius. As the score stood, he stood to take the biggest
beating of his life, but he sat smiling calmly and thinking,
"That's my boy."

As the second half started, Molinas reached out and
grabbed Cousy to interrupt a Celtic fast break. The next
time down the floor he went for a steal and fouled Bill
Sharman. Birch yanked him and he sat placidly on the
bench the rest of the game, watching Boston come from
behind to win 82-75. Hacken left before the Knicks game
began. He had no action on that one, and he'd already had
a banner win—but not the kind you hang from the rafters
in the Garden.

Jack celebrated the holidays on the basketball court,
starring against the Celtics on Christmas Day and the
Lakers on New Year's Eve. And Joe, taking inordinate pride
in all of Molinas's skills, celebrated vicariously—even
though those were the only two games the slumping
Pistons won as they went to the all-star break just one
game over .500.

Molinas was on top of the basketball world, just as he
knew he should be, when he was chosen for the West All-
Stars. But Hacken was every bit as high and mightily satisfied as the player, and it seemed that in his way he suffered
even more from the blow that kept his boy from ever playing in the NBA All-Star Game.

Chapter 16:
Blind Justice

As soon as the report on Molinas came to Podoloff, the decision was instantaneous. Molinas was out. Podoloff would tolerate absolutely no overt connection with gambling in the NBA. He had earned a law degree at Yale in 1915 and practiced for a while, specializing in real estate law, before his own real estate activities led to the purchase of the New Haven Arena with his brothers Nathan and Jacob. But "innocent until proven guilty" was not a principle of the justice that President Maurice Podoloff applied to the American Hockey League or the National Basketball Association. When it came to gambling, a verdict of guilty and a sentence of exile would be made on the submission of any evidence in accusation.

As president he was a hanging judge. He was absolute and he was absolutely consistent, even if he carried his conviction to a questionable extreme. Big Bill Spivey of Kentucky was an extreme case. Implicated in the college scandals of 1951, he was guilty by association and perhaps only by association. His jury was hung, 9-3 for acquittal, and he was never retried. Polygraph tests supported his claim of innocence. But he was guilty of not reporting what he might have known about some of his teammates. Podoloff kept him out of the NBA through appeal after appeal.

A decade later, Doug Moe was banned. Called the best high school player in New York City history—better than Cunningham, Alcindor, the Hawk, even better than Molinas—

Moe once during his North Carolina career accepted $75 in expense money from Aaron Wagman, who later confessed to participating in fixes. Moe never played in Podoloff's NBA, though he finally made it as a coach under the administration of Walter Kennedy, of whom Podoloff said, "He began his life as a bartender and reverted to type." As long as Podoloff ran the league, an NBA player, like Caesar's wife, must be above reproach for the appearance of wrongdoing in the eyes of the public—as Maurice Podoloff interpreted the public's view.

Why weren't more players and other personnel around the league on Podoloff's enemies list and dispatched in disgrace? Because Podoloff didn't have such a list. He never believed in witchhunts or purges, never looked for trouble, and was probably both extremely naive about the whole gambling scene and unwilling to see what didn't have to be seen. Not until Pete Rozelle's NFL regime was there a chief executive in American sports who understood the gambling dimension of the sporting life. But when information was brought to Podoloff's attention he acted immediately.

This wasn't the first time he'd heard anything about Molinas and gambling. Ike Gellis of the New York *Post* had phoned the league office weeks before and said he heard on the street that something funny was going on with Fort Wayne, that there were unnatural fluctuations in the betting line. Two inferences could be drawn from that phenomenon. One was that big money was being bet on games involving the Pistons. The other was that inside information about the team was getting out. Podoloff had called Zollner right away, an owner whom the president regarded—despite his playboy reputation—as a gentleman sportsman. He reported Gellis's tip and asked directly if he knew what was going on. Zollner said that they had already started an investigation. Podoloff asked if any players were involved.

Zollner said they didn't know for sure, but that they were suspicious of Jack Molinas. Podoloff asked for a report as soon as they had one, and this was the report that was now on his desk. By the time he saw the player he also had on his desk Molinas's statement of limited admission.

From the league office in New York he placed two phone calls and dictated a telegram to his secretary. The wire was to Carl Bennett of the Fort Wayne Pistons. It said simply that Jack Molinas was suspended indefinitely. The first call was to Fred Zollner, telling him that the telegram had been sent, thanking him for the thoroughness of the report, assuring him that the matter was closed and the action final, and arranging for the club and the league to confer before issuing statements to the press as soon as possible. It was a long conversation, serious but cordial, with mutual regrets expressed. At the end, Podoloff told Zollner that he planned to see Molinas privately, but that there was no possibility of a reversal. Zollner was relieved.

Meanwhile Molinas was waiting on hold on the other line. Podoloff assumed that Molinas already knew what had happened, but he didn't really care. The conversation was brief. Podoloff took an avuncular tone, his usual jovial heartiness with players now muted with sadness but, he thought, with a trace of indulgence. Molinas responded in monosyllables, a chastened cadet. Podoloff would see him next day in his office. Molinas was to be accompanied by his attorney and his father. Podoloff was very insistent about that, and Molinas readily agreed.

Molinas had great cause for grief. The past two months had been the best of his life, better even than when he was whipping a game on the world at Columbia. Best of all, it seemed that his joy could be sustained for years to come. Now it was as if they were threatening to take all his pleasures from him at once.

And yet he found reason for optimism. Just as he thought he would escape punishment at Columbia for a thoughtless stunt, he thought he could cop a plea here and be reinstated. Podoloff's request for lawyer and parent seemed significant to him; it meant that there was going to be a lecture and a negotiation. "I'll do all right," he told Hutchins before he left. "I always do. I'll make out all right and I'll be back."

The scene with Podoloff could have been played for broad comedy. The president, sometimes affectionately called "Poodles" and occasionally the Fiorello LaGuardia of sports, stood barely five feet, round of head and trunk, with prominent features. But at 63 his presence, his sense of command, his presiding voice, made you forget the person and accept the personage. And here was Molinas, towering, powerful, confident, and handsome, brimming with positive energy, having to pretend not only submissiveness but contriteness: the sheepish boy before the all-powerful shepherd.

Podoloff had come out from behind his desk and sat facing Molinas in a small circle of chairs. Molinas, flanked by his father and Irving Waldhorn, thought this was a good sign, that it would have been easier for the president to wield absolute power with the executive desk enthroning him. Louis Molinas sat on the edge of his chair, his anxious face darting somber looks back and forth and around the room during the whole meeting, hanging on the words and trying to understand the nuances he thought were there but that he was missing. He didn't speak after the formalities of introduction, but his manner expressed sad wonderment at where he had gone wrong with his son.

Nor did Waldhorn speak. He seemed unconcerned with the matter at hand and barely followed the conversation. He was, in fact, awed at the scene and trying to act casual. Waldhorn was a hack, a neighborhood plodder who had

known the Molinas family for years around Creston Avenue
and the Grand Concourse. He was there because Podoloff
had asked for an attorney and Jack knew Waldhorn would
be available at short notice. He also knew he'd never have
Waldhorn representing him or his father in any legal proceeding. For all intents and purposes, this meeting was
Podoloff and Molinas, one on one, and the others were just
part of the stage setting.

"Jack, you're through with basketball."

Molinas heard it but didn't believe it. Why the lawyer? Why
his father? The old man was going to start from the worst and
then move away from it. Good negotiator, he thought, but
what does he hope to get from me in negotiating?

"At least as far as the NBA is concerned. We're in a bad
way, Jack. Our whole future is on the line. The league lacks
credibility with the public. It's not going over as entertainment, and we've got to maintain this television contract.
The current rules don't allow for the game to be seen at its
best, and we're hunting for ways to fix that."

What's this to do with me? Molinas thought.

"Now what does this have to do with you, Jack? Well, a
report has been made, certain activities have been uncov-
ered, you have admitted them, and it will be made public.
Your contract, all league contracts, specify an interdiction
of gambling activities and associations."

Molinas had a sinking feeling. Now he knew why he was
supposed to have a lawyer there, to confirm that he had no
legal recourse. And Podoloff wanted to have the semblance
of a fair hearing. Still he hung onto the hope represented
by his father's presence.

"We've always enforced this rule, Jack. Now more than
ever we can't afford *not* to enforce it, even if we wanted to.
And if it were up to me, we would enforce it forever."

Is that an imperial we, Molinas wondered.

"You've admitted betting on games, isn't that right?"

OK, here it comes. "Yessir."

"Why did you do that?"

"Admit it? Because it's the truth."

"No, I mean, why did you bet?"

"I didn't think it was wrong, as long as I was betting on my own team to win, and as long as no one knew about it." He had to bite his tongue to keep from saying that everyone did it and everyone knew it.

"Others had to know about it."

"What do you mean?" This old man knows more than he's letting on.

"Well, your friend in the Bronx through whom you placed the bets knew. And whoever accepted those bets knew. Don't you see? You were not only doing something illegal, you were providing information that could be used illegally by others."

"I just didn't think about that, sir. I didn't think it was a serious thing. It certainly wasn't serious money. And I thought it was common practice among the pros, that that was one of the big differences from college ball."

Molinas was lying, thinking hard, maneuvering for position, looking for the best balance of lies to get out of this. He knew that Podoloff knew he was lying, but he didn't know just what fabrication Podoloff would be satisfied with. He didn't know whether he had anything to offer Podoloff in this negotiation. And he couldn't tell whether Podoloff was lying.

"No, Jack, in that way it's just the same. We can't tolerate gambling anywhere in sport and hope to convince the public it's still honest sport." Molinas stifled the urge to laugh at that. "And we don't know of any other player who has been betting. If we did, he'd be out too."

"I was wondering if you had decided to make an example

of me, and I wondered why." This was a touchy area, and
Molinas was looking for an opening to score. He suspected
that he was singled out because he was a Jew, and that
Podoloff might feel pressured as a Jew not to go easy on a
landsman. In a league where Ben "the Burgler" Kerner
and Eddie Gottlieb were mainstays, and where Danny "the
Hood" Biasone and his coach Al Cervi along with Lou Pieri
of Providence provided the Jewish Mafia with some traditional Siciliani flavoring, there might be a certain dignified
sensitivity about "ethnics" among people like Zollner, Birch,
Walter Brown, and Clair Bee.

Podoloff was slow and deliberate in answering, taking in
Waldhorn with his glance, and for the first time measuring
his words. "You're an example because you're in the public
eye. You're an example for young people. Every player is.
But so far as the league is concerned you are an individual
player who has violated his contract and broken a basic
tenet of the league. Any individual player who perpetrates
that violation will be dealt with in the same way. There can
be no compromise of that tenet. As of now you are the only
individual player we know of who has actively compro-
mised it or the league's integrity."

Now Molinas was faced with a major decision. He could
see an angle he might use. In the silence that followed that
speech, Podoloff seemed to be savoring the effect, and
Molinas thought the whole thing through before he spoke.

He knew that a lot of people around the league were betting. Joe Hacken had been telling him that for years, even if
he didn't see telltale signs of it himself this season. If he told
all he knew and told them where to look for the rest, he
could take the whole league down with him. Podoloff must
know that, too, but why wasn't he saying anything? Maybe,
if he began to say what he knew, Podoloff would realize that
he had to negotiate after all. That's a kind of blackmail he

might understand. I could say, Take me down and I'll take a lot of other people along. And let's see how the public eye sees that. But maybe he already knows that. He's seeing if I'll keep quiet. That's what I have to offer him, my silence.

Unless it's information he wants from me. I could give him names and games, but that doesn't figure. Why should I tell him what he probably already knows? He's got to know. They all know. Shit, I knew a month ago that they were investigating and it didn't stop me from betting. Why should it have? I knew they were onto me after I shaved that Boston game in New York—and scored 20 points doing it. The whole world was onto that one.

Wait a minute. If the Pistons were checking, and they already knew I was betting, why did they go ahead and trade Share for a guard and then sell Schaus? It doesn't figure, unless they thought that it wouldn't matter either. They knew I would be around anyway. That's the clue. If I play along with their sham, make them look good to the public, after a while they'll reinstate me. But of course he can't tell me that, certainly not in front of witnesses—such as they are.

Cautiously, he said, "Mr. Podoloff, if I could tell you about others gambling, players or coaches, should I tell you or would it seem like sour grapes?"

"Of course you should tell me, if it's true. But be certain of this: it can't do you any good. There are no deals here."

Molinas said nothing. In the pause he thought again that he didn't know why his father was there. And then Podoloff said , "Let's run through the facts and see if we have them straight."

"OK."

"According to the report, you were betting through a friend in the Bronx, and you don't know where or how he placed the bets."

"Right."

"That was Stanley Retensky who helps his father run a candy store."

"Yes."

"They do not book bets in the store."

"No. I'm sure they don't."

"Would you know if they did? Do you know any bookmakers in the Bronx?"

"I don't know any bookmakers anywhere, Mr. Podoloff," and as he was saying this he was wondering if Podoloff actually knew about his connection with Joe Hacken. "Why, until this basketball season I never bet on anything in my life," and then he looked over at his father and smiled, "except for some two dollar bets at Hialeah on a trip with my dad." Mr. Molinas eagerly nodded, in grim affirmation of that happier time. Louis Molinas had always tried to project the image of a strong disciplinarian, a model of honorable values for his family, but Jack knew him as a sentimental man he could always manipulate, so strong was the father's vicarious pleasure in the son's successes.

"You bet on ten games, always on Fort Wayne to win, in amounts from fifty dollars to two hundred."

"Right."

"You didn't always win."

"I won six, lost four."

"Your net profit was about five hundred dollars?"

"Barely."

Podoloff looked up slyly from the report. "That's just the size of the bonus you held out for before signing with Fort Wayne, isn't it?"

Molinas had a genuine smile this time, just a brief flash of the charm that everyone loved—except the ones who hated him. "That's right."

"Well, Jack, I'll accept your word on it. That's the way it's going to go down." There was relief in the way he said it, and Molinas felt that they had an unspoken understanding. In time there would be reinstatement.

"Now I have to ask you some nasty questions because I know you're going to hear them over and over." He was the lawyer now, preparing his client, rehearsing testimony. "Have you every deliberately tried to lose a basketball game?"

"No, sir."

"Not in the NBA, or at Columbia, or at Stuyvesant, or in the summer leagues?"

"No."

"Have you ever tried to hold down a score, control the margin of victory?"

"Still no."

"Have you ever been asked to do so?"

"No."

"Either lose or control margin of victory."

"Absolutely not."

"Do you know anyone—a player, a coach, an official, a gambler—who has been involved in any such activity?"

"Not that I know of." .

"When you were a sophomore at Columbia and you heard about the scandals, how did you react?"

"I was shocked. I didn't know any of the guys involved, never played with them—or against them—but I just couldn't imagine how they could do it."

"In moral terms or practical?"

"Well, both, sir. They would have to have no self-respect or regard for others. And besides, a team sport is a team sport, no individual can control the result. There are too many variables."

"Good. Now back to the list of games. You include two games against Boston, December 3rd and 25th, which you won, but you don't include the game against them on the

15th in New York. Why not?"

"I didn't bet on it."

"Why?"

"I was nervous about it, my first NBA game back in the Garden. I knew I would be pressing. Besides, I was tired and the team was not playing well. I had scored 20 against the Knicks in Fort Wayne but we lost anyway. I didn't have a good feeling about that game."

"You scored 18 points in the first half. Why didn't you play much in the second half?"

"You'd have to ask Coach Birch about that."

"Didn't you?"

"Me? I'm just a rookie. You don't question your coach as a rookie in this league."

"Our reports say that the point spread moved from 3 1/2 to 7 favoring Boston in that game, that the bookmakers took a beating on it, and that Fort Wayne was what they called 'off the boards' after that. Do you have anything to say about those reports?"

"No, I don't. Those things don't concern me at all. But frankly it sounds like irresponsible talk by irresponsible people." As he was saying it, he felt suffused by an inner glow of satisfaction. He loved it when the bookies took a beating, as they had in that one, as long as he was on the winning end. He was letting them know that Molinas was back in town. It was almost as good as the second Yale game in '53, where they had taken a huge bath and he and Hacken had made a big score. But his face betrayed nothing, nor did his voice, and Podoloff regarded him with a look that suggested approval, or at least satisfaction. Molinas felt that he had passed a tough exam.

The examiner relaxed in his chair and said, "And now I want to give you some advice." For the first time Podoloff looked directly at Louis Molinas and then back to his son.

Jack's confidence plummeted. Now he knew why his father was there. Podoloff was going to speak to him *in loco parentis* and what he was about to say was what his father, more than anyone, wanted to be said.

"I understand you have an interest in the law."

"How did you know that?"

"You'd be surprised how much we know."

"Well I have looked into law schools and I'll probably start at Brooklyn very soon."

"That's fine, because you are a bright young man. But I want you to understand something, Jack. You are through in basketball. Put it all behind you. Devote yourself to your studies. Please, for your own sake, forget all about basketball. Don't ever touch a ball again, don't step foot on a court, don't go to a game, don't even watch it on television. It will be the best thing in the world if Jack Molinas never gives another thought to the game of basketball."

His father nodding emphatic agreement, the lawyer trying to be blasé, Molinas heard this *obiter dictum* with sinking feelings and bowed head. But what he was thinking as he started to leave the office was, "We'll see, Putz, we'll just see about that."

Waldhorn and the senior Molinas had already passed into the outer office when Molinas turned, almost filling the doorway with his frame. Standing tall, he looked down a foot and a half at the man who had taken the best part of his life away, and said, "Mr. Podoloff, when I appeal for reinstatement—and you know I will, and I believe you'll give me a hearing—might you give me a second chance to play in the NBA again?"

Podoloff looked burdened just to hear this, but he brightened quickly and said, "Would you in my place?"

And Molinas said, "No, it would be too big a gamble," and shut the door behind him.

Chapter 17:
In the Swing

During Jesse's years in graduate school at Brown, his obsession with Molinas receded to a kind of occasional preoccupation. He still kept track of the general outlines of Molinas's life; several people who knew of that interest would fill him in with details as they picked them up or even rumors as they surfaced. At the same time, his fixation on Rachel, which culminated in a hasty but convenient marriage, also receded into a vaguely disturbing or frustrating sense of misgiving, disappointment, befuddlement.

The fact was that Jesse was extraordinarily happy in graduate school. He felt as if he had come home, had found out what he was all about. To spend his time reading and writing, talking and thinking about literature, and have that be considered an occupation, was almost too good to be true. The actual courses were slight inconveniences, brief interludes in the days and weeks, but useful both as punctuation and structure for his studies. And the classes he himself taught to undergraduates he learned to teach as extensions of his studies.

The game-playing aspects of graduate school also appealed mightily to him: adjusting to the ways individual professors interpreted the rules so that each performance was not only excellent but appropriate, that is, excellent in context; adjusting to each assignment so that the accomplishment would serve the future purposes of publication and advancement. Of course, it was as satisfying as it was, in part, because it was very easy for him, and it was as easy as it was, in part, because he had no serious distractions or pressures on him.

Rachel's father had been generous about the marriage, arranging to pay Jesse directly the kind of stipend that put most graduate fellowships to shame, and it took years for Jesse to realize, with more sorrowful surprise than bitterness, that the man had made a good deal for himself—paying Jesse to take a troubled, troubling, and very expensive responsibility off his hands. But for the time being it was a blessing for Jesse to be able to do what he loved doing without having to worry about finances, and without having to dissipate energy in social and sexual pursuits. And when, within the space of fourteen months, Rachel delivered two boys, Jesse's cup ran giddily high.

Later he could easily rationalize his failure to deal with the marital malaise that came almost immediately after they settled into an apartment. Rachel's dark beauty, exotic and erotic, was not, after all, all that had enchanted him. There was also the elusive quality of mystery, the allure of pregnant silence, a stillness he read as gentleness and depth. Once they were married, he began to experience her distance as withdrawal, her passivity as almost punishing in its coldness. This was also a challenge, but when it deepened into depression after Nathaniel and Jeremy arrived he was frightened about the way her attitudes toward him were extended to the boys as well.

Yet he was happy. He was juggling a number of appealing and rewarding activities. He was an acknowledged success in graduate school, his schedule allowed him to spend a great deal of time with Nat and Jem during these early years when they were an unmitigated delight, and he still had the leisure to keep up with his other interests in music, movies, politics, and sports—he would read three or four newspapers a day, *Variety*, and *The Sporting News*, as

well as the professional journals in his own discipline. If the
marriage itself seemed uncomfortably peripheral to his life,
so be it. His life was full without it. Clearly the danger was
that inattention to Rachel and the marriage could only
make things worse. Jesse sublimated, he rationalized, he
avoided, and ultimately he denied what he looked at in her
and about her and would not see.

What he thought of as his clever and successful juggling
gave him a privileged vantage to appreciate the greater juggling that Molinas was performing. Jesse had been hit hard
by the suspension, especially after he had experienced
Molinas's early successes in the Pistons camp and his grow-
ing successes in the NBA as triumphant justifications of his
own expert judgment, or even redemption of his faith. Now
he continued to follow pro basketball while looking out for
the eventual reinstatement, or resurrection, of his hero.

By another rare stroke of good fortune, Jesse shared an
office at Brown with another graduate student who shared
his interest in basketball. Stan Karlsberg had been an outstanding schoolboy athlete and a varsity basketball player
in college, but he had met his match in Jesse when they
talked the game, as they did for hours, in their office—literature and student papers be damned. Stan, who had been a
ball-controlling guard, railed against the heresy of the 24-
second clock when the NBA adopted it in 1954, but Jesse
hailed Danny Biasone of Syracuse, who proposed it, as the
savior of the league. Stan called it the greatest travesty in
the game; Jesse praised it as the single most important
rules change since the team of five was instituted sixty
years before.

"It's necessary and it's right," Jesse said.

"It cheapens scoring, like pinball machines," Stan
answered.

"Overnight NBA basketball has become a game of superlative skill and excitement, unmatched as entertainment."

"That's the problem, Jesse. It's entertainment values placed above athletic ones, and why would anyone play defense?"

"See, that's where you're wrong. In time, the ability to play defense for 24 seconds will separate the good teams from the great, because these guys will always be able to score. The only thing that bothers me about it is that Jack Molinas, who was perfectly made to play the game at these new heights, can't."

"Yeah, well, he'll elevate the coal towns of Pennsylvania."

Many a night Jesse and Stan drove up Route 1 to Boston where they put all their differences aside in a shared love for the first great Celtics teams led by Bill Russell, who made it possible for Tom Heinsohn and Bob Cousy and Bill Sharman and Sam Jones and K.C. Jones and Frank Ramsey and Jungle Jim Luscutoff to do all those wonderful things. They even shared the wish, seemingly perverse in Boston fans, that someone would shove that goddamn cigar down Red Auerbach's throat. Many years later, Maurice Podoloff endeared himself to Jesse when he confessed to just that wish as antidote to one of his major annoyances during his NBA reign.

Once in a while the old Molinas obsession would get the better of Jesse and somehow throw his priorities off balance. For example, when Rudy LaRusso matriculated at Dartmouth after a high school career in Brooklyn reminiscent of Molinas's, Jesse would set everything aside—kids, papers, classes—to see his alma mater play, not just in Providence, but Cambridge and New Haven as well. Taking advantage of his familiarity with the Payne Whitney gym he once was able to corner LaRusso for a conversation about a legendary game on the playground court in Kelly Park back home.

"You've got that right," LaRusso said. "Molinas scored 50

points, and I know because I had to guard him. I was still in high school, but I was already bigger than Jack. And I thought I could handle anyone, but Jack Molinas was unstoppable. He made every kind of basketball shot you've ever seen, but none more impressive than the hook, from deep in the corner when I had him perfectly defensed. The crowd was shouting like crazy and everything he threw up went swish."

That game had been played during the summer of 1954, the first year of his exile, when he was a star attraction wherever he played while attending Brooklyn Law School and making up for a lost semester at the same time. The juggling started in earnest when he graduated, on time with his class, and began to practice law while playing and coaching basketball in the Eastern League. Stan came back to Brown from a Christmas vacation visit to his folks in Scranton with some fresh material to tease Jesse about his idol.

"They say that for a small-time lawyer and minor-league basketball player he talks the biggest game in North America."

Jesse always rose to such bait. "Now, wait a minute. He plays in the Eastern League because he's blacklisted in the NBA. He may make less than a hundred dollars a game, but even as a player-coach he still averages almost 40 points. You know as well as I do he belongs under the big top, not nickel-diming at some sideshow in Williamsport or Hazleton."

"Sure. Big man. First-class all the way. Do you know what his legal practice consists of?"

Jesse winced and shook his head. He couldn't stomach the image of that great stiff-kneed Molinas stride chasing ambulances. The report he'd heard was that he was specializing in accident negligence cases. "Goes after insurance companies, right?"

"Twenty-five thousand a year, Jesse, tops. Small-time and bottom of the barrel."

"It's just a game for him. The money doesn't matter. The sport is nailing the companies."

"One story I heard is that Molinas goes around bragging about the time in Wilkes-Barre when his own car spun out. He was barely scratched but the woman with him had a slight neck injury, and they made a big score on the insurance company."

"That's what I mean. The kick was suing his own insurance company on behalf of the victim of an accident in his own car which he was driving."

"But I've got news for you. Levy and Harten, the firm he works for, is filing suit against the NBA and Maurice Podoloff for three million dollars in damages. They claim Molinas was deprived of his right to earn a living through ban, boycott, and blacklist."

Now Jesse's spirits lifted. "All right! Now we're getting somewhere."

"Not yet. They don't expect to win this one. But when they lose, then they can go for the jugular: a multimillion-dollar Sherman Anti-Trust proceeding."

"I get it, the college draft—it's an illegal device to maintain a monopoly. No free market situation. By blacklisting him, the NBA acted in restraint of trade."

"Jesse, if it was anyone but Molinas you'd laugh at that. Don't you think they had the right to do that after what he did?"

"Look, he's paid for that. He's lost a lot of money and a lot of years from his life, his career. He's got to be clean, now. The grand jury dismissed all charges against him in '54. In '56 he passed the bar with a clean bill of character and fitness. And ever since he's gone through proper channels to be reinstated. But is there due process? No. They frustrate him every time. What else can you call it but a league-wide conspiracy?"

"Hold on a minute, Jesse. Don't get carried away with how clean your man is. Of course he's ready to go into court and swear under oath that he never dumped games or shaved points. Do you believe that? And now he'll also say that he knows absolutely nothing about the rumors that it's going on again, bigger than ever."

"Now?"

"Now. They even know it in Scranton. And if it's true, do you really believe that Jack Molinas knows nothing about it?"

"Oh, my God!" Jesse said, and it was almost a wail. His recovery was weak. "Stan, listen. This is not about fixed games of basketball. This is a legal game, and in court you've got to play by their rules. You go all out, make the system work for you, and maybe you can win. All he wants is to be given a chance to play *that* game by their rules."

"He can't. They won't let him. Someone's got to bend the rules for him to win, and he won't be satisfied unless he's the one doing the bending."

"Is that the conventional Scranton basketball wisdom?"

"No. It's what I learned from reading Joseph Conrad. What a thesis this will be."

The Karlsberg thesis on Conrad didn't work out too well, but he was certainly right about the Molinas case. It took two years, but when the process had run its course Molinas had lost both the preliminary suit and the Anti-Trust case. The courts had simply refused to consider the substantive issue of whether the NBA was operating in restraint of trade, which pissed Jesse off because he believed it was. They also refused to address the larger philosophical issue of treating players as chattels disposable according to whim if not conspiracy. This saddened Jesse because he saw little chance of changing such attitudes and values. Yet it was hard for Jesse to refute what the last court had pointed to as the central matter of fact: Jack Molinas was an admitted gambler. Federal Judge Irving Kaufman, in denying the suit, called the NBA rule against gambling "about as reasonable a rule as could be imagined."

When Jesse completed his degree, he applied for teaching jobs only in the New York metropolitan area. His own thesis would soon be a book, and he probably could have done better academically (once he had been turned down at Columbia), but he was drawn to the city. He had not yet fully realized the hollowness of that vestigial hunger for fame that made him want to be where the action was. Despite the great satisfaction he took in what he was doing, he felt that in New York he might yet entertain the possibility of pursuing some other career. Rachel had been almost positive about the move, once the City College offer came through. One final fringe benefit—that he would be at the very Mecca of basketball, teaching in the institution that Nat Holman had immortalized—was, however, undercut by a single regret: he could go to Madison Square Garden all season and never see Jack Molinas on the floor.

Chapter 18:
Fox and Dogs, Running

For Jesse, teaching at City College meant that he could be in touch with the current talk on the street. And no sooner had he begun his duties than he began to hear hot rumors of another major basketball scandal. In time even the newspapers picked up the rumblings. There was talk of a vast network and a New York mastermind at the controls. The papers began to mention a "Mr. X." On the street it was wisely and widely conceded that Jack Molinas was—or had to be—the mastermind, Mr. X.

Jesse was appalled, but if he had allowed himself to think about it, he would have realized that Molinas was just amused by all of this. It made him laugh out loud when he heard the latest rumor or when he read the freshest item in the paper. The joke was not how uncannily accurate the New York street talk could be, if you walked the right streets, but how incredibly slow the emergence of the truth was in the fastest of lanes. Molinas had been fixing college games for five seasons before most of this talk got around.

Molinas had done more than open a law office in 1957, he had renewed his partnership with Joe Hacken. He was not only playing and coaching in the Eastern League, he was also very active in the schoolyards around the City. He played everywhere, knew everyone. Anyone who had any active interest in the game of basketball knew Jack Molinas. With his big flashy car and his big flashy good looks, he was a charismatic figure to the high school and college players.

He'd outplay them, slap their backs, take them places, fix them up with hookers, slip them money, give them tips on horses, and lend them his car. And always he'd introduce them to Joe Hacken.

Joe Jalop, too, was well known in basketball circles. It wasn't just that he was the guy who booked bets on Creston Avenue for Jack and friends like Aaron Wagman and Joe Green when they were still schoolkids. He had also coached a team, sometimes called the Hacken A.C., that came within two points of beating the Cinderella City College team that had just won a national championship. It was Joe Hacken who would eventually talk point-shaving to the kids as well as ask to meet other interested players.

Molinas and Hacken were middle-men. They didn't have the kind of seven-figure bankroll it would take to pay out the bribes and spread the action around the country to make it really worthwhile. What they did was set up the games and sell the information. Their first big customers were in St. Louis—Dave Goldberg and Steve Lekometros, who Molinas thought were backed by the mob. Meanwhile, Wagman and Green were working the same street, on a smaller scale, sometimes through Molinas and Hacken, sometimes selling games on their own.

Hacken liked things the way they were, neat, virtually undetectable because they attracted no attention. But Molinas was always thinking bigger. And in time they went from middle-men making a clear, safe profit to men in the middle out on a limb, taking big chances and occasional big losses along with big payoffs. Molinas was intoxicated with the machinations of moving big numbers around.

He started selling games to people in other cities, Pittsburgh, Boston, and especially Chicago. Some of the games he sold were guesses, not fixes. That way he'd pocket the bribe money as well as the information fee, and if the game went bad he'd have to lie his way out of it. But Wagman and Green started selling games on their own too, and sometimes they were working at cross-purposes. Hacken and Molinas lost as much as $80,000 on a game they thought was locked up because they had paid off three players to lose. The trouble was that all five starters on the other team were dumping the other way.

College basketball was not their only arena. They sold "opinions" on college football and NFL football. Molinas let people believe he had NBA personnel he could count on, but he never seemed to sell any NBA games, apparently because he was still suing to get back into the league. In time it was college football that was their undoing, though basketball remained their mainstay.

Molinas kept dodging the bullet and laughing his way out of trouble. He nearly came a cropper with some Chicago maneuvers. Lefty Rosenthal was booking a lot of his action and was sometimes caught short and slow with his payoffs. So Jack got even in his own way. He touted Lefty on a game that was fixed and gave him a New York number where he could get down for forty dimes (a $40,000 bet). Molinas had the game fixed the other way. Shortly thereafter, Tony Dicci (di Chiarinte), another Chicagoan who was as they say connected, called Molinas about a football game he was touting but Dicci called a phony fix. Jack was summoned to Miami.

He went, despite warnings, saying he knew he could straighten things out without getting hurt. He couldn't tell if Rosenthal was behind it, but he hoped Lefty hadn't found out that the New York bookie who took his forty grand was fronting for Molinas. In Miami he was taken for a civilized ride by people he didn't recognize. He got a reasonable lecture, the text of which was that from now on he should "play straight with the boys at all times." And then, as a small sample lesson, one of the gentlemen took a sap to the back of his hand, breaking one small bone.

Molinas was incorrigible, however. He sold a game that went bad and was invited to a meeting in a fifteenth-floor hotel room in Pittsburgh. There his big athletic body was held out the window by his ample feet held by two big unathletic bodies, until he swore that it would never happen again, promised to make restitution for the loss, and acknowledged that another mistake would be fatal. Of course that was after he had bellowed, "You can't hurt me, I'm Jack Molinas." There is no witness to record how the famous Molinas grin looked upside down fourteen and a half stories up.

The bookies of America were getting hurt too bad by the fixes. No one depends on honest sport more than bookmakers. When they were finally convinced that the whole business was rotting away with a very loud stench, they began making noises of their own in the vague direction of law enforcement. But it wasn't until late 1960 that the law found an opening through which to begin to take action.

Aaron Wagman was in Gainesville, Florida, trying to make sure that the Gators didn't cover their 13 point spread against Florida State. He offered Jon MacBeth the Florida fullback $1,500 to fumble a couple of times. It was hardly a major tragedy, but MacBeth told his coach, the coach told the police, and Wagman was arrested. Within the week, another Hacken-Molinas operative, Dave Budin, once captain of the Brooklyn College basketball team, made the same mistake, in Ann Arbor, Michigan with an Oregon halfback, with the same result.

Now the fun began. With Wagman and Budin out on bail, their trails led to Hacken and Molinas. From then on every move they made was under surveillance, and they knew it at once. For Molinas it was a signal to increase his activities, step up the action, show the fuzz what it was like to be a high-roller. It was also a signal to press on with his suit against the NBA. He thought the league would run scared because of the noise in the street and come to terms with him. And he knew that in New York State he could never be convicted entirely on the testimony of co-conspirators. Since he talked only to gamblers and never mentioned gambling to players, he was in the clear.

A scene from those days: Molinas is having a drink with big Sid Youngelman in the Left Bank across from the old Garden. They are at the bar talking, in a preliminary way, about setting up a sure thing on an NFL football game. Molinas gives Youngelman a cigar, takes one himself. From his other side a man resembling a New York version of Christopher Plummer reaches across with a lighter and lights both cigars, looking Molinas straight in the face. It is Vinny Richter, one of Hogan's chief investigators, who helped crack the Carbo boxing case and would now be instrumental in breaking the basketball fixes. Neither man shows a flicker of recognition.

Twenty years later, Richter would insist to Jesse that Molinas could never have known they were that close to him and still carry on the way he did, incriminating himself. Jesse knows Richter as a canny, savvy man, but he also knows that Richter is an eminently rational man. Molinas, on the other hand, may have been a pathological liar, claiming that he knew all along about the investigation, or he may have been pathological about carrying on in full view of police surveillance. Or both.

Molinas loved those games. He thrived on the attention, the angles, the excitement. He was everywhere in those days, playing ball, watching games, trying cases, partying at the Copa with stylish broads. If there was a spot for action, Mr. X marked that spot. And he was betting with both fists and reaching out with both hands to receive payoffs for his information or opinion. He was a masterful juggler and he was putting out extra hard in his performance for a special audience, the investigators who were tapping his phones and shadowing his action night and day.

That was his special angle, his ace in the hole. "Listen," he said to Hacken, "they're never gonna stop us."

"Why not?"

"Figure it out. They're tapping our phones, right? It figures that they've gotta be tapping into our action. They hear us talk about a few games that are in the bag. They check them out. Now whenever we mention a game they call their friendly neighborhood bookie. You think cops don't bet?"

"Everyone bets. But I still think we should back off, cool down the whole operation."

"Joey, where's the Joey I've always known? I've gotta be right on this. If we cut back, we'll be cutting down on the extra income for the cops. We've gotta make it worth their while to let us stay in business."

"Well," Hacken said glumly, "I don't like it. I like privacy. But at least if they're gonna arrest us I'll know in advance. I've got someone on the payroll in Hogan's office."

"Fine, but it'll never happen. By the way, I was right about the NBA, too. They want to settle out of court."

"Congratulations."

"Forget it. I'm going all the way with that. If they're so afraid of the Anti-Trust angle that they'll settle with me, they must be sure they'll lose in court."

"What if they offer you a big number?"

"No deal unless reinstatement goes with it."

"Jack, you're almost thirty years old."

"Shit, are you kidding? I can still beat those guys' brains in. And I prove it every time I play."

Molinas carried on on all fronts. He even carried on conversations with the wiretappers. He'd call Hacken and talk about how those clowns and fools working for the D.A. were getting rich off him but couldn't arrest him even if they wanted to because they had nothing on him that would stand up in court.

The investigators were betting all right, but they were betting too much and too early. Molinas and Hacken would discuss a game on the phone and by the time they would call their contacts to get down on it themselves the line on the game would have moved a point or two or even three. That meant that the information had spread quickly enough through the gambling investigators for one-sided action in six figures to change the point-spread. It was only a matter of time before Molinas got hurt on a serious bet because of a big shift in the spread.

He was furious. He dialled Hacken's number but he spoke directly to the tappers. "Listen, you sons of bitches, listen good this time. I'm giving you valuable information and you don't know how to handle it. How dumb can you be? You're cutting my throat with it. You better wise up and knock it off or your source of golden information is gonna dry up in a big fucking hurry. Talk about killing the bull goose!"

Maybe those detectives who were betting didn't have the resources at their disposal to wait until near game time and spread their money around through a transcontinental network. Or maybe they didn't care enough to bother. Or maybe they wanted to get their own bets in early before the lines changed. Or maybe they just resented Molinas's attitude and wanted to show him they shouldn't be insulted that way. In any case, the very next week the very same thing happened.

Molinas's fury turned to icy resolution. Two big losses in a row seriously damaged his cash-flow situation. But this time instead of blowing up in anger, he designed his revenge.

He told Hacken in advance, in person, to be ready for the switcheroo and not to be fooled himself. And then he set about fixing a game in Philadelphia that would be the lock of the century.

He took painstaking care of this game. He had three players on one team dumping. He had two star players on the other team primed to go all-out, protecting against any counter-fix. And he had the best guarantee in the world to control a basketball game: he had bribed both officials.

On the phone to Hacken, he said excitedly, "Joe, I've got the all-time lock on this game. I've got three and two and the tooters. This is going to be our biggest score ever." Only, when he named the team, he named the wrong one, the sure loser.

The betting line on that game began to move immediately, half a point, a point and a half, three, four and a half. Only Molinas and company were betting the other way. The investigators were going for it, going big, betting their bodies and souls. One detective took a second mortgage on his house.

Molinas went to Philadelphia himself to field-general the whole operation and to watch the show. He had all of his people instructed to keep things close in the first half and then put it away safely in the bag in the second. In fact he let them know he wanted them to rub it in as bad as they possibly could.

The plot worked to perfection. As he walked around the Palestra that night, he said later, he saw that "half of New York's sleuths were there. But they weren't watching me. They had eyes only for the game." The game was played according to Molinas's scenario. He and Hacken made a big score, and for once the bookies did all right because the whole world was betting the other way. But that wasn't the measure of Molinas's triumph. All the way back to New York and for days afterward he savored the expressions on the faces of New York's plain-clothed finest, the first-half excitement, the second-half horror.

Trouble was it worked too well. They had been hurt too bad not to hit back, particularly the detective who had lost everything and now owed an extra eight thousand on his house. They had been caught in a losing game and it was time to close the book on Molinas and company. They neither admired sublime roguishness nor forgave self-destructive bravado, and they didn't much care which had been at work in the doublecross.

Hacken's man in Hogan's office got the message to him: they are preparing to bring players in for questioning. The advance notice should have been all they needed. Hacken dispatched Wagman and Green to speak to every player they had ever used, to warn them (their foreknowledge should have been a convincing demonstration to the players of their influence and power) and to tell them that if they admitted nothing there was no problem. Deny everything. Lie and keep lying. There was no admissible evidence. Without admissions there was no case. And that was all true.

It was March 1961 when the roundup began. Hacken and Wagman were arrested. Dozens of players were brought to New York from all over the country. A parallel, cooperative investigation in North Carolina corralled many others. The frightened players proved easy pickings for the interrogating police. They sang like Whiffenpoofs, poor little lambs led astray, and in time so did the gamblers, except for Hacken. Joe Jalop was old school; he'd rather do his time with a clear conscience than rat on a business associate.

Molinas was still in the clear. His operation was fully exposed but he could not be connected directly to any players, only to co-conspirators, and so he could not be convicted. But once again he went too far in trying to show up the law enforcement system, and he overextended his amazing high-wire juggling act: he decided, against Hacken's sage advice, to act as attorney for one of the fixers. The prospect of going into court and defending a player against charges of fixing games, when the court and the world knew that he was the master-fixer, was irresistible to Mr. X.

Billy Reed was a nervous kid from Queens. When he went to Bowling Green to play basketball he was all set to do business with Molinas. He idolized him, and Molinas took advantage of his charismatic hold over him. In fact, he was so sure of Billy that he broke his own rule against talking directly to a player about point-shaving. And now, more nervous than ever, Reed had come to him for advice, help, legal counsel before being questioned.

Molinas wanted to make doubly sure that Billy would accept his guidance, so he took him to another lawyer in his building to tell him that if he admitted nothing to the police and weighed his answers to the grand jury he couldn't be touched.

"What should I do?"

The attorney looked nervous himself and said, "I advise you to tell the truth, the whole truth, and nothing but the truth."

Molinas jumped up, took his associate by the arm into the next room, asking, "What gives?"

"I think he's wired," was the frightened answer.

Molinas threw his hands up in disgust and led Billy back to his own office. Could he have misunderstood the other lawyer's warning? Did he think he meant wired as in drugged up rather than wired for sound? Did he mis-hear "weird" for "wired" as one newspaper report had it? No, he simply didn't believe that Billy would do that to him.

Yet he knew that his own office was bugged. He turned on a radio, loud, and then took Reed into a closet. Over and over he told him not to say anything, not to admit anything to the grand jury.

"But what if they really know? What if they ask me if you personally paid me money to fix games, if you personally told me to shave points, if they know the games and the dates and the amounts of the bribes."

"You lie, Billy. You say no. They really don't have anything unless you break down and confess. So you don't. You lie."

They were closeted for over half an hour. The tape ran 42 minutes. A couple of months later, on March 16, 1962, Molinas kept a public-speaking date in Washington, D.C., with a New York detective in the audience, as usual. The title of the speech was "The Integrity of Basketball." The next day, back in New York, Molinas was taken into custody. With Reed's evidence to open the way, Wagman's testimony could convict him.

But Jack Molinas kept smiling. He announced his engagement to an elegant young Park Avenue woman from a family of old New York German-Jewish money. Indeed, some of that money would pay for his defense. Molinas was not such a fool as to have himself for a client.

Chapter 19:
Trial and Errors

Jesse's disenchantment with City College began almost as soon as he started teaching there. The school had come a long way since earning a prodigious academic reputation in the twenties and thirties, most of it downhill. Recent revisionist history tells how the open-admission policies of the seventies ruined a great institution, but it ain't necessarily so. When Jesse got there in 1959 the faculty was just a shadow of the distinguished, vigorous, intellectually adventurous and groundbreaking entity it had once been. It had been democratized to a faretheewell and become a comfortable sanctuary for mediocre lockstep timeservers, a living argument against the tenure system.

Even the student body had deteriorated from its glory days. Admissions policies still kept out marginal students but the good, prestigious schools creamed off the top with scholarships, so that what was left, for the most part, was the second level, the over-achievers, no less aggressive but somewhat less brilliant. They did not make up for the poisonous atmosphere, but Jesse felt more comfortable with them than with most of his colleagues.

At City in those days the game in residence was not basketball but character assassination. In the faculty dining room even the bland or crudely salted food was less offensive to Jesse's taste than the malicious gossip. Conversation lacked even the saving grace of cleverness. For a time he abandoned the English departmental tables and joined the limp-wristed theater circles, where the wit was quicker and pleasure was taken with the most demonic of British crosswords. But before the end of the fall semester he quit the whole room, preferring to join groups of students in the massively unappetizing commons room for lunch and conversation, knowing that his absence would make him a ready target for the faculty defamers.

For two years Jesse struggled to stay afloat at City, but the truth was that his life was falling apart and he didn't want to see it. At school he avoided all the cliques, holding himself aloof from the politics and paying the double price of no support and charges of snobbishness. On one opinion he joined the majority: he didn't belong there. Nevertheless, he got the needed votes for tenure and assumed that when he came up for promotion next spring he would get it. He was, after all, publishing regularly and getting feelers for jobs elsewhere.

At home his comfortable assumptions could only be sustained by inattention. Because he had to teach extra evening courses to pay the suburban rent, his time with the boys was severely curtailed, and Rachel's withdrawn silence and coldness kept him in the dark about her. For all the energy he had put into the family, he had begun to feel like an outsider.

The Molinas trial, then, provided a perfectly timely distraction. Preoccupation became obsession. Jesse lost himself so thoroughly that it amounted to an escape from reality. Colleagues and students alike shook their heads over his compulsive rehashings and interpretations of the trial.

The press gave full daily coverage and anyone who sat at Jesse's table in the college cafeteria got the benefit of a thorough collation plus commentary. The reporting he liked best was that of Milton Gross in the New York *Post*. Gross had been close to the case, and to Molinas, all along,

and Molinas respected him despite Gross's assumption of
his guilt. Six months before the trial Gross had done a
series called "Inside Story of Jack Molinas," based on several interviews. Whenever there was a new development in
the case, Molinas would call Gross to talk about it.

Though Gross had long since identified Molinas as Mr. X,
he also printed Molinas's disclaimers: that he was innocent
except that he knew all the gamblers and players, that he
was an inveterate—but not big—bettor himself who took
advantage of any inside information that came his way, and
that Hogan might seek to embarrass him because he was a
lawyer but couldn't get an indictment just on association.
That was the Molinas party line but Jesse may have been
the only one who swallowed it.

Gross reported that one gambler had said of Molinas,
"You could chill a bottle of beer with his blood." But Fran-
ces Kahn, who was his attorney at the original bail hearing,
said that he was in a state of shock, not coldblooded but
scared. Hacken said the same thing; he believed that the
grin was a mask, that Jack was always scared inside. Now
Gross called Molinas a "study in impassiveness in court."
With rings under his eyes and "sallow-faced by nature" he
still showed no concern or emotion.

While his fiancée waited off to the side, Molinas talked
with his attorney, the distinguished Jacob Evseroff, and
Gross during a recess. "I quit going to the Garden for basketball games after the scandals of 1951," Evseroff said.

Gross said, "You saw a lot of games, Jack, more than
most, didn't you? That could be part of your trouble."

"Yeah," he grinned, "I've probably seen more than most."

"Well you've got chutzpah, I'll give you that."

"I will too," said his lawyer, but he didn't make it sound
like an asset.

The prosecution case was outlined for the jury in the

opening remarks of Assistant District Attorney Peter Andreoli. For two and a half hours he told them he would prove a) that Molinas, Hacken, Green, Wagman, and others had conspired to bribe 22 players from 12 colleges to lose or to shave points in 25 games over four years, b) that Molinas personally paid three separate bribes of $1,000 each to Billy Reed, and c) that he tried to get Reed to perjure himself before the grand jury.

Evseroff's opening statement was brief but emotional. In fifteen minutes he outlined the thrust of the defense: Molinas is guilty of nothing but guilt by association with people like Wagman, Green, and Hacken. Those men are parasites who used their friendship with Molinas to gain access to college players who could be bribed. The only witnesses who will testify against Molinas are crooks, chiselers, thieves, and corrupt college kids, people who will say anything the District Attorney wants them to say in order to save their own skins.

"The jury won't buy that," a student said to Jesse at lunch.

"Well it just might," he muttered, with an elaborate rationalization. Since the others had all pleaded guilty, the jurors would have to satisfy themselves that there was a reason behind it. In the light of the discrepant plea, they could accept a presumption of innocence not despite the coordinated testimony against him but because of its carefully orchestrated, conspiratorial nature. There must, it was Jesse's fond hope, be an element of paranoia in the minds of juries, too.

The possibility and the hope gained strength, in Jesse's desperate thinking, by the prominence of Aaron Wagman at the beginning of testimony. Wagman occupied the witness stand for seven full court days and seemed to enjoy almost every minute. He had bargained himself into the position of being able to brag about all he had done, to be a big man for the first time in his life, without worrying about having to pay too big a price for it. He had already been convicted in Florida, had been sentenced to 5-10 years, and was out pending appeal. Unfortunately for him, two teammates of Jon MacBeth had taken the money before the fullback said no and blew the whistle. Now Wagman had pleaded guilty to 38 counts of conspiracy and bribery, but if his testimony convicted Molinas he'd get off with a suspended sentence of 3-5 years contingent on his doing time in Florida.

For seven days this former Yankee Stadium souvenir vendor told about what a big shot he was, while putting down Joe Hacken as Molinas's "errand boy," and for almost two weeks Jesse cursed him as a star villain in a travesty of justice. Wagman didn't claim to have originated the idea for the fixes. He said that Joe Green had come to him in September of 1957 saying he had met two college players who were interested in throwing games for a price. Wagman then started looking for backers. After several people in the Bronx turned him down, he approached Molinas who jumped at the chance.

On cross-examination, Evseroff asked Wagman how he knew about fixing games. The answer was, "I heard about it in the neighborhood." And when the attorney rose to the bait and asked, "From whom?" the trap was sprung. "From Molinas," he said, "in 1954." That was no ad lib but a carefully rehearsed line, and it got the anticipated laugh in the courtroom.

It seemed to Jesse a terrible mistake for Molinas's defender to make. The one thing you don't want to do, he told anyone who would listen, is score for the other side. Not if you're trying to win. The proper question after that testimony, Jesse proclaimed, should have been asked quickly and without a hint of surprise: Why did you approach so many

other people before you got around to him? He kept fanta-
sizing being a lawyer, defending Jack Molinas in court.

Wagman's narrative was colorful, graphic, and detailed.
Several of the episodes he described had the ring of truth
about them, particularly when they played down the brag-
gadocio. But at other times the twists of the plotting added
up to a loss of credibility. In their second season of fixing
(1958-59), Wagman said, while Molinas was getting money
from one backer to bribe the players that Wagman had
lined up, he started selling the games himself to a second
backer and pocketing the bribe money. When Molinas
found out and confronted him, they agreed to share the
extra revenue from both backers, each of whom believed
he had exclusive information.

Leonard Kaplan, playing for Alabama, was a contact
Molinas had developed in the New York schoolyards. For a
game against Tulane, Frank Cardone of Pittsburgh had paid
for Kaplan to make sure Alabama wouldn't win by four or
more. By the time Molinas tried to sell the same game to
Dave Goldberg in St. Louis, the line had dropped all the
way to one point. Goldberg didn't like the odds, so he
instructed Molinas to tell Kaplan to win because he was
betting on Alabama. Kaplan's performance that night was
worthy of Molinas himself: he was the high scorer of the
game with 27 points, sank the last-second basket to win by
two for Alabama (and Goldberg), but kept the spread
under four (to win for Cardone). Molinas told Kaplan he
wanted him to play on his Eastern League team when he
was finished in Tuscaloosa.

Wagman testified how he and other fixers, once they
knew they were under investigation, kept moving around
and working out of pay phones in candy stores, hotels, and
bus stations, concentrating on games outside New York.
Here again Jesse faulted Evseroff for missing a golden op-

portunity. He could have gotten Wagman to testify that Molinas, unlike the rest, never played the part of a drug-store bookie.

Instead, Wagman went on bragging about the time he set up four fixed games in one day from a pay phone in the Henry Hudson Hotel in the Bronx. Columbia against Penn in Philadelphia was to be controlled by Fred Portnoy, Mississippi State against Auburn in Montgomery by Jerry Graves, Tennessee against Vanderbilt in Knoxville by Richard Fisher, and North Carolina State against Duke in Durham by Anton Muehlbauer and Stanley Niewierowski. Neither Portnoy nor Graves, however, prevented their teams from covering, so the fixers won on only two of the four games. If you can only break even betting fixed games, Jesse told the lunch crowd, you're in the wrong business.

Evseroff redeemed himself in Jesse's estimation before his cross-examination of Wagman was over. He had the wit-ness, by turns, claiming to be a wily operator on Molinas's level of intrigue and confessing that he was a fool who never made any money out of all the plotting because he lost so many bets on games that weren't fixed. Probably most damaging to Wagman's testimony, Evseroff got him to admit that, yes, Molinas's phone conversation with Leonard Kaplan was actually about playing in the Eastern League after college but that the conversation "wasn't really about that." Wagman seemed too eager to claim that Molinas later met with Kaplan to bribe him, although he admitted he didn't know for a fact that that meeting took place.

At one point in his testimony, Wagman was asked to iden-tify Joe Hacken in the courtroom. Gross reported that Molinas didn't even look toward his loyal old friend. When Hacken walked by during a recess Molinas looked away, but Gross caught his eye and raised his brows questioningly. Jack shrugged and said, "It wouldn't look good for the jurors to see us talking."

Jesse found it comfortable to see Wagman as the heavy in the scenario, deflecting whatever anger and shame he might have directed toward Molinas so that he could still cling to a heroic image. It was much later that Jesse heard a different version from Vinny Richter. For seven months in the Tombs, according to Vinny, Wagman had been as loyally uncooperative as Hacken, until he learned that Molinas had let him down. He had promised Wagman he would take care of his wife financially as long as Wagman protected him by stonewalling, but Molinas couldn't acknowledge even that debt of honor. "Just a bad guy," Vinny said. "We knew Wagman would finally talk, but when he did he surprised even me—he was a brilliant witness with a sharp, unshakeable memory for detail."

Wagman supplied the facts in court, but it was Billy Reed who gave them credibility. The whole case turned against Molinas with Reed's testimony. Wagman could be doubted, impugned, perhaps even turned to Molinas's advantage, but Reed gave compelling drama to the special audience of twelve.

First of all, he was in uniform, on temporary leave from Army duty in Germany. Then, instead of trying to make himself look good, he became an object of pity, choking up as he described his acceptance of bribes to shave points in six separate games, and finally breaking down on the stand. The tape corroborated what he said, in Molinas's voice as well as his own.

Everoff fought that tape all the way, but Andreoli got it admitted, bringing eight witnesses to establish its authenticity and accuracy. Then, on the day that the corollary trial opened in North Carolina, Everoff presented an affidavit signed by Reed swearing that he didn't throw games, that Molinas didn't bribe him but was just his friend and attorney. It was a desperation ploy. Judge Sarafite hesitated to admit it as evidence. Reed acknowledged that he had signed something in Molinas's office that day, but hadn't read it and remembered neither oath nor notarization. This was too obvious an attempt to muddy the waters and probably worked against Molinas because of sympathy for Reed.

The rest of the prosecution case seemed weak, but Jesse knew he was clutching at straws. He hoped that Andreoli's strategic arrangement would backfire by leaving the doubtful parts in the minds of the jury just before the presentation of the defense. For example, Tommy Falentano, a teammate of Reed at Bowling Green, had been named by Wagman as another player enlisted directly by Molinas. But Falentano said he'd met Molinas only once on a New York playground court and hadn't been asked to fix games or been given any money by him.

Leonard Kaplan was also a weak link because, after his testimony implicated Molinas directly in bribery, the defense introduced its own tape, secretly recorded by a private detective at the Pimlico Hotel owned by Kaplan's family. On it, Kaplan admitted to Molinas that "it could be the truth" that the money Jack gave him was a bonus to play pro basketball.

Three other former players were called, Gary Kaufman and Leroy Wright of College of the Pacific and Barry Epstein of Utah. Wright told of plotting with Molinas but not carrying it out because of injury; Epstein told he had been recruited by Kaufman as well as Hacken but refused involvement; Kaufman, who lost credibility through Epstein's testimony, told of aborted fix attempts arranged by Molinas and subsequent threats by Molinas. Then came the final taped evidence of the trial, a ludicrous scene recorded in Kaufman's house, with a transmitter in the basement TV set and the D.A.'s detectives upstairs with receiver and recorder.

It was like a soundtrack from a grade C gangster movie or a Sid Caesar parody. Molinas warned Kaufman that no one should ever implicate him or any backers in any connection with a fixed game. "They'll get shot. They get killed. I'm not kidding... It's the old Capone mob from Chicago... Don't ever identify them... Regardless of what you do, don't ever do that, for your own good."

Evseroff wisely ignored this part of the prosecution's case, hoping it would seem to the jury as to most of the courtroom audience as too hokey to be true. After sixteen days of methodical if inconsistently effective testimony from thirty witnesses, Andreoli rested the prosecution's case. Commenting on the total presentation, Jesse said that the whole thing smacked of obvious conspiracy and Molinas himself would surely give the lie to it, turn the whole game around when he had his chance to play to the jury.

It was clear as soon as the defense began that Evseroff had elected to play for contrast, in form as well as substance. He refused to have Molinas testify. He had twelve witnesses on the stand in less than an hour, including the father of the Molinas bride-to-be. He established a quickly-drawn character portrait of Jack Molinas that boldly distinguished him from the other fixers, and he stressed the point that Joe Hacken, who by the prosecution's construction was close to the heart of the operation from the beginning, had never implicated Molinas.

He made one mistake. He included Carl Green, who played with Molinas at Williamsport, as a character witness. Green was the only one cross-examined by Andreoli, because it gave him the opportunity to establish that Jack Molinas had been kicked out of the NBA. That was a counterproductive character reference in itself, and Molinas had yet another reason to curse Maurice Podoloff's summary justice.

Waiting for the jury's decision, Molinas told Jimmy Breslin, "This is murder. I wish I had the verdict right now. Bang! Get it over with."

But he didn't have long to wait, about as long as he'd have to wait for a result of a basketball game he'd bet on. He was already thinking appeal when the foreman announced that he had been found guilty on three charges of bribery, one of conspiracy to bribe, and one of subornation of perjury. Clearly, Billy Reed had done him the most damage in court. He could get up to 36 years, but he'd have to wait a month for sentencing.

Jesse had anticipated the decision and was fully prepared with an attitude in response. Grimly, almost belligerently, he went around saying, "It's one thing to get a conviction, quite another to get Jack Molinas to prison."

When sentence came, Jesse indignantly castigated it as unconscionable. Molinas was going to jail. Here was a first offender, convicted by questionable methods of questionable police and the testimony of confessed criminal conspirators, and they were throwing the book at him.

Consecutive sentences of 5-7 1/2 years were imposed for each of two bribery charges. State Supreme Court Judge Sarafite called him "a master-fixer, a completely immoral person, and the ringleader of groups that corrupted college ballplayers to dump games for money." It would be seventeen months before he'd begin his sentence. Repeated motions for appeal would be denied, but the Supreme Court of New York eventually would reduce the sentence to 7-12 1/2 years, after the Appellate Division called the 10-15 excessive.

Over and over Jesse shook his head over these decisions. Then he shook it again and his vision cleared. The dramatic distractions all dissipated and he could suddenly see what had happened in his own case. The opposition to him had solidified in the English Department. Like Molinas he had gone along believing nothing could touch him, and now he was informed officially that the vote had gone against him for promotion, unofficially that it wasn't likely to change for a long time and he'd be well advised to move on.

Driving home to confront Rachel with an impending uprooting, he came to his own decisions with a new clarity. First, of the job possibilities that had opened up for him, clearly the best was the University of Georgia. It wasn't just the idea of academic advancement with early promotion and a decent graduate program that was appealing, but the idea of making a home in a livable place like Athens.

Thinking about how to present this decision to Rachel, he realized that he had more to confront her with than geographical dislocation. Focusing on their marriage, he suddenly saw emerge a clear picture of infidelity. Molinas had let him down, the legal system had proven a sham, his colleagues had turned on him, and his wife had surely betrayed him. Why was this man smiling?

He was, in fact, pleased that he was moving, moving on, getting on with what was to be his life. This would be an opportunity for both self-knowledge and enlightenment about other people. He wondered if Molinas would be able to take similar advantage of his time. Prison, like a new environment of freedom, or exile, can furnish perspectives for growth, after all.

Rachel surprised him. Not by denying everything—he'd expected that. Even the slightest expression of jealousy on his part always brought the counterattack that he had to be crazy to think such thoughts—a behavior aptly called "gaslighting" by mental health professionals. She did admit, however, that she had been considering leaving him and the children. But she had nowhere to go, she said, so if he still wanted her they would go to Georgia as a family.

There came times when Jesse would blame himself for taking the easy way out and accepting this lame expression of commitment. At other times, when he wasn't full of bitterness at her blatant denials, he would condemn himself for his own blindness to the truth and failure to accept the opportunity, the challenge really, implicit in her response: take your sons and go to hell in Athens. But there was another truth that took precedence, a light for him in those dark days: he knew he was capable of change, and he believed that therefore she must be too.

Chapter 20:
Odd Couplings

For Jesse, Athens, Georgia was a perfect place to experience the 60s. When he'd say that to friends on occasional visits back to the Northeast, if they knew him well enough to tease him, they'd say, "Oh, sure, compared to Attica." But he meant it, with or without any odious comparisons to Molinas and with or without reference to the filth he'd left behind in New York.

It was certainly a good place for political re-education. Movements came late there, change slowly. It was small enough for abuses and injustice to be dramatically visible, but large enough for groundswell activism to be organized and effective. The presence of the university helped because in time, even among that conservative, apathetic, football-and-fraternity-oriented student body, there were just enough concerned students to get things going, enough aware faculty to support them, and enough responsive people in the community to give substance to the numbers.

And it was just a good place to live, with four clearly defined and leisurely seasons, with relatively healthy atmosphere and environs, and with a heartland-America attitude toward sports that enriched Jesse's understanding from new perspectives. It was a good place for him to grow and for his sons to grow up, he thought. And when Rachel in a moment of weakness yielded to his pressure and took one last chance at producing a daughter—with Susannah the blessed result—Athens became the promised land of humanization for him. Later he would joke about the foreplay leading to Susannah's conception: two years of begging, three years of pleading.

But whatever its magic was, it didn't work for Rachel. She was depressed, more withdrawn than ever, and so withholding as to make them all feel the chill of unloving. She never could or would say what was wrong. Jesse guiltily assumed that she was hurting because she wasn't sharing in his growth, his opening up. The more he urged her to come along with him, the more she resisted, sticking closer to home and pushing him out. She accused him of wanting more than she could give him; he reaffirmed his commitment to her, but agreed that he wanted more from her. He wanted companionship; he wanted to feel loved.

Ironically, it was she who needed what he couldn't give her, feelings of superiority that came from brief periods of adoration in metropolitan anonymity from the occasional janitor, stockboy, or butcher's assistant she'd indulge. In the small-town, college-campus atmosphere of Athens, there were far fewer opportunities, and she missed them. There may, too, have been an element of guilt in her depression, because she couldn't acknowledge what had sustained her through the graduate school and City College years.

Jesse was selfish: he didn't allow the frustrations in that central relationship to get in his way. Most everything else in his world was going too well (which Rachel must have resented) for him to dwell on the problem at home. But what matters most to this story is a pair of other relationships from his Athens years, two people who helped him learn certain things about himself, and illuminate certain aspects of Jack Molinas's life and death: Eddie Vennor and Millie Chandler.

*   *   *   *   *

Eddie Vennor was a soul of honor and a fount of wisdom. It was not just a matter of information or expertise, but of principle, philosophical acceptance, and consistent application. The better Jesse knew him, the more he admired his self-contained lifestyle, the breadth of his knowledge and interests, and his comfortable way with himself and the world. And none of this had anything to do with their professional relationship. He was Jesse's bookie.

Jesse met him within a couple of months of moving to Athens. He had found someone willing to accept a modest World Series wager from a newcomer, and the man had suffered a crippling stroke before the sixth game. A week after Jesse's team had won, he learned that Eddie Vennor was paying off all the invalid's debts.

At that time Vennor operated out of a trailer parked behind the American Legion post west of town. Periodically he would move his phones back into the city, depending on whether he could get better protection from the city police or the Clarke County sheriff's office and on whether the political situation called for a "clean-up" campaign in either city or county. But from the first time Jesse stepped inside that trailer, he had the sense that he was a welcome guest of a quietly warm, genuinely humane, confidently humble man.

Much of what Jesse learned about Vennor personally came from other sources. He had been an outstanding premed student on scholarship at Emory, but had been even more successful in Atlanta's very active gambling community. And when he started in the medical school there, he was already a marked man. While most med students eked out a meager subsistence, sometimes supported by ambitious wives, Eddie drove a Cadillac to school while his wife's main occupation was to answer the phones at home. The good fathers of Georgia's close-knit power structure deemed him unsuitable Hippocratic material, and thanks to a complaisant physiology professor who failed him twice, they saw to it that he would find another profession.

He already had one. Eddie shrugged, came home to Clarke County and Athens, and set up shop. He never talked about that experience, neither expressed nor showed any bitterness, only rarely saying with a wistful smile, "I should have gone to Tulane." And he never talked about his two ex-wives, his current wife, or any of those women's children. Yet on the subject of his business he was perfectly open with Jesse and discoursed freely on any subject he had some familiarity with. He had no opinions on matters of which he was ignorant, but he had many strong opinions.

Ostensibly Jesse's visits to Vennor's trailer, or later to his office in the oldest part of town not far from the famous hedges of the stadium, were to settle accounts. But his action was so tiny that Eddie could have carried him for years without settlement. It wasn't really worth his paper work to have Jesse as a client, but it provided a pretext for conversations mutually enjoyed by the college professor and the bookie. The ritual was firm; they never met in another context, never met each other's wife or children or even friends—not until Millie began to take part in many of their discussions.

Eddie taught Jesse the mechanics of his business, exploding some cherished myths in the process. For example, the days of balanced books and guaranteed profit margins for bookmakers were long gone, so that despite multiplied opportunities for lay-offs, most bookies had to be gamblers, had to adjust their own betting lines from the national spreads in order to influence their clients, and were vulnerable to getting hurt by one-sided plays or coups. Besides, in this enlightened age, organized crime no longer controlled or wanted to control all illegal gambling, so that Mafia bookies and independent entrepreneurs existed peacefully and cooperatively, laying off big numbers back and forth for the usual charge (the vigorish), and trading services and information—if not collection efforts. It was a rare independent bookie who had the bankroll to survive without access to mob operations, but the mob itself profited from the enormous proliferation of friendly neighborhood bookies trying to make a decent living from an ancient system of honor, fair play, and credit.

In Clarke County, unlike other parts of the state, the mob did not have major gambling interests. They seemed content to allow Vennor to be the local bookies' bookie, and he was always cordial in his dealings with them on a statewide basis and occasionally across state lines when the risk of federal law enforcement was dictated by the higher risk of being wiped out by an extreme, unbalanced book. It was through those networks of mutual interest that the fixed games of the scandals were first detected. Eddie showed Jesse how easy it was to smell a rotten game when unlikely numbers came in from unlikely places.

When a football coach in another state, say Indiana, was betting a game, Eddie and his people in Athens would know it soon enough to take the game off the boards before noon on Saturday—the rush hour for the betting crowd. But he would never take advantage of this information or his inference by betting the game himself—you didn't stiff another bookie with a fixed game, and you didn't fleece your customers by taking bets on only one side of a fixed game. It was a matter of honor—or enlightened self-interest—because you couldn't stay in business for the long haul any other way.

Eddie also taught Jesse about the structure and hierarchy of organized crime. He had many friends in the outfit, and though he cherished his own independence he had no contempt for them. The idea of bureaucratic Big Crime went against his grain almost as much as bureaucratic, intrusive Big Government and bureaucratic, conspiratorial

Big Business, yet he argued persuasively that society needed a Mafia as a protection against chaos, a provider of
needs and services that would otherwise engender anarchy
or tyranny. "Better the Mob," he used to say, "than mobs."

Later, when Jesse needed help in getting close to the
Molinas story and its denouement, it was Eddie Vennor who
opened the right doors and loosened the right tongues. As a
favor. It was on his recommendation and on the basis of an
old friendship, finally, that the source Jesse called Deeper
Throat cleared some remaining mysteries for Jesse.

Just five or so years Jesse's elder, Eddie seemed to him
of another, older generation, a latter-day version of North
Georgia rugged individualism, a traditional libertarian/
Republican mountaineer. Millie, a decade Jesse's junior,
was of another generation too, an Old South belle turned
new radicalized youth. Before leaving Athens, Jesse came
to identify himself with Millie's positions, but he never lost
his respect for Eddie's. And in time he would need the
lessons of both to distinguish his place from that of Jack
Molinas in the generation between, just as he would use
the help of both to tell his story.

*   *   *   *   *

Millicent Chandler was, by turns, Jesse's student, his
teaching assistant, his friend, and his lover. When he first
arrived at Georgia, she was enthroned as Queen of the
Stacks. She held court among the philological quarterlies in
the library, and the English graduate students attended her
like so many ladies in waiting. With sweet brown eyes and
matching hair of Tupelo honey, Millie was not only one of
the smartest people around but also glibly sharp-tongued.
She had most of the faculty cowed and most of her classmates buffaloed. The inner circle around her was made up

primarily of those good-looking, fine-mannered, young southern men of questionable sexual preference who seem to gravitate toward the fine arts or belletristic areas of academe. Protected by this coterie from what might be unseemly or threatening in the world, Millie ironically grew far beyond the provincial attitudes that most of them clung to.

She had come to Athens as a new graduate student, fresh out of the University of Arkansas at 20, a year before. Young as she was, there was already a Tennessee Williams aura about her of wistful tragedy. The story was told in hushed tones about an engagement to a poetic New Orleans boy who had drowned himself a week before their wedding, with the implication of sexual confusion. A harsher version had her scorning him to death for inadequacies that were as much intellectual as sexual.

Neither was true, but she did nothing to dispel the rumors. She played both the lady and the wit as she lorded it over her fellows. But in Jesse's class she played it straight. She was in his first graduate seminar at Georgia, probably the best group he ever taught, and she was one of the best of them. With Jesse, from the start, she dropped any act of coquette, vamp, or ingenue. There was no batting of eyes, no tempting sidewise smiles. She simply worked hard to compete in class, to impress him with the quality of her work and her mind. Beyond that, outside of class, there was only an ongoing exchange of badinage that was intended to demonstrate an extra-scholastic worldly-wise brightness. It was being cool and talking fast and loose at the same time, and it was the closest they came to a flirtation—though Jesse caught glimpses of her going through all the southern-feline species of allurement with others.

The following year, by the three fates who ran the graduate program, Millie was assigned as Jesse's teaching assistant. She had a lot going for her. She knew he was attracted to her but instead of carrying on a flirtation she adhered strictly to a professional relationship. Yet they were together enough for him to learn that she wasn't like the usual run of graduate students in English, women who think a penis is just a phallic symbol. She fairly shone with sexuality but seemed to be trying to keep it to herself for the time being.

As soon as the academic year was over and spring quarter grades turned in, just when a flirtation might have begun in earnest, a friendship blossomed instead. Jesse was nominally her advisor since she was considering the medieval period as her field of specialization, but they talked little about her work. She made him her confidant, narrating the saga of her perilous escapes from involvement with a number of men.

He played lay therapist with her, as teaching careers seem to demand, and led her to understand that she was encouraging that kind of attention because she was afraid of any genuine (or, the implication was clear, consummated) involvement, and she could effectively deal with inappropriate overtures from essentially unavailable men. But it was a two-way therapy street. Jesse opened up to her about Rachel, and she tried to reconcile her own impression of the aloof wife with the image, the myth really, projected by Jesse and reflected by Rachel.

During those parties where some junior faculty were welcomed among graduate students, though, Millie and Jesse often demonstrated affection by touching or hugging, and occasionally exchanged sweet and sexy kisses. Still, however it may have looked to others, they maintained a protective distance in the mutual knowledge of her hangups and his unavailability.

More and more of their time together, during the next phase, involved discussions that set literary and personal matters aside and went directly to social issues, to political and philosophical values. Her consciousness was a half-rung ahead of his in most ways. Only in the fight for racial equality had he come to "the movement" ahead of her. She was feminist first, anti-war sooner, and equally anti-establishment. And she was way ahead of him in experimenting with drugs; while he was just trying, ineffectively, his first marijuana, she was testing the non-addictive psychedelics. Amazingly, the conservative old-timers in the department still saw her as a fine young southern lady, white gloves and Presbyterian Sundays—and Jesse as a Yankee radical.

Visits to Eddie Vennor became highlights of their weeks. The dialogue was dynamic and intense, but always good-natured. They met on the common ground of love of freedom, and between Eddie's humane acceptance of corrupt human nature and Millie's romantic notions of working toward perfectability Jesse found himself shifting priorities from defending individual freedoms to achieving liberation of masses.

Millie and Jesse talked, joked, fantasized, and gradually attained an easiness of intimacy. The one intimate thing he never discussed with her was Molinas and the one thing they avoided was physical intimacy. Until the following November, when the South Atlantic Modern Language Association met in Greenville, South Carolina at the old Jack Tar Poinsett Hotel. That's old as in old, not good old. Jesse believed he had discovered in his room the ur-indoor shower, a bare nozzle and hose mounted twelve feet above the floor with a drainage system as primitive as the outdoor latrines at the Baths of Caracalla in Rome. But the shower was the least of the surprises in store for him in that room.

The last night there, Millie and he had drinks and dinner and began making the rounds of the publishers' parties. Millie was drinking her way into a state of happy expansiveness Jesse hadn't seen before. Every gesture ended in a touch, and as they went through the hotel she insisted on walking arm-in-arm.

The Harcourt party had spilled out into the corridor, and there they saw Duke's Trygve Erickson leaning against a wall, flanked by a couple of admirers, his normally florid face glowing in extravagant flush. Erickson may well have been the most influential Anglo-Saxon scholar in the region at the time. If there is such a thing as academic clout, he had it, regardless of whether the reputation was merited.

Millie sashayed up to him and said, sounding more like Arkansas than ever, "Why, Professor Erickson, it's a pleasure and an honor to meet you, sir. I just had to tell you how much I admire your work."

Since he was already crimson it was hard to see that he was blushing, except that his cheeks took on such a purple tinge that Jesse thought for a minute his face would begin hemorrhaging. He drew himself up to all the courtly height he could muster, looked up at Millie who at sixty-four inches plus three-inch heels seemed to float over him, and tried to say something courtly.

Then Millie's voice dropped an octave, the Arkansas honey turned to lemon juice, and she said, "I thought you'd like to know that we have some Old English going on over at Georgia, too. What do you think of this?" And she proceeded to recite a passage from the *Beowulf*, the part known as "The Lay of the Last Survivor," in perfect metrical cadence, just as Jesse had taught her it should be scanned.

Erickson's mouth fell open. It was a stunning performance. He could find nothing to say. Millie chose to interpret this as meaning he didn't recognize the poetry. She said, "Well, perhaps you'll be familiar with this." And she began reciting *The Wanderer* from the beginning.

Again Erickson just gaped. After half a dozen lines, she broke off and said, "Well, at Georgia we are learning to appreciate the poetry, not just the words in it," and glided on into the Harcourt suite. Jesse couldn't have been more gratified, not just because she had learned so well what he had taught her, but because he knew that she had done the whole number primarily for his sake.

When they finished up at the McGraw Hill party, they were close to his room, and there they went for a nightcap. "Well, Jesse, it's late," she said, after barely sipping the short drink he had poured. "I'd better get to my room." She got slowly to her feet.

"OK," he said, following her to the door. "It's been a lovely evening."

Millie turned in the doorway to say goodnight, and he said to her, "Aren't you going to give me a goodnight kiss?"

"Oh yes," she said in a long breath that ended up more a sigh than a word.

It was a long kiss, full of longing, lingering with lips and tongue but still light and without accompanying embrace. At the end he said, "Please stay with me."

And she answered again with the word that turned into a sigh. Then she sat on the bed, curled up her legs, and lay on her side with her eyes closed.

*   *   *   *   *

Jesse half expected that they would both treat that night as an aberration, that they could pretend it hadn't happened, that the status quo ante would be restored. But Monday morning she called him at the office and said she had to see him, to come to her apartment as soon as he could. When he got there, her first words were, "What are we going to do?"

He knew he should have said, "Nothing. Let's just forget about it." But he couldn't. Just being there in her apartment with this pretty, desirable girl who was showing emotional excitement was a sure turn-on for him. It was easy to convince himself that he loved her. So he said, "What do you want to do?"

What they did was get into bed, make love, and agree to a "clandestine affair." The phrase was hers, one of the surprises of the afternoon. She told him finally her sexual autobiography, and it was a slim volume. She had told only externals before; now she was turning herself inside out for him. All of her experience before had been hurried, frightened, frightening, and unsatisfactory. She had never achieved orgasm until that night in the Jack Tar. Her fiancé had been a fool, his death an accident on a sailboat in the Gulf. She felt that with Jesse she had taken a significant turning in her life toward maturity. And she thought she loved him.

All this was a tremendous ego-trip for him, and he willingly went along with her mood and her scenario. He made a very formal profession of his primary commitment to Rachel and proclaimed that he would permit nothing to interfere with that. But if that were understood he saw no reason why they couldn't discreetly attempt to please each other since he was "so drawn to her" and felt that he already "loved her a little." The truth is that he had thoroughly enjoyed the Jack Tar night, that he was flattered at the role of sexual developer she had cast him in, and that he believed he could meet any demands she *and* Rachel might make. In other words, he thought he could satisfy his egocentric lust and get away with it. He even had a ready-made rationalization in Rachel's coldness; but the other side of that coin was the guilt he felt so keenly that he would in time believe Rachel's accusation that he *caused* her coldness by his desire for others.

Millie was freshly, refreshingly innocent. She had some

literary notions of sexuality but no experience. She was willing to learn though somewhat squeamish about tangible trying. Jesse didn't have all that much to teach. They tried and tried, but never recreated the splendid exhilaration of their first coming together. Still it was fun doing it and apparently getting away with it.

In some ways, though, she was wise beyond her experience. Once, as they lay on their sides, she gently disengaged herself, looked over at him, and said, "You're not doing this because you enjoy the sex all that much, are you?"

"No," he said, after a beat in which he realized how precisely she had caught him.

"Then why?"

"Just to do it, I think, because I can and because it's supposed to be part of it."

"Then why me?"

Jesse smiled. She was letting him off the hook. "What other bright, beautiful, sexy woman can I talk basketball with after we've made love?"

It was true. Millie not only appreciated but even shared his passion for basketball. When they read in the paper about how Adolph Rupp's Kentucky team responded to Ray Mears' patented 1-3-1 trap zone at Tennessee with a match-up zone of his own, Millie actually understood what had gone on on the tartan floor. She, too, could soften her focus so as not to zoom in on the ball and thus take in the patterns of movement and grace in the entire court of play.

Up to a point, Jesse and Millie were playing a game of clandestine affair, Jesse's role being the oh-I'm-being-torn-apart-by-loving-two-women one so dear to the heart of country-western songwriters. He played it with dramatic intensity to a very appreciative audience of one. But the game, the roles, the playing, gave way to genuine feelings. And so instead of a formal closure to a scenario, the reality of the loving in the affair produced a crisis of conscience.

Jesse knew that Eddie was embarrassed by being drawn into their dilemma. But the bookie never let on that any discussions, however frank, fazed him. His advice was in the form of generalized, gentle suggestions, phrased as questions: What are your priorities? Where do you want to invest the burden of your committed selves? What is central to your lives—to the practical living as opposed to the passional experience?

Those weren't his exact words, but his sentiments were clear. Thrice-married and not really involved in family living, Eddie knew that Jesse placed the highest values on what for him was peripheral. What he didn't know was how loving Millie somehow made Jesse's love of wife and family so much stronger, an active emotional elevation of every positive relationship. And what none of them knew, except perhaps Millie at some instinctual level, was that Rachel herself had for years been using casual relationships with others to prop up her passive and flagging commitments to children and husband.

"Is she worthy of you, Jesse?" Millie asked in the long afternoon of their parting.

"Of course," he said, thinking himself unworthy, knowing Millie was a more congenial companion, hating himself for knowing that, feeling his need to hang on to his children as a weakness.

"Does she appreciate what she has in you?"

"Maybe not, but that's my fault for not showing her she has me enough."

"Then there's nothing more to say. Thank God I'll be getting my degree and leaving here soon."

"I'll always want to know where you are and how you're doing. Will you keep in touch?"

Her smile and little movement of the hands said she

didn't know if she could. In fact, it took a while. He kept up with her indirectly. The genuine affection and mutual respect were sustained without contact. But once he had relocated and she was settled elsewhere, they made contact. And when they met again, years later, she brought him a surprise bonus gift of new insight into Molinas.

PART V:
Reunions

Chapter 21:
Forking
Paths

Jesse went to the national MLA meetings in New York in 1968 knowing it would be for the last time. He had lost all interest in a convention that is supposed to exist for the purposes of scholarly presentations and job interviews, but really thrives on academic free-loading and careerism at its worst. And he was more than a little frightened at the prospect that he was turning into one of those insular, self-important, senior men who took themselves and their increasingly narrow subjects with monumental seriousness.

More than that, he was disgusted with the Association's failure to confront issues of war and peace, civil and human rights, or even (in enlightened self-interest) self-determination and labor relations. The academy was earning the disrespect of American society as a whole, because instead of asserting its role as a leader out of darkness (see the roots of the word *educate*), especially through the Humanities, it was a bulbous tail being wagged with ponderously slow motor reflex by distant institutions in control of the beast. The academy led no movement, but only moved when change had already taken place. And the MLA was a belated fart at the end of the bowel movement of social history, a fetid, officious afflatus.

How shall the world be saved, Jesse wondered, echoing Augustine and Chaucer's Monk, when the American academy was more removed from reality than the most cloistered holy orders? Bobby Kennedy was dead, and with him,

Jesse felt, the sole remaining hope for millions who wanted emotionally active participation in the political process. Martin Luther King was dead, and with him, Jesse feared, the already faded dream of racial ecumenism in this country. A breath of freedom had been sniffed in Czechoslovakia and snuffed out as summarily as it had been in Hungary a dozen years before. Riding the crest of all this misery, the improbable Richard Nixon had been elected president and, to cap a year of watershed wretchedness, was bringing the impossible Spiro Agnew with him.

Jesse was sharing this lament with Tony Exeter, a friend from graduate school days, a Victorian literature specialist who was pursuing an interest in thoroughbreds while teaching at his hometown Bluegrass University. "We'll have to start meeting some other way," he said, "because this is my last MLA."

"Well, everything's changed," said Tony, who could find irreverent humor amid any solemnity, twirling his class ring on his finger in a familiar gesture of nervous energy. "I was in New Haven the other day and found out that Mory's had been sold and turned into a Japanese restaurant." Jesse waited for the other shoe to drop, and Tony said, raising his glass in mock solemnity, "O tempura, O Mory's."

"God," said Jesse, "you're as bad as my colleague Russ Jackson," and told him Russ's long, rambling narrative about a trip to Mexico and a search for a bar run by a gringo named Turner, all designed to produce the inevitable groans when finally a native is made to understand and says, "Ay, cantina Turner."

It was precisely at that juncture that Jesse first met Arnold Burr. Walking by, he had spotted Tony and come over to say hello. Jesse was struck right away by two things about him. One was the way he moved, as gracefully as if he were dancing, despite the great mass of weight he carried, like Gleason moving around the pool table as Minnesota Fats in *The Hustler* or Fat Jack Leonard doing a soft shoe. The other thing was his deep tan, especially noticeable on his absolutely bald and shining pate, here in New York in the week between Christmas and New Year's.

It was surprising that he had never met Burr, who seemed to know everybody at the convention. In the ten minutes they sat there, feeling virtuous for buying their own drinks in the convention hotel, thirty people must have gone by. Nearly twenty of them Burr hailed by name and usually with a wisecrack. The other dozen he also identified, turning his back on them and directing his remarks about them to Tony and Jesse.

He also tossed off three drinks. In the years since, Jesse had many occasions to observe his prodigies of eating and drinking, concluding that Burr does both not compulsively but absently and without apparent effect. It is as if the masses of flesh on his large frame simply absorb anything taken into his gastro-intestinal system, just as his mind seems to absorb for instant recall the name, face, and academic affiliation of anyone once seen. But while the absorption of food and drink is accomplished without pleasure, the accomplishment of systematized information about the world of MLA is relished. The wisecracks were his way of deprecating at the same time as he demonstrated his championship form in the game of Who's Where.

Just before he left, he casually but convincingly suggested that Tony and Jesse meet him later that night at a non-MLA party uptown. When they expressed genuine interest and grateful relief, he insisted that they all meet in the lobby at nine and go together.

Jesse didn't know what to expect, but really didn't care. Any opportunity for pleasant company outside the associational compound was worth taking. During the cab-ride uptown Arnold had little to offer by way of preview. It seems that he had visited his grandmother earlier in the week, struck up a mailbox and elevator conversation with an attractive young woman in the building, and come away with a good impression and an invitation to this party. He had threatened to bring some people with him, but no matter, she had said, it was to be a big party. All this, Jesse learned in time, was typical of Burr: attractive women, wangled invitations, and accompanying players brought along to any social performance.

The building was one of those old, dark-brick, low-rise apartment houses on Riverside Drive not too far from Columbia. They age well because the brick weathers nicely, ivy and other greenery give class to the exterior, and the rent control over apartments of six, seven, and eight rooms encourages people to invest in the interior as in long-range home planning. It even lacked that characteristic smell of old apartment buildings.

It was a big party all right, but the rooms gracefully accommodated a gathering of seventy, maybe eighty people, without the sense of wall-to-wall bodies. It was clear at first glance that this was a party where conversation was the main thing, though there was ample booze, a reasonable spread of food, and good jazz on the stereo. Arnold plunged right in. Giving a perfunctory greeting to his hostess and waving toward Tony and Jesse by way of indicating that he had carried out his threat, he was off making the rounds, lining up potentially available women as he glided through the rooms, tossing down drinks, canapés, and crudités as indiscriminately as he tossed off wisecracks to clustered groups of strangers.

Jesse and Tony moved more slowly, gradually introducing themselves to a few people who included them in their conversations. It was a relief to find no MLA types, though some of the theater people there would have been right at home at the convention. Gradually, Jesse became aware of a persistent, intrusive sound. It was a voice, a loud, good-natured but raucous voice, roaring out from the kitchen over all the other conversations in the apartment, roars of approval, of contempt, of laughter, of punch lines.

"What the hell is that?" he asked a woman he had just met.

"Oh," she said, "you'll have to make allowances. He's obnoxious, but he's got his reasons. That's Jack Molinas and he just got out of prison."

Jesse recoiled as if sharply struck, but no one seemed to notice. He could not have defined his feelings, because he was numb, his emotional reaction delayed, suspended in the shock. He moved purposefully almost as if under hypnosis toward the kitchen and the hero of his youth, the great Molinas.

He was sitting at the kitchen table with half a dozen people gathered around, including the hostess. Two other women were also sitting there and Molinas would reach out with the big hands and the long reach to touch, nudge, embrace them in punctuation of his remarks. He looked great, as if he were still in playing condition, except that his hairline had receded alarmingly. Instead of a sickly prison pallor, his color radiated health. He was nearly as dark as Burr and just as glistening.

Jesse resisted the urge to rush up to him, to thrust aside those others, unworthy as he thought them. But he saw that Molinas appreciated his little audience, and he was putting himself out to amuse them, especially the attentive women. Yet the performance had the air of naturalness and spontaneity. Jack Molinas was the life of the party.

In time Jesse was introduced, by name, and insisted on the formality of a handshake. He said, "You know, for most of my life, you've been my alter ego."

"You look more like alter kocher to me," he snapped back and sent another burst of laughter roaring through the rooms.

To be the object of the Molinas laugh was not to be hurt, or even to be offended. It felt more like being graced, taken in by a kind of heroic acknowledgment.

Jesse wasn't to be put off.

"Really, even before you went to Stuyvesant I was hearing about your game, your moves, your hook, your smarts. When I was very young I used to be compared to you all the time, my accomplishments put down next to yours, by my cousins. Remember the Miller twins, Stanley and Marvin? Well anyway, if I had been a foot taller I'd have been you."

"And what would you have done with it?" he said, smiling sardonically but really testing, curious about the answer.

"Whatever I could have," Jesse said. He knew it was the right answer for Molinas, but he didn't have to think before he said it. And Molinas bought it.

The conversation meandered. Molinas was open, effusive. When the subject of recent political history was mentioned, he had no hesitancy in talking about how he and others in prison reacted to cataclysmic news events from outside. "Doesn't mean shit," he said. "Time marches on? Forget it. The only time inside is the time we're doing. And none of those things really matter anyway. Inside or outside, nothing changes. People get sent away, people get offed, and who cares? Other people move right in. The only thing you have to know is that what goes around comes around."

"That's another joke, another pose, right? I mean, I suppose that for career cons, lifers, etcetera, the only world is inside. But for someone like you, a first offender, someone who knows he'll soon be back in the world, surely what happens outside matters."

"No, it doesn't. The only thing that would matter is if

they changed the rules, and they won't do that because the ones that make the rules do all right the way they are. They know how to get around the rules they have, and they're not gonna change things."

"You learned that inside?"

"Hell, no. I knew all about that going in. But I did learn new ways to enjoy myself." He caught Jesse's startled look and quickly misinterpreted it. "And I don't mean with queers."

"Enjoy?"

"Yeah. I wouldn't *choose* prison, but I made out all right."

Jesse couldn't let go of the issue of Molinas's nihilism, even at the risk of seeming a prig. The other people were drifting away, but Molinas didn't seem to mind. Jesse surely didn't and hoped Molinas was enjoying this conversational game.

"Wait a minute. Do you mean to say it would make no difference to you if Bobby Kennedy were going to be inaugurated next month instead of Tricky Dicky?"

"Not a bit. Neither one of them ever learned to laugh, especially at himself. People like that think they're fooling everyone because they take themselves seriously. The trick will be on Nixon when he finds out that nobody's fooled."

"It may be too late."

"For what? No one in power would change things if they could. That's suicide. Jack Kennedy knew that. He didn't make a difference, but he didn't care. He was enjoying himself, making the most of his time. He laughed and people laughed with him and nobody was fooled. Besides," and here Jesse heard the Molinas laugh again, this one a warm, indulgent bark, "I liked his taste in women."

"Jackie?"

"I said women, not wives." He grinned, preened a little, rubbing a hand across his thinning hair and obvious hairpiece. "Your President Kennedy and I shared half a dozen broads."

Jesse wondered how he knew that, but he was hanging onto the hope of genuine intimacy, not locker-room stuff. They were alone in the kitchen now, and he wanted to make the most of this. "I must admit that when he was president I liked his style but not his substance."

"Well, that's what I mean." Again the grin.

"At least he seemed to be surrounding himself with the best available people. And after he was killed, it was the loss of that community at the center of things that hurt most. Even though Johnson got more of the so-called Kennedy program through than Kennedy would have. But in those days I hated Bobby. I thought he was arrogant and abrasive, the Camelot hatchet-man for his brother."

"Jack had to have someone he trusted to do the dirty work so he and the rest of those best people could have their fun."

"But Bobby changed. You see, it does happen, sometimes in important ways. I'm not ashamed to admit that I loved him, that I still weep over his death. He learned to hear people, to respond to needs that were more than just economic or practical. He developed this extraordinary perception and sense of compassion."

"Compassion, my ass. He learned a new way to win. You make it sound like a fucking religious conversion. Who was it said that Christianity is just a trick on niggers?"

"Flannery O'Connor."

"Right. Same one said, I been believing in nothing since I was born."

"Her best one is this sermon: Where you come from is gone. Where you think you're going never was there. And where you are ain't no good until you get away."

"Hah! I like that."

"But wait a minute. There's a big unspoken *unless* at the end of that little sermon. It says everything is rotten unless you believe in something—no matter what. Doesn't have to be religious faith, just belief in the reality of experience or the value of art or people or compassion."

"How about believing in yourself? Suppose you know that all those things are phony, just games that people play at your expense?"

"Despair."

"Doesn't have to be. Because if you know it, you can go ahead and play your own game, the one where you make up your own rules."

"When they kicked you out of the NBA they made you play by their rules."

"They made up new ones for me. But I was just doing what everyone else was."

"But you were too open about it?"

"Right. If you do go your own way, you can't let on. You have to pretend you're going along. But I made a mistake. I thought I had been accepted in a club, when actually I had been blackballed."

"What do you mean?"

"Well, you know they came to me, the guys on the Pistons who ran things, and told me to cooperate and I'd get my share. I didn't say yes, I didn't say no. But when I saw that they were laying down in a game, the next game I'd bet my lungs on us because I knew they'd be hustling their ass out there so as not to look too bad two games in a row."

"Did they know what you were doing?"

"I think they found out and decided to get me."

"Who was in on the fixing?"

"At different times, the whole team. Shit, the whole league for that matter."

"Did you tell Podoloff that?"

"Are you kidding? That would guarantee that I'd never come back. Either that or there wouldn't be a league to come back to."

"But, Jack, those players on your club, Andy Phillip, Larry Foust, George Yardley, they all had good long careers. If they were dumping or shaving, wouldn't it be obvious? Why would they risk their lives like that?"

"Why? To make a year's salary in one night, with very little risk. But let me give you a better example. You didn't mention Mel Hutchins, the best all-around player on that team. I lived with him that season—the straightest, nicest guy you ever saw. He played his best to win every game, did everything asked of him. Probably the best defensive player of his time. He could shut down a high-scoring guard like Carl Braun one night and the next night totally dominate a hotshot forward like Paul Arizin. And he'd always get his own points."

"I know. I saw him do that."

"Now Fort Wayne wins the West—this is under Eckman, not that fool Birch. And they go against Philly in the finals. Hutch shuts down Arizin to tie the series, and in the next game, with the title on the line, Arizin's open all night and Hutch can't do a thing. How do you figure it?"

"Do you know what happened?"

"No, but I have a good guess. And I think Fred Zollner had a good guess too because that's the last game Mel Hutchins ever played for the Pistons."

"Maybe he was just disappointed he didn't win the championship and had to shake up the team."

"Come within one game and trade your best man?"

"Owners often make mistakes. And coaches. Look at Auerbach and his reputation."

"Hah! You ask Joe Hacken about his friend Arnold sometime."

"For a guy who's supposed to be a genius on talent, he's been off more than on. He guessed right about Russell and that got him off the hook for all his mistakes."

Molinas looked at Jesse with some new respect. "I can see you're not so dumb about basketball...just people. You're too willing to trust, to give the benefit of the doubt."

"I get disappointed that way, it's true," Jesse said, chagrined to hear himself sounding like a wimp again. "But without the capacity for disappointment there's no pleasure, either, no positive anticipation."

"No, you keep the right to get your brains beat, your heart broken, and your pocket picked."

"Is everyone corrupt then?"

"Corruptible."

Jesse took a chance on ending the conversation. "As long as someone like you is around to do the corrupting?"

But Molinas laughed. He was actually enjoying this, while Jesse was losing his taste for the whole thing.

"The world's already corrupt, don't you see? Human nature is corrupt. All I did was make my knowledge of the corruption pay off for me. I didn't corrupt anybody. I just made it possible for some corrupt natures to make a little money."

"Connie Hawkins?"

"We never had a chance to get to him. He was so dumb he didn't know we were setting him up. But we used him to meet some players who did buy in."

"Everyone's not only corruptible but contemptible, right?"

"Hold on. You seem to have a healthy amount of contempt yourself."

Jesse had never underestimated the Molinas intelligence or quickness, but he was still surprised to be caught like that. "You've got me there. But I'm working on it. You see, I think things are changing, Jack. And I want to change too. I've been very lucky, watching my children grow and being close to generations of students who want more and more to change the world they're gonna live in, to make it better, to make it whole."

"I've been around a lot of kids, too, inside and outside. I don't see any essential change. But I sure as hell see a lot of new angles."

This conversation was depressing Jesse, devastating his stubborn grip on an object of hero-worship. He might take some delight in the game of iconoclasm, but not when his own idols were torn down. Maybe he had done the very thing he laughed at others for, taking a personage who performed heroic deeds and ascribing to him a heroic nature. Now he was feeling about this man, with whom he had fantasized a spiritual intimacy for most of his life, that he had flown poles apart from him.

"What about people? Think of all those people who have helped you and supported you and made you the center of attention, the object of adulation. What about them?" Jesse was getting carried away, excited by his own sense of loss, of acute grief. "I've talked to people who were around Columbia in '61, when you'd be at most of the games, and you had Portnoy, and probably everyone knew they were dumping and that you were flashing the big roll along with the glad hand and the smile, and that you had been banned for life by the NBA, and that you had worked over the insurance companies, and that you did whatever you wanted no matter what or who got caught—and you were still the best-loved guy in the City. Didn't you feel like you owed something to those people who loved you? Didn't you have anything to give to them?"

That performance didn't put Molinas off at all. He said, "I did give it to them. I gave them more than six six and a quarter. I gave them a figure taller than life to love."

And there he gave Jesse a possible way to preserve that part of himself he had invested in Jack Molinas. Molinas seemed to know it, too. They both smiled.

"You're consistent, all right, all of a piece, and what a piece of work. You know what you are? You're the rogue hero, the trickster. In order for the trickster to work, for his doings to take hold in our imaginations, there has to be a belief in a consistent world, a corrupt human nature. The trickster can only play his games with the world's knowledge that rules are made to be broken. Rules are made because without them nature would impose chaos. The trickster reminds us of that. He constantly tests both our acceptance of rules and our understanding of rule-breaking. That's what you are, Jack Molinas. You can still be a hero for me."

His grin was broad enough for the five boroughs. "A legend in my own time."

"More than that. The embodiment of a myth, a walking, breathing myth among us."

"And as good as a mile?"

"As a league."

"Eastern or NBA?" And they laughed together.

"And that's what you were doing that night when the verdict came in, standing in the corridor of the Criminal Courts Building on the thirteenth floor, telling that Laurendi, the detective who arrested you and who hated your guts, that it didn't matter that you were going away, that you'd do all right anyway. You were making an epic boast, as any self-respecting trickster hero would."

He seemed to take as a matter of course that Jesse knew the details. The startling thought occurred to Jesse that what he had experienced within himself for more than twenty years—a part of him projecting the image of Jack Molinas and identifying with it—could be accepted by Molinas himself within the space of a single evening.

"I'll tell you something better than that, old sport." Jesse gasped at the echo of Gatsby talking to Carraway, but he never had a chance to find out whether Molinas was deliberately alluding to a parallel that was deeply entrenched in Jesse's consciousness or, more likely, making fun of his literary background. "I made good on that boast. In spades, which is the only way to do it in Attica. Does that make me more of a hero or less of a trickster? Don't answer that. Do you want to hear about it?"

"You bet."

"Well, I would if I were a betting man."

Chapter 22:
Jailhouse Jive

Jesse Miller sat in that kitchen on Riverside Drive, having long since ceased to be aware of the sounds and presences of the party, and Jack Molinas told him the story of his prison term. At times he seemed to Jesse a modern version of ancient royalty schooled in the arts of performance, at times a mythic figure reporting episodes from his own legendry, at times a teller of tall tales in the American frontier tradition, and at times a braggart, a brigand, and a bastard. But at all times he spoke with an ease undisturbed by modesty or mockery, smoothly presenting a balanced overall view of those years. Yet it was an unrehearsed, spontaneous performance, and he enjoyed the telling.

But for Jesse it was more than enjoyment, though finally much less. Despite the differences between them, despite his distaste for a lot of it, he felt blessed, graced in his role of special audience. It wasn't that he was overwhelmed by the magnitude of all Molinas had done, but that he was presenting it all to Jesse. It was the gift of his intimacy that was overwhelming. It was the feeling of special privilege to bear solitary witness to this testimony, that in some strange way (it was Exley, of course, whose drunken brilliance set him up for this) Molinas was Jesse's own fame. It was a feeling, however, anticlimactically, that failed to survive the performance.

"In the first place," Molinas began, "I went in prepared. I wanted to set myself up right away, set myself apart as far as the prisoners were concerned. I'd have no trouble with guards or officials. I knew that. I had money and I was famous. But it would take more than that to deal with the inmates. Power, power that can be applied on the inside, and privilege, privilege that could be extended to them, was all they understood.

"So I came in with some practical plans and with some goods. But I counted on my preliminary detention and processing taking about seventy-two hours, certainly no more than a week. I was prepared for Attica, but something happened that first day on the yard at Sing Sing that set me back several weeks.

"I was just standing there, minding my own business, taking in the scene but not paying too much attention because I wasn't gonna be there long enough to really study the setup, when I saw this little Puerto Rican guy coming toward me. Well, coming isn't the right word. He was sort of floating, staggering slightly, nodding his head in time to some rhythm of his own. I was fascinated by his eyes because they were fixed on mine in a glazed way. I figured, oh boy, this junkie's just had some kind of fix.

"Then he starts mumbling or chanting, 'Hey, man, you too big, you too big, hey, man, you too big.' I just stared at him. I was smiling but didn't say anything, and when he walked around me in a circle, sort of sidestepping in that crazy rhythm, I kept turning to face him. All of a sudden he lurches forward and takes a swing at my head. He never reached me, but when he swung again I caught hold of his wrist, then the other one. I'm just holding his arms away from me, wondering if he's gonna start to kick and what the hell I was gonna do with him now.

"Suddenly he throws his head back and lets out this high piercing scream: 'Too bi-i-i-ig'. Two guards run up and take him off my hands, and I say thanks. They're dragging him away and they invite me, very politely, to come with them. And the next thing I know I've been sent to solitary for fighting in the yard, and no one wants to hear my side of the story. There's no due process, just rules and punishment.

"I expected some kind of culture shock in prison, but nothing like this. Four blank walls and a can. At night they throw in a blanket and in the morning they take it away. That's your mattress and pillow and you love it. It's all you have. There's no window so all you can do to survive is take out your mind and play with it.

"Sometimes, though, your mind is playing with you. I started thinking about that spic. If he has access to junk that means there's a live drug market going on inside. I didn't want any part of that, but I figure if there's drugs there has to be gambling, and if there's gambling somehow it's gonna be mine.

"Then, on the other hand, I think, Why me? And it occurs to me that there's no drug market, that I was set up. They want me punished. No model prisoner shit for me, they want me to do bad time. They gave that guy a fix and told him to pick a fight with me. They've got him sleeping it off somewhere and they've got me where they want me, in solitary. He didn't mean I was too big physically. He was just repeating what they told him, that I'm too big and they want to cut me down.

"But I wasn't about to let them beat me that way. I'd just be Cool Hand Luke pretending to play by their rules but playing my own game all the time. Some people can do what they call good time, but I knew that I'd have to do it my way.

"The secret to doing good time, Joey Hacken told me, is to accept the sameness of the days and avoid all thoughts about duration and continuity and counting on a calendar. Hacken could do that. Just keep his nose clean, not get tight with anybody, keep his mouth shut. He'd read a lot and ignore the fact that every day is just like every other day.

"He has that kind of discipline, but he's sentimental too. He's different from me. One time he went up to Boston to fix an MIT game and when he met the kid who was gonna dump for us, the kid was wearing an ROTC uniform. So Joey came back to New York and said he couldn't do it. The kid looked so good in his uniform that he didn't have the heart to bribe him and corrupt him.

"I knew I couldn't do good time Hacken's way. My way would be to make sure that the days would not all be the same. Four days in solitary was all the sameness I wanted to handle. So I would look for action, for movement, for change—anything that would fight against monotony, so long as it didn't interfere with any shortening of my sentence. Because that would be the basis of a lot of activity, looking for ways to get out. You didn't have to be a lawyer in jail to be a jailhouse lawyer, but I was both.

"Sing Sing bookmaking was a joke. The currency was all cigarettes, and one small syndicate handled it all. They booked baseball games and got the results at eleven-thirty at night on a radio wrap-up. But I found out that one of the permissible activities was raising pigeons and you could give the pigeons to visitors. It was so simple it was ridiculous. I started betting with these guys, a carton here, a carton there. I don't even smoke and I'm playing for cigarettes. Then one Sunday I have a guy give his wife this homing pigeon that he's trained, along with instructions.

"The wife goes back to New York, listens to the Mets beat the Cubs, wraps the results around the pigeon's leg, and off he flies to Ossining. Hours before the bookie gets the scores I bet so many cartons that they're out of business without even knowing it. No sweat. Two weeks later I was on my way to Attica anyway.

"This was what I had prepared for, and even though I couldn't take all my cigarettes with me I had enough to start booking right away. I also had plenty of other stuff to make me a celebrity as soon as I walked inside the walls. I checked in with about five hundred dollars' worth of athletic equipment—uniforms, balls, shoes—because, you know, sports is a really big deal at Attica. And I had all these magnetic hangers to attach to the ceiling of my cell, and it looked like a fucking close-out sale of sport shirts, even though everyone is supposed to wear standard issue.

"And every month, when you're allowed to receive a food package, I would get like a boxcar-size package with booze and the best deli. Only I got it every week. I never had to eat the prison food, and some of my friends ate with me, but usually it was a good idea to be seen in the messhall at mealtime anyway. A lot of business got done then, and that's where your status was clearly established, more so than on the yard. Shit, I was a hero at Attica from day one."

He leaned way back on the kitchen chair, a gloating smile on his face, and balanced himself on the back legs with one foot and then the other. Jesse recognized the scene right away. It was Henry Fonda as Wyatt Earp in *My Darling Clementine*, only Molinas's huge feet would never have fit inside Fonda's cowboy boots and his hair and hairpiece, though equally glossy, did not reek of lilacs.

He looked so pleased with himself that all Jesse could think of was the waste, putting out the effort to make himself a prominent con in Attica—and for what?—when he could have been and done anything in the world. And then Jesse's own sense of Molinas as hero took over and he answered his own question—what Molinas wanted in Attica was what he had always wanted, to be himself, to assert the identity he had projected for himself, to retain his notion of personal integrity with the public image that satisfied his private conception.

"I could get anything I wanted. They absolutely forbade hair stuff with an oil base, but all I used was Shontex. So I had my girlfriend fill Colgate tubes with it, put a little toothpaste at the top and send it up. They never even checked.

"Sports counted for so much at Attica, even more than outside, I knew I'd have it made. Other guys with money and connections got cut down to size by the cons whenever there was exercise time. I was thirty-three years old but no one could stay with me. I was the king of that asphalt basketball court. They'd try to muscle me, but I knew more dirty tricks than they had ever heard of. Some of the spades could outjump me, but if they had the rhythm I had the timing. I could bother their jump shots and no one could stop my hook. But I'll tell you, some of those boys were better than a lot of pros I've played against.

"But at Attica—this was a surprise to me, even though I had the equipment for it—football was the big thing, not basketball. The hitting was something fierce. Those mothers got off a lot of their hostility playing football. The screws loved it, it made their jobs easier because of the so-called healthy release of tension, and the warden was a fanatic about it. Organized a regular cell block league. And never missed a game. Of course there was a lot of betting on the side and the only problem was that if a guard on your block lost a bet he might ride your ass pretty hard.

"Every team had the muscle men to block and tackle. There's enough hard guys in Attica to stock two NFLs and the Canadian league thrown in. But when I came on as D Block's wide receiver we had the talent at skill positions to score on anyone, because we had a precision passer. If you ever read Breslin, you know who I mean. It's Fat Thomas's brother, a friend of mine because he's done some booking himself.

"Not one of those cons could stay with my fakes and they weren't big or smart or good enough to knock me down, so whatever pattern I run I'm open, and the ball is there on the money. We had an unstoppable play on a down and out, where the ball is thrown right at the fucking wall at a spot where only I can go up and get it on a timing pattern.

"Of course we had to lose a few times to make things interesting, and there's some dissension on the team when they think we're betting the other way. After all, I did have some reputation in this area. But when the warden challenges an all-star squad to play against a team of screws with a few ringers thrown in things really get interesting.

"There's plenty of action on this, both ways, and we figured we'd have to lose it just to survive. We'd blow the game, but meanwhile we'd get some satisfaction just beating up on some of those bastards physically. But we couldn't do it. I mean, we saw we could win and the feeling was so strong, with pride on the one hand and humiliation on the other, we had to try. We went the length of the field to beat them and only used one play. I'd fake a post and go down and out, the ball would be there, and I'd step out of bounds. We ran it seven straight times and covered eighty-four yards for the winning touchdown. Christ, they ought to make a movie about it."

Jesse could see the comic film potential right away, all the possibilities for rough-and-tumble slapstick, passes thrown into the groin, colorful language, bit parts for famous players, and satisfying dramatic suspense with good-guys-overcome-adversity-to-win-against-all-odds-in-the-end. Soon to be a major motion picture. But Molinas had already moved on to another movie.

"I started getting some breaks around that time. First they reduced my sentence. When you think about it, I shouldn't have done any time at all—a first offender, a non-violent crime—but I was a practicing attorney, so they originally gave me what the appeals court finally ruled was an excessive sentence. I was still looking at a maximum of twelve and a half, but seven to twelve and a half sounds a hell of a lot better than ten to fifteen. Besides, the fact that for the first time a ruling had gone in my favor gave me new hope for other avenues of appeal I was pursuing.

"Then I got close to a guy who could teach me something. He was doing fifteen for a stock swindle and he was the sharpest market analyst I ever met. He read the *Journal* every day and would pore over *Barron's* and a dozen Wall Street tip sheets. He worked in the library and all he did was study the market. The warden and other people in the penal system were making money listening to this guy.

"I listened good myself. Every night he'd brief me for half an hour on what was happening, and he'd tell me how to anticipate what would be happening. Best of all, and this was information he'd give only to me, he showed me how to spot scams and conspiracies. I had an arrangement with Red Benjamin in Brooklyn. His firm couldn't accept my business, but Red set up his own account which was all mine except for his percentage. And he'd make plays that I instructed him to make, according to a code we had set up. We made some good scores, especially playing with platinum futures.

"Word got around that my opinion on the market was at least as good as my opinion on sporting events, and then all of a sudden I was put in a position to have my opinion do me some good. I was engaged at that time, a real classy broad but crazy. Her old man paid for my defense. Anyway, when the news started to break about that million dollar Mays Department Store swindle, the phony check deal, this broad made a discovery. The names in the papers matched names on a list that I carried around, and she realized that those errands she used to run for me, picking up envelopes from strange men on street corners, weren't part of the normal practice of law. She had been a bag-woman.

"Actually I wasn't part of that caper. But some of the guys were gambling clients, and I just handled a lot of the money. My fiancée thought she'd better go to the D.A., unless I could clear her, and, by the way, the engagement was off. So I talk to some people and in a matter of hours I'm on my way back to New York to the Tombs.

"That may sound bad, but it wasn't. I mean the conditions are foul, but they bent some rules for me. I was on the move. And I spent more time outside than I did in a cell. I told these detectives everything I knew, and I told it in great detail because the interviews took place in some of the best restaurants in Manhattan. What I didn't know about the case I pieced together and told them as if I knew. In the end, what they got from me was a detailed account that substantiated everything they had from other sources —but nothing new. So I was never called as a witness. But the detectives and I sure feasted at those meals.

"Meanwhile, my stay at the Tombs was prolonged for another reason. A very high official in the criminal justice system had heard about my expertise on the market, and he decided to put me to work. Twice a week a limousine would pick me up at the Tombs, one of these hideaway jobs with a bar and stereo and TV and thick curtains in back, like a drawing room on a train with total privacy, and I would be chauffeured to Wall Street.

"I was playing with two and a half million dollars and was doing very well for him. For myself I was playing for cigarettes, but enough cigarettes to buy anything I wanted in the Tombs, and I was also getting days of freedom and good food outside, and about once a week there'd be a broad in the limo for me. The chauffeur would pick me up at the closing bell, I'd step inside and close the curtains around me and the broad, and he'd drive around in rush-hour traffic before delivering me to the Tombs at six with a shopping bag full of good deli for my supper as an extra reward. Of course, he was playing a smart incentive game: when I didn't have a good week with his money I got no goodies. But most of the weeks were fine."

Molinas was oblivious of Jesse by now. He was grinning but not for an audience. He was himself the audience for these remembered or fantasized scenes. His eyes were shining with a kind of glaze, as he paused for a drink and then went on.

"The Supreme Court declined to review my conviction, and while I contemplated my next legal maneuver I was shipped back to Attica. It was business as usual there, but by the time I had finished my first year inside I knew that I had to find a way back to the Tombs. There was no such thing as good time for me in prison, only ways of angling to get out for good or for a few good hours—while doing what I could to amuse myself in the meantime.

"I applied for release and was turned down again and again. I had to keep trying. I had been convicted on evidence improperly or illegally obtained and the testimony of confessed conspirators. Of course I was guilty, but that's not the point. The point of law was that it was a bad case and a bad conviction. The legal challenge still excited me. Then, in late summer of '66, I got another chance to cooperate in an investigation. My old friend from the Mays case, Aaron Koota the Brooklyn D.A., found my knowledge of fixed harness races to be accurate and useful. I was on my way back to the City again.

"They couldn't bury me in the Tombs quickly enough to suit me. I figured I had Wall Street and the broads to look forward to again, but things were much less open this time around. Security was tight because they were dealing with big-time criminals, not a one-shot operation, and they thought I needed protection. For reasons of my own I didn't want to discourage that thinking.

"The story went around that my information triggered the whole investigation, but everyone on the inside knew better. Over a year before, Koota had started a large-scale investigation of o.c. in Brooklyn, trying to crack down on their infiltration into a number of legitimate businesses. As usual they tapped a lot of phones and in the course of this court-authorized surveillance they got their first inklings of conspiracies to fix races at Yonkers, Roosevelt, and Monticello.

"Actually this sort of thing was ancient history—everyone knew about it—but now they had hard evidence that it was being done in a comprehensive, organized way. OK. I had the details of the scam from a lot of sources, and when I heard that they had arrested Carmine Lombardozzi with a bunch of his boys in Sheepshead Bay I figured they had their case. Now I could go before the grand jury and tell them what they already knew and get all kinds of credit as a public-spirited whistle-blower risking the vengeance of o.c.

"It didn't help my final shot at a Supreme Court review. In March they declined to give the case a hearing, by a vote of eight to one, but I figured the odds were longer than that anyway. As the harness case dragged on, so did my time in the Tombs. I had my old food privileges, but not much else.

"The detectives must have loved the cloak-and-dagger stuff, because they kept devising new schemes to spirit me away from the jail and conduct their interviews with me in out-of-the-way roadhouses or hotel rooms that I'd get to through private entrances and service elevators. One time they gave me a phony beard and fatigue hat and took me to a hotel on Lennox Avenue in Harlem as if I was Castro's big cousin or something.

"I don't know who they were trying to fool, but they enjoyed their game. I did too. It kept me moving around. It got me out on the street, wearing decent clothes, eating pretty decent food. But the best part of it came when it was over. They took their sweet time about it—hell, it was good duty for them, and I had to hand it to them, they made the most of it—but last May it was over and back I went to Attica. Only this time no sports, no socializing, no gambling. I had done what could get me killed in prison—I had ratted on o.c. They had to put me in the protection gallery.

"Now I knew I had them. I was eligible to come up before the parole board for the first time, and there was no way they could deny me. I had been practically a model prisoner. But more than that, now it was a nuisance and an extra expense to keep me inside. Some of those people hated me, had it in for me, I know that. But they probably figured I was a dead man as soon as I hit the street in New York. If I had been a betting man I'd have bet my lungs I'd walk.

"The funny part of it was that I was perfectly safe, inside or outside. I hadn't betrayed anyone. No o.c. guy got in trouble because of me. All I did was give them what they already had and dress it up with some colorful wrinkles. Everybody knew Jack Molinas, and Jack Molinas wasn't gonna be touched for anything said or done. But when I went before the board I had to put on an act. I had to be both chastened and frightened, eager to go straight and make amends in society and anxious to avoid contact with any criminal element.

"It was a breeze, routine, no contest. I think it was all decided before I even went into the room. They only kept me a few minutes, and none of them looked me in the eye. July the second I walked out, free—if you can call parole freedom. And it's gonna be forever before they have me again."

In the silence of the kitchen Jesse heard the tired hum of the refrigerator motor and gradually became aware of party sounds in the other rooms. He felt numb, empty inside. On faith, for years, he'd protected the image of this man in his heart and his guts, and there was nothing left to defend. Jesse was swallowed up by the realization that he couldn't believe a word Molinas said. Molinas, too, seemed spent, absent, almost wistful, as if he didn't know where he was at that moment or that anyone else was there.

"Jack?"

"Huh?"

"Jack," Jesse said, as slowly as he could while they both got reoriented, "what will you do now?"

The smile came quickly back and all the wistfulness was gone in a flash. "Enjoy living my life."

"How do you do that?" Jesse's voice sounded hollow to himself, faking a concern as shallowly as Molinas faked pleasure, and with an undisguised edge of sarcasm that he knew Molinas would take for granted anyway.

"Beautiful women, fine food and wine, good cars and clothes, playing some basketball. And fuck anyone who gets in my way."

"No responsibilities, no obligations, right?"

"What are they? Stuff like that gets in the way, too, so fuck them."

"Come on, those common pleasures aren't what living really means to you."

"You're right again. Those things are just what come with living a good life. The side dishes, the fringe benefits. They make the good life better, and they're always there if you are really living. But the main courses are Movement. Action. Control. Living for Jack Molinas is moving big numbers around and leading the dance among them."

"Grand Master of the Jugglers' Ball, eh?"

Now he was his laughing self again. "Yeah. Having a ball at the ball. Having the balls to have it. And giving it to them in the balls if they don't like it."

"Will you stay in New York?"

"No way. I'm gonna get out to the Coast where I can move some numbers without them breathing down my neck. And it might be fun to go to a Lakers game at the Forum and give Hawkins a hug or shake hands with Mendy or Manny or some other official and palm him a C-note."

"Good luck."

"I'll make out. I always do."

Chapter 23:
Revisions

Driving to meet Millie for the first time in years, Jesse reflected with just a trace of irony that this time she was married and he was not. She was the one who had to fabricate the cover stories, and the plans had been many months in the making.

She had left Athens, degree in hand, and for two years he hadn't heard from her. Then she had written, having settled into a small college faculty in Indiana, and from then on their old intimacy had been restored, mostly by mail but with occasional phone calls. She had interrupted her academic career for three semesters, most of that period of silence, to do some other kinds of things.

For a year and a half she had divided her time between the mountains and Manhattan, doing social work in Appalachia or odd jobs in publishing or P.R. in the City. It wasn't that she'd been holding out for the right kind of academic offer, though that had been part of it, but that she'd felt she owed herself some time out to devote to causes she believed in. When the teaching job did come up that second spring, she felt that she'd grown a lot—to the point of being ready to settle down.

She had gone back to teaching and scholarly research with new enthusiasm but remained politically active, caught up in Kent State and the women's movement. It had all made Jesse proud of her. There had been several men, of course, and when she'd committed herself to a man in the school of social work and married him, he'd been even prouder. She'd earned tenure in her department and found time to produce a baby as well.

Meanwhile she'd been a constant source of support for Jesse through changes and troubles. Returning to a metropolitan area, he had unwittingly hastened the collapse of his marriage. Rachel had moved quickly back into her old patterns, but she'd made two serious mistakes. First, she'd tried to resurrect relationships from the past. And then, when one of them had threatened to get serious and she'd backed off, the man had reacted with stereotypical violence.

As devastating as the resulting revelations had been for Jesse (it was a police detective who'd told him he had a habitually unfaithful wife who "liked to play games with men"), they had been catastrophic for her. Unwilling to face his hurt and anger, and maybe unable to bear any of the guilt she'd always piled on him, Rachel had run.

Foremost among those who knew him, Millie had spent hours practically holding his hand through the long distance phone line, talking him through suicidal weeks. And in her long, intelligently caring letters during the following months, she had helped him understand many things: that he was not diminished; that his children needed him to be strong, all the more in the light of their mother's weakness; that he should now be able to understand much that had baffled him in the past; and even that Rachel's behavior should be seen as reflections of Rachel, not of his own unworthiness.

And now here he was on his way to see Millie again, driven not by his own loneliness but by her need to validate their importance in each other's life. He was her sounding board as she sounded the depths of her maturity. She had arranged to attend professional meetings at West Virginia, and he was driving to Morgantown (having once flown into that nightmare airport, he knew he couldn't do it again, not even for Millie). Carefully she had worked things out with Bob and childcare for Cleo at home, and she had also arranged to disappear from the meetings for thirty-six hours and be covered by friends. It was easier for Jesse, with the boys away at school and only Susannah to make arrangements for.

He parked in the hotel garage, right on schedule, and she was waiting. She looked wonderful, more womanly and with shorter hair, but somehow more youthful than ever, less vulnerable, less fragile, healthier, warmer, more fully alive. But as they clung to each other in a long hug, she felt just like his sweet honey Millie once more.

"I'm in your hands," he said. "Do with me what you will."

"I will," she said. "But we're gonna pay a visit first."

Her months in the mountains had led to some good, lasting friendships. And the arrangements she'd made for them came from those connections. First there was the borrowed Ford pickup, in which they headed straight for the hills. The roads were anything but straight, but she drove them fast. Millie at the wheel is a confident pilot, almost serene in her knowledge of back roads, seeming to compose self and truck and road and terrain into a single continuity, an experience rather than a pattern of process. It was as if she *lived* that pickup through the hills and woods to Ed and Julie's house.

Jesse had heard a lot about them. They affected a hippie life style but, because Ed had a straight job, lived it very well. They had a superior sound system and the best dope available, and they were free and easy with food and drink so that many of the freaks in the area congregated at their house, a rough and rambling, overgrown, high-ceilinged, log cabin but comfortably furnished with an abundance of textures in rugs, hangings, and cushions. Millie was very much at home there, felt comfortable about bringing Jesse in, and so he felt at home too.

They got soaringly high right away and laughed a great deal. Ed gave Jesse a backgammon lesson. Julie one-upped everyone, even Millie, with acid one-liners. Some neighbors came by, and for the next few hours Jesse rejoiced in the mellow camaraderie of the group, enriched by the almost tangible beams passing between Millie and him. And then finally she stood, came across the room, took his hand, and said, "Come on, I'm taking you home."

Home was a cabin she had borrowed. It was further up in the mountains, but she had gone up earlier in the day to get it ready. The ride took forever over roads that felt like the back ways to back ways. The truck jounced, recoiling as the roads coiled, and climbed steadily upward as Millie pushed it to the limits of the conditions. They were quiet most of the way. Jesse's eyes were closed a good part of the time, not because he was tired (which he was), not because he was anxious (which was the farthest thing from the contentment he was feeling), but the better to enjoy the trip, the sensation of being taken higher and higher toward a promised end. Every time he looked at her, when the bright night gave him an angle to see her face, he saw the same shining smile. There was the suggestion of antici-pation there but, more, the look of control of a musician playing through a virtuoso performance.

Finally they were there, the candles lit and dimly fra-grancing the bed that dominated the little cabin. It was as if they had come to a place separated from the world for their lovemaking, suspended in time and space beyond reality, where all but their conjoined selves was removed. They moved without transition, as in a dream, into mustily warm depths of embraces. Like the drive, this trip went on and on, higher and higher. At a point of supreme suspen-sion, with Millie convulsing in orgasm, Jesse let completely go of voluntary physical control and felt his body convulse with hers in a miracle of total oneness, precisely rhythmed in the intricacies of spontaneous sympathy.

If there was anything that undercut the perfection of that reunion it was the shared sense that there was something frightening about how good it was. Jesse sensed some relief in the strict time limit imposed on them. They slept briefly and then, finally, began to talk. It was as if they were ready to share their lives with each other at a new depth of intimacy, to see everything and themselves with new clarity.

For both there was more than reaffirmation of their importance to each other. There was also an element of demonstration: see how far I've come, they were both saying, not surprisingly expressing a mutual satisfaction sexually. In the morning, he learned that she had developed incredible muscular control and coordination. Crouching over him as he lay supine, she seemed to suspend herself so that only their genitals touched and her whole body weight was brought to bear, exerting a constant, rhythmic pressure where it would do them both the most good.

Remembering an exchange a decade earlier, she slowed way down, smiled down at him, and said, "You really like this now, don't you?"

"I love it," he said, not missing a beat.

It was all different, not just the joy of sex but the pleasure they took in liking each other so much more. She had become a warm and loving person; she seemed to sense that he had, too. Sexually she had become delighted to give and share; she said that he had, too. She expressed appreciation at the way his rhythm suited hers, gratitude to him for her orgasms. When he came in a full rushing single explosive release, she thanked him for that, too, holding him with calming certainty as he gasped back to breath and voice and pulse within a normal range, and she said, "It's only me."

It was only Millie, completely fulfilling for the moment but with a paradoxical sense of permanency. Later that day she spoke, with what was almost reverence, of the way they had survived the relative shallowness of their early affair and its inevitable transience.

"It's funny," she said, "but I relived that whole time in just a single weekend. It was during my months in New York. This guy came on so strong, so dominant, he couldn't be denied. He reminded me so much of you."

Jesse's little laugh had a question mark at the end.

"Oh, he was completely different, of course, a loud, coarse man, but obviously quite bright. And he was huge. I never knew his name, never wanted to, but he was supposed to be a great athlete in his time. From his size and build, I'd say a basketball player—and you know how I love basketball."

He sat up suddenly in the bed, his head throbbing with an odd sensation. "Describe him." ·

"What's the matter? Oh, I can't give you his measurements, or his uniform number. That's not the point anyway. I want to tell you about the old you I saw in him."

He let it go, for then. It was enough that it *might* have been Molinas. He didn't want to ruin it either with confirmation or rebuttal.

"Just a shadow of my former self," he said.

"Yes, given an extra foot and about eighty pounds. But he had to have me, just had to. And then when he did, it was like it didn't matter anymore, not for a minute. I swear he didn't even enjoy the sex. All I could think of was that time in Athens when you admitted it. In my mind I kept asking him the same question, and he kept giving the same answer. Except when he came to the part about why. In my head, then, the answer he gave was a kind of trochaic trimeter refrain, 'Why not? Who cares? I'm me.'"

"Spondees."

"Maybe, but not the way I scanned it in my head."

"I'll take your ear's word for it."

"But that's just the way you were, Jesse. It was this big guy screwing me, or screwing me over, but it was your old voice in my head saying, 'Why not? Who cares? I'm me.' God, I'm glad you've changed, I'm glad you care now, I'm glad you don't have to demand your identity like that any more."

"But I'll bet he never changes."

"Who?"

"Never mind. Why didn't you tell me about that guy before?"

"I had to be with you."

"But why were you with him, anyway?"

"Oh, Jesse, I had to try out everything that I thought would help me grow in those days. It felt right. I was very drawn to him, the power, those dark eyes always laughing. He was charismatic, beautiful in a way."

"I know."

"What do you mean?"

"I think I know who it was." And so Jesse told Millie about Molinas. Through precious hours of their second and last night together he told her much of the story rehearsed in these pages. And it seemed to him she understood it all, whether or not Molinas had indeed been the man she knew for a weekend. Millie had recognized in Molinas something of an otherself for Jesse, and so she understood his compulsion to tell his story.

"And why didn't you tell me about him before?" Jesse matched her smile. "I had to be with you—the way we are now."

Shortly before they had to leave the cabin to return to Morgantown, Millie redirected the focus.

"Jesse, in these few years since Rachel left, you've had

several women. Were you trying to prove, as you were with me, that you could be loved by more than one woman?"

"You mean like Molinas? Maybe I was."

"Then you should have been happy to prove it. Instead you were depressed. You're not like him at all. The question then becomes, why can't you come to happiness as a man who loves more than one woman at a time, who needs to love more than one, and who knows that?"

He thought a long time before saying, "Because it just doesn't work that way. To have more than one woman is to be essentially a man alone. Some people, of course, have role requirements for wife and mistress."

"Victorian gentlemen."

"And mafiosi, too, proponents of an individualist ethic. Freedom from restraints, for them, implies the need to be free from commitment. So they compartmentalize activities in their lives to protect what they think is the integrity of their intrinsic individual selves."

"Fragmentation."

"Yes, which is disintegrative and destructive."

"Then why is your Molinas so full of himself?"

"There's enormous potential for loss of self there. If he keeps escalating the compartmentalization, he'll end up atomized. Maybe he has to be alone, to be in control of the myriad parts so that no one can reach or touch or identify his essence."

"Protean?"

"And chameleon and ubiquitous. Until he gets blown away, like motes of energy a-beam in the wind."

"But that's not you, after all."

"I'm no rogue-hero and was never meant to be a trickster. No, I don't want to be alone. If I am to come to happiness—I like your turn of phrase—it will be as a committed sharer."

"And why hasn't it happened?" She spoke gently, without any of the acid bite that once had been her trademark.

"Jackpot question."

"Do you still love Rachel?"

"I suppose so, but I hate her, too. There's no commitment left; that would be totally empty. But what really matters is that other women see me as still committed. I think I'm ready, but their perceptions deny it."

"Self-protection, Jesse, not rejection. We're afraid to be the second woman, however exciting it may be. I knew that ten years ago with you."

"And now?"

She smiled. He smiled back, and they held each other in a long, firm embrace. Nothing more had to be said. Jesse had given her the really important thing she sought from him, verification of the significance of their relationship, and Millie gave it, unasked, back to him. He knew they didn't have to keep seeing each other to sustain an emotional closeness. Without having to make an effort he had supplied her with validation, because he genuinely shared that feeling.

Jesse went home feeling enormously gratified. Those hours of dynamic intimacy had brought him closer to Millie, without a hint of threatening the separate integrity of their lives. He thought it unlikely that they would see each other again, but he was pleased to know they were permanent parts of each other. That closeness could grow because their ongoing epistolary conversation would now touch the connected roots of their living spirits. And if they were to see each other again, it wouldn't have to be called reunion, because the union had been saved and confirmed. Besides, he regarded it as no inconsiderable bonus that Millie had given him new glimpses of and insights about Jack Molinas and what he meant to him.

Chapter 24:
Paved with Gold

Molinas sat across the table from Bobby Kraw, grinning as usual and stuffing his face with tacos and burritos, but sizing up his old Brooklyn acquaintance for what use could be made of him.

"Bobby, seeing you again makes me realize how much time has passed." Kraw was the one who looked as if he'd done time, his skin drawn tight and coarse like a lifer's, the smile revealing rotting teeth.

"You look the same to me, Jack. Are you Dorian Gray or what? But please call me Norm."

"Where'd you get 'Norman Arno' anyway?"

"Saw it on an architect's sign when I first got here and I needed one quick."

"I guess you did." Kraw had been indicted in North Carolina during the basketball scandals but somehow had evaded arrest. "You also needed a good lawyer," he said, turning the grin up a notch.

Kraw laughed, remembering Molinas defending him in a negligence case. No money had changed hands. As a book-ie back home the only way he could collect from Molinas was by hiring two thugs to relieve him of whatever cash he was carrying. It usually covered the tab, and they never discussed those transactions.

"Now here we are in sunny California, Americans are walking on the moon, and you're meeting with Joe Pasternak to talk a movie deal."

"The moon shot is moon shit, if you ask me. I'm gonna

find out what studio they used to fake that one."

"You don't believe anything is straight, do you?"

"I know better."

"And what do you think is going on this week at Woodstock?"

"Another fake, with enough dope to keep all the kiddies happy and all the right palms greased."

"With that attitude it's a wonder you believed I could set up a meeting with Pasternak."

"That's different. I've got something real to sell. The true life story of Jack Molinas is better than fiction. You know it has to be a hot item or I wouldn't have gotten a six-day pass from parole, right, Bobby?"

"Norm, please. But if nothing comes of this meeting, I've got lots of other contacts in the business too."

"I'm counting on you," he said, knowing that everyone in a fifty-mile radius of where they sat claimed showbiz connections, "and for contacts in other business as well."

"You better steer clear of the rackets, like me."

"Bobby, Bobby, you don't fool me. This is where it's happening. I'm not talking demographics or population shifts. I'm talking shifts of power and pressure and focus and attitude. That adds up to opportunity. I can hear it knocking all around me here. Knocking? Hell, it's ginning out, in spades, across the board, Hollywood on a schneid. And you think o.c. doesn't know that? They're opportunity's sweethearts, always have been."

"It's not so simple out here. Sure there are families in Frisco and L.A. and San Diego, but they're all loose operations. They don't even know what's going down in their own area, no less control it. They seem to concentrate on specific interests, not geographical rights. Only San Jose is tied up—the Cerrito family."

"Do you know the way to San Jose? Well, forget it. That's

nowhere."

Kraw laughed, his con-like face breaking up into a hundred narrow fissures. Molinas went on, more serious, more vigorous.

"But they're all out here, moving in from all over the country and from Mexico, moving their money this way."

"Right, but it's mostly into legitimate businesses, using their labor union connections."

"All the better. Ownership goes unchallenged here. It's all a front. What's up front is all that counts. Listen, you know how things are in New York? The five families always had almost everything locked up. You couldn't get too friendly with one without offending another. Now after Apalachin and Valachi and the Banana War, it's worth your life or your freedom just to talk to a soldier or an old friend on the street."

"No wonder Joe Bonanno himself took Greeley's advice. Now he's taken over in Arizona and Colorado."

"And you know the real reason he's persona non grata with the commission? Because they know he was moving in the right direction. They'd all like to be here. The old industrial Northeast and Midwest are dying, and o.c. has its own notions of manifest destiny."

"So where do you come in?"

"Wherever the action is, Bobby baby."

"You already sound like you belong."

"I do belong. And when I'm here to stay I'll show you how to make it pay for both of us."

*   *   *   *   *

Red Benjamin was anxious to see Molinas after his six-day furlough to Los Angeles, to see if he had cooled down and could stay under wraps for a while, if the chances for a future deal would sustain his sudden surge of good feelings when the prospect first opened up. Instead, what he encountered was the old Molinas, only more so, a manic ebullience that could only lead to trouble for both of them.

"Red, I've got to get out there for good. It's where I belong."

"What are you going to tell the parole board? That you have to be transferred in order to make a fast buck?"

"This particular fast buck, yes. The deal's practically in the bag for book and movie rights to my life story. It's got Hollywood written all over it."

"OK. Say they buy it. It's still a one-shot thing. What happens then?"

"Are you kidding? It's wide open out there. All you have to do is look good up front because no one looks underneath. They build on the San Andreas fault and when o.c. money gets laundered it looks as clean as anyone's."

"If you're thinking about gambling, Jack, forget it. If you're so much as seen talking to a bookie you'll be sent away. You know that. Don't you think they're just waiting for you to make contact with Joe Hacken?"

"Red, you worry too much, just like Joey. Haven't you always done well with me?"

"So did Joe until you went too far. Look, I'd like to see you stay out, and that means staying clean. As far as the rackets are concerned, these days are different from the ones we grew up in. Everyone used to accept the mob and their activities as a given of society, the dark side of the establishment, a genuine part of law and order and the status quo.

"But that's all changed. The media have educated the people and there's a new attitude. Remember Kefauver? You know what Bobby Kennedy's Justice Department was like? They declared war on organized crime."

"Headline-grabbing, budget-building bullshit."

"Right, but it focused attention. Even Ramsey Clark, with all his concern for defendants' rights, citizens' constitutional rights, carried on the campaign."

"That was yesterday, old buddy. Today is a new day again. What goes around comes around. You talked about gambling. You think it's like old times when Mickey Cohen had a lock on L.A.? No way. It's every man for himself. And Nevada's worse, I mean better. I can hardly wait."

"I heard Meyer Lansky's people and the Chicago crowd— including your old enemy Lefty Rosenthal—are everywhere."

"There's enough there for all the families and plenty left over for anyone who can nail down a piece of the action."

"According to Vinny Teresa you can't make an illegal buck in Vegas because the feds are swarming all over the place trying to see how the mob skims from the casinos."

"Wherever there's a spotlight of attention, there's plenty of shadow to move around in."

"You still have to be extra careful. That war is paying off. Nixon's hard-line law-and-order posture has got him record budgets."

"That's bullshit too, Red. Nixon's using that budget for what he calls national security. The enemies of the people aren't o.c. but the political dissidents, the rights activists, the war resisters, in other words, enemies of Nixon."

"I suppose you got that right. It's the old Nixon, the young Commie-hunter, coming back in the new mask of Nixon the crime-fighter."

"I hear all the boys, the friends of friends, are delighted with this administration. They say you can do business with a John Mitchell Justice Department, and that if you can't do business with a Vice President Agnew you just don't know how to do business. On the Coast they claim to have a book on these guys Haldeman and Erlichman in the White House, and the text is cooperation in the interest of mutual profit, common cause against common enemies, and increased power to maintain and secure the present order. Hell, they say those weekends at the western White House in San Clemente make Apalachin look like a boy scout jamboree."

"Just don't get carried away, Jack. You're starting to sound like your old self."

"It's the broads out there, Red."

"You don't like what I lined up here for your party?"

"Listen, there are all these super-fresh and healthy-looking teenagers who know everything. Know what they call a blow-job?"

"Going down?"

"Not any more. It's 'giving head'. And they all love to do it."

"As long as you don't get yours handed to you."

"They all give head to Jack Molinas. And Jack Molinas's head floats above it all."

*   *   *   *   *

Molinas was on a high roll. This was going to be the second best day since he was paroled. The best of course was February 25, 1970, the day his parole was officially transferred to L.A., and he had been out of town before sundown. Today he was going to introduce Bobby Kraw to Junior Torchio.

Those last months in New York hadn't been all that bad. He'd knocked out an outline for Pasternak within a month and then used it both to get up a book prospectus and to show his parole officer that his activities were legitimate. P.O. Horman was impressed by it, as he was by a letter from attorney Harold Messing expressing confidence about the movie deal and saying that Molinas should be in Los Angeles for the negotiations for rights to the story of his life. In his formal request for transfer, Molinas presented

Messing's bill, from the firm of Greenbaum, Wolff and Ernst, a ploy that gave Molinas an extra reason to smile, because he never paid that bill.

He had flaunted his confidence in the transfer by drawing attention to himself in public, especially at Knicks games in the Garden. Neither Podoloff's edict of exile nor the State's terms of parole could prohibit that. And just in case his presence might pass unnoticed he paraded about the arena with his regular date who looked like she had stepped from the pages of *Playboy* in her tight tops and miniskirts and was indeed known as Annie Fanny.

When he got to the Coast, after a brief stay with Kraw he had moved into Annie Fanny's one bedroom apartment while she pursued her own interests in New York—and vice versa. He had adapted to a southern California life style as if born and bred to it, but everywhere he went there were familiar faces from New York. He was at home in L.A. but it was old home week from New York too.

Nothing had come of the movie deal, despite meetings with Pasternak and Marty Ritt and others. But it had served his primary purpose, getting him out there, and now he was in the movie business anyway. He and Kraw were partners in Jo Jo Productions, porn-producers. It was a sweet deal. Kraw worked hard while he did the heavy thinking, quickly. A friend of Kraw's, Tony LaRosa, lined up the broads, called starlets. They shot wherever they could and sold 16 mm. prints on a strictly cash basis to exhibitors anywhere.

Molinas had quickly revolutionized the business. By accepting post-dated checks from exhibitors he could move Jo Jo's X-rated movies in volume instead of two or three at a time. The instant success of this innovation brought him a lot of money but also the attention of the competition. He had received both a direct warning and an

invitation to share Jo Jo's profits for the privilege of staying
in business. He had ignored both, never mentioning either
to Kraw.

And now he had solved the problem with Junior Torchio, a
small-time hood from Brooklyn, not a made member but connected to the Joe Columbo family. Molinas liked his colorful,
loud, flashy style. He was like an Italian Molinas without
brains, and Jack enjoyed baiting him at every opportunity.

They drove up La Cienega Boulevard, better known as
Restaurant Row, in Junior's Caddy, top down, to the storefront headquarters of Jo Jo.

"Bobby, shake hands with Junior Torchio. Junior, this is
Bobby Kraw."

"Norman Arno's the name, Junior. Jack likes to make jokes."

"So I hear," said Junior. "Pleased to meet ya, Norm."

"Junior here is your new partner, Bobby," Molinas said
and relished the shock freezing Kraw's ravaged face—a little fringe benefit of this maneuver.

"What?"

"I've sold my share to him." Junior did a little oafish
dance, waving some documents in his face. Molinas had
drawn them up himself. "But don't worry, everything will go
on as usual."

"You could have discussed it with me. Or is this another
joke?"

"No joke." He knew the deal—and Junior especially—
would stick in Kraw's throat.

"Then why?"

"It was time. That's all. I've got to move on to other
things."

"What other things? Gambling? Shylocking?" Torchio,
still clowning around the office, gave a hoot at that. In
California, as in New York, porn movies, loan sharking, and
bookmaking were often interlocking operations.

"What amazes me," Molinas said, looking anything but amazed, "is that there's always so much money around out here but everyone seems to want more cash. Small businesses get in credit trouble with the banks. They'll pay my rates—a point or two under the street rate—and take my terms. I get a guarantee of cash return from regular receipts regardless of net profits or losses."

"What do you do for cash to lend out?"

"If I don't have it, I get it from a loan shark." He grinned. His debts were building rapidly. It made him feel like a rich man.

So the deal was made, but Kraw didn't know that the paper transaction was not the reality. Molinas could still draw money from Jo Jo. When Kraw and LaRosa were arrested on obscenity charges a few months later, Molinas produced those same documents to show that he was not an interested party.

He wasn't charged, but then neither was Torchio. He never explained it to his old crony, Bobby Kraw a.k.a. Norman Arno. The police had cracked down on Jo Jo at the request of their o.c. competitors, who didn't like being undercut by such unfair business practices as credit. Any credit should be extended their way, through their loan sharks. Torchio, though, was one of their own, a friend of friends. And Molinas? He led a charmed life, and the charm was all his own.

Chapter 25:
Togetherness

L ydia knew he was special the first time she saw him. It was between takes on the set of "Rainy Rossini," and she was perfectly at her ease, reclining naked on a couch, turning the pages of a book on Magritte. She did nothing for effect, only what felt good and natural, but the effect was striking: a luxurious young body and that rare Sicilian combination of blue eyes, golden hair, and smooth bronzed skin.

She felt him take all of her in, but then almost everyone did, even the faggots. The difference was that she perceived an aura of intelligent excitement about him, a palpable charge of high energy. Even before she saw him drive off in a gold Caddy (Torchio's rented wheels, as it happened), she had decided to call him. She was broke and asked him for a loan, but it was only a pretext. He was more than twice her nineteen years, but age was no consideration either.

Two months later she moved in with him. Skinny Vinny Montalto, just out from Queens to practice his trade in stolen credit cards, was sleeping on the couch. But she didn't mind. When they moved from Annie Fanny's apartment out to Ridpath Drive in Laurel Canyon their combined gregariousness had attracted a large and varied acquaintance: musicians and actors between gigs, gangsters, gamblers, visitors from New York. They both seemed to thrive on it.

Lydia was proud of being the first woman he'd ever lived

with. She knew what it was about her that he was taken
with—he was an expert in phoniness in the world's capital
of phoniness and she was totally, healthily open and honest. She knew what she was and what she liked, and she
didn't mind telling anyone. She got him to try vegetarian
cuisine and marijuana, but neither was to his taste. She
hated his hairpiece, talked him into going without it for a
while, and burned it when he was out.

He didn't share business details with her but she had a
general sense of what he was doing—moving in and out of
financial arrangements like Buster Keaton in a revolving
door. He'd get into a troubled business, find a way to turn it
around on a short-term basis, and get out with a profit
before the expedient device exploded in the owner's face.
The idea seemed to be more than just making money; Jack
wanted to be making it as quickly and in as many different
ways as possible.

The most fun, still, was gambling. Using the popular blue
boxes to avoid paying the phone company for long-distance
calls (and to avoid self-incrimination by wire-taps), they
would spend most weekends calling around the country for
information on sports, making bets, taking bets, following
games three or four at a time on radio and TV. The action
was frantic. Molinas thrived on it, and Lydia grooved on his
energy. They were also running over to Vegas fairly often,
violating his parole each time, but he was doing that every
day in a dozen ways.

He was a whirlwind and she was intoxicated by it. The
manic zaniness of his personality made a commonplace
drive to the airport an adventure. It was another game, to
see how close they could cut it, stopping for fried chicken,
tossing the bones on the freeway. Of all his business activities, the only one that turned Lydia off was the one that
Molinas pursued with a special vengeance. He hired himself

out to a lawyer to do what he called paralegal work. The lawyer listed him as a clerk.

Molinas was under the illusion that in time he could become a member in good standing of the California bar. Some money in the right palms, some connections in the right places, and his knowledge and experience would do the rest. He could not yet be an officer of the court, but in doing this work he was paying court to the system by demeaning himself. That was bad enough in Lydia's eyes, but then he decided to make it pay, too, as long as he was playing the game.

With his connections among insurance adjustors, he would get lists of accident victims, sign them up as clients for his boss, and take a cut of a third out of the settlements. It was a sophisticated form of ambulance-chasing, profitable, and of course illegal. Ironically, what put a stop to it was the lawyer's discovery that Molinas was also using the firm's phones to make and book bets.

If there were any depressed valleys in his high manic plateau, Lydia was the only one who saw them. She told friends that sometimes when they were alone, Jack would be withdrawn, abstracted, cold, unresponsive. She thought it was that he had so many things on his mind. But he'd always snap out of it with a laugh and a suggestion for some kind of fun.

She could not get him to share her concept of a completely intimate relationship; he could not match her steady giving of warmth or her healthy appetite for exclusive sex. When she realized he was seeing other women, they didn't fight about it. She just started seeing other men. Once she stayed out all night and when she got back in the morning he told her calmly to pack up and leave. But when she pointed out that he had done the same thing, he just grinned at her and said she was right. Even when they were most incompatible they were compatible.

When she suggested a trial separation she knew it was a calculated risk, but if you couldn't take a gamble you had no business being with Jack Molinas anyway. She told him she wanted to spend some time up north and he seemed pleased with the idea, said they needed a break. He gave her the feeling that when she thought of it she had been reading his mind. She enjoyed that feeling but didn't share it with him. She knew he wouldn't appreciate it, especially if it were true.

*   *   *   *   *

Mickey Zaffarano was one of the few people Molinas had some respect for and could trust with serious conversation. He always looked forward to his visits, and especially this time while Lydia was away. He knew him from Coney Island, where he had run a parking lot near the Eagle Bar. He was a made member of the Bonanno family, but he had survived the war on good terms with all—a man of integrity respected by the commission. On his last visit to the Coast he had arbitrated a dispute between Torchio and other porn distributors. The interest-free "loan" of $7,000 he received from Molinas, ostensibly for an investment in a Brooklyn restaurant, was Zaffarano's arbitration fee.

"Moving up in the world, eh, Giacomo?" Mickey said as they drove back from the airport in the Mercedes 450 convertible that Molinas had unloaded the Eldorado for. Then he repeated the question when they arrived at the new house, on Thrush Way in the Hollywood Hills.

"Life is beautiful, Mickey. I'm on top of my game."

"Lydia?"

"Fine. We're getting along better than ever now that she's moved to Frisco. Visiting back and forth, you know.

She's twenty-one now—I'm not twice her age any more."
They both laughed. "She'll be moving back soon."
"And?"
"We'll see."
"Well, Giacomo, I wish you luck. Now there are two serious matters of business we must discuss."
They sipped their twenty-five-year-old scotch. Molinas appreciated the shift to formality in Zaffarano's tone and diction. He regarded the older man as a kind of Italian Dutch uncle.
"First, tell me of the book."
"The Jack Molinas story? Mickey, it's a good one. It'll be a movie yet."
"I suppose you took pleasure in performing with a mike and tape recorder, inventing yourself for artistic purposes."
"Right. What I didn't like was the editing, emending, correcting, cutting, and amplifying that Gross wanted at first."
"Why did you make a deal with Milton Gross?"
"He was perfect, Mickey. Of course, I'm prejudiced because he supported my campaign for reinstatement in the NBA. But he's honest and he works hard. I hated him when he'd try to pin me down to be accurate, to eliminate what he saw was contradictory or preposterous. I'd be joking around about things he knew for himself and he'd take it seriously. But he got it done and, besides, he got the contract from Bantam."
"Did you get an advance?"
"Blew it in Vegas in one weekend. But the real money's at the other end, in sales and the movie."
"When will it come out?"
"Pretty soon. It's in production now. But there's a clause in my contract that says I can stop publication at any time before release."
"I've never heard of that."

"It's unique, except that I used it before, years ago, with Patsy Flynn, when she was a writer. But I wanted to see if they'd go for it. There are penalty costs, but how would they collect?"

"Jack," he spoke more deliberately than ever, "your family does not want the book. Your father is very unhappy about it."

"I know, I know. My mother talks about it all the time."

"They feel ashamed. It would bring it all back and make it worse."

"I keep telling them that my side of the story will clear the Molinas name."

"You don't believe that one yourself. But your family is not alone, Jack. My family, too," and here he smiled briefly but sadly, "and their related families do not want this book."

"It won't hurt anyone."

"But it could hurt you. They are sensitive to your track record. They believe you would point the finger—or give it—to anyone if it would do you, or your book, some good."

"I've gotten similar messages from other sources—organized sports, the insurance business, the world of high finance—everyone is afraid I'll blow the whistle on their good things."

"A mutual friend asked me to suggest you stick to bookies and leave books to others."

"I'm still having second thoughts, and third. The thing is, I may have painted a good picture of myself but I've also painted myself into a corner. Put down between hard covers, I'd never be able to re-invent any of my stories."

"My recommendation is to stop the press, though it would be too bad for Milton Gross."

"That's his problem. He knew the risk all along."

"Now let us talk of a more pressing matter, where I understand a great deal of money is involved. Tell me about your fur business."

"I invested fifty thousand with Bernie Gussoff to form Berjac, Inc. I liked his style. He's ten years older than me, captain of the Brooklyn College basketball team in '43, and he stays in great shape, dresses right, lives with a former beauty queen. The goods."

"How did you make the connection?"

"Through Junior Torchio."

"You know, of course, of Junior's associations."

"Yes. Hell, he fronted for me in Jo Jo, had the right connections in New York with the Perainos."

"Let us be clear on this, Jack. Torchio is on the payroll of Bryanston, Louis Peraino's film distribution company. It was Louis's father who was the original angel for *Deep Throat*. Both Perainos are associated with the Profaci family."

"And since Joe Columbo was left a zucchini?"

"Not funny, Jack. The boss is Thomas DiBello, no better, no worse. Now you see what you are dealing with."

"I'm dealing with a successful guy in the fur business."

With a warehouse full of furs. Where did those furs come from?"

"I didn't want to get into that part of the business. I handled the money, Bernie the furs."

"And what guarantee did you have that your truckloads would survive hijacking for delivery?"

"That didn't worry me either. What worried me was that not enough were sold to warrant delivering truckloads. There was no cash flow. I borrowed twenty thousand from the Bank of America, then sixty thousand from City National."

"But it was not enough, so you went to Bryanston."

"They came through with almost a quarter of a million, $247,000."

"You cannot bail out of that one, Jack. Here is what you must do. Get a secured loan elsewhere to pay that one off.

Your partner will have to put up his Canadian property as collateral. He will, because he understands what and who he is dealing with. Do it soon, but as a first step, before approaching potential lenders, you and Mr. Gussoff must take out insurance on each other's lives, say half a million. That you can do tomorrow."

Molinas nodded, waiting to hear if there was any more, if there was a hidden agenda here. But Zaffarano had shifted gears again. It wasn't that he was an inscrutable catechist, just that the business session was over.

"And now, Giacomo, just one more question before I say goodnight. When is your parole over?"

"In a few months. I never even think about it any more. I've never felt so free in my life."

"Then let's drink to a long life of freedom."

Chapter 26:
High Times

It pleased Red Benjamin to see his friend Molinas doing so well. The convertible Rolls seemed emblematic of how far he had come. What disappointed Benjamin was Jack's waning interest in the market—his opinions had been good for both of them. But Jack said that the action was too slow and constraining for him.

As he described his business deals Red heard a dizzying story of numbers being moved around at breakneck pace. Molinas was making more, spending more, and owing more than ever. No one could fathom the intricate pattern of blinds, dummies, and dodges. Benjamin gave up trying. After all, he was visiting mostly for fun, and there was always a succession of parties among the wheelings and dealings for Molinas.

Two bits of unpleasantness marred this visit. In one, just after he arrived, he had been an unwitting contributor to a domestic quarrel. In the other, just last night, he had probably been an unwilling witness for an alibi. Now, flying back to New York on the red-eye, the late editions of the L.A. *Times* and *Examiner* on his lap, Red had occasion to ponder both those scenes.

The day after he'd arrived, he'd been in the house with Lydia when her friend Barry showed up. He looked like a beach bum or a surfer—long hair and golden-brown glow all over and a generally mellow demeanor. Barry's attitude ran a short gamut from happy-go-lucky to spaced-out, but he was in fact a shrewd businessman. He was a careful, selective dope-dealer who often angled in on interesting investment opportunities to put his profits to work. Benjamin liked him more each time he saw him, was flattered that he picked his brains on money matters.

"Red, my man, glad to see you."

"Hey, Barry, looking good."

Barry reached into his pocket before shaking hands, palming a small brown wad into Benjamin's unsurprised grip.

"A little welcome-back gift, like, a dash of opiated hash."

"Celebrating some good news, Barry?"

"Just high spirits, man."

"I was going to compliment you on the return you got from your investment with Zaffarano."

Lydia walked into the room at that moment and saw the blank look on Barry's face. They all realized at once what had happened. On his last brief visit west, Mickey must have paid Barry off by giving the money to Molinas for him, and Jack must have pocketed the money.

"That's all right, man. It's cool. Nothing ventured, you know. It'll work out."

"Yeah," Lydia said, "like Jack always says, what goes around comes around."

She had been calm until Barry left but then had stewed about it all afternoon. When Molinas came home she lit into him, shouting, "Cheating my friend is like cheating me, worse, because it makes me out to be a cheater, and now it's cost me a friend."

He shouted back, "That's my business you're talking about, none of yours, and you better not interfere."

Her anger was genuine, but his, Benjamin thought, was not. Later Jack told him he wanted to pick a fight with her, because he wanted her to go away again for a while. Lydia, shaken by the scene, confided in him that it was their first real fight since she'd come back. She really didn't understand it, she had said, but Benjamin thought now he understood it too well.

Then, on Benjamin's last night in town, Molinas hosted a party at the Polo Lounge. Red wasn't exactly privileged as guest of honor. Jack had parties because Jack wanted to have parties. Any pretext would do, and he'd just as soon invent one. In leisure suit and white shoes, he was his most expansive and obnoxious self. He just had to let the whole world know he was there. At one point, apropos of nothing, he held forth to Benjamin on the subject of Bernie Gussoff.

"Son of a bitch is supposed to know furs and he makes one mistake after another. I had it with him when he started unloading the inventory at huge panic discounts. I pulled out of Berjac and left him to worry about the Bryanston loan. With Torchio on his back for starters, he had plenty to worry about.

"I had another lender set up to get him out of that bind but he blew the deal. Now the prick thinks the business is gonna make a comeback and he's flying to Europe tomorrow to buy furs. I hear he's been calling everyone he knows to advance him some money. Well, bon voyage, Bernie."

Benjamin, on his own plane flight, kept coming back to that valedictory. Molinas's language echoed in his ears and he kept reviewing the gloating attitude for signs of something unusual in Molinas.

Gussoff, it seems, had missed his plane flight. According to the papers on Red's lap, sometime during the previous evening, in his room at the Oasis, the furrier had been strangled and beaten to death with a blunt instrument. Why both? Neither police nor press had an answer to that.

Red couldn't avoid uneasy thoughts. He knew that Molinas had half a million dollars coming from a life insurance policy on his ex-partner, Gussoff. He would certainly be suspected, having that much to gain. But he would be cool, dismissing any accusation with a laugh and a sneer. Benjamin could see him now, and he also knew that he himself could testify—along with a hundred other people—that Jack had been in the Polo Lounge all through the time-frame of the murder.

Had Molinas been celebrating his inheritance in advance? Some people might think so, but Red thought he knew better. At least he kept telling himself, "No, that party was his normal behavior." Only occasionally in the months to come did he wonder just what was "normal behavior" for Jack Molinas, but he was always able to push such questions aside.

And as for Molinas, as soon as Red was on the flight he was out of mind. The same was true of Gussoff. He was gone and forgotten; the money was just money, a good return on a clever investment.

Every morning he woke up on an instant manic high, and as the day went on he just soared higher and higher. Racing from meeting to meeting, in a dozen cities, in several countries, on three continents, he tapped a store of energy that was frightening. He felt so keenly alive, so balanced on the sharp edge of full living, that he could appreciate, as if seeing it from above, his capacity to juggle more and more without losing sight of any one item of the whole intricate pattern or the pattern itself as a whole.

And from his vantage he could yet be introspective, examining his feelings for Lydia. What he found on examination was ambivalence. He loved her body; it was the one that suited him best. She reminded him of Patsy Flynn, but there was passion and spontaneity in her moves, rather than workmanlike skill. And yet there were times when the familiarity of it turned him off and he wanted something different. Her face was not beautiful, but he didn't tire of looking at it, with its expressive openness, its generous features.

He liked her youth, but he often felt out of touch with it. They were products of different times, they had too little in common, and yet they enjoyed many things together. She was bright, quick, lively; but she lacked sophistication, subtlety, class. She was devoted to him, but he sensed her capacity to transfer that devotion to someone else if he didn't keep working at receiving it.

The odd thing was that the more he thought positively about the relationship with Lydia, the more he thought of Sharon. All his life he had used women, getting in and out when the getting was good, just like his wheeling and dealing in business. And now that he had found someone he might change all that for, he was thinking he could do better with someone else.

Sharon had the complex intelligence and sophistication that Lydia lacked. But maybe she didn't have the spirited spontaneity and openness of Lydia. Sharon was beautiful in a classy way; Lydia would always be ogled, but Sharon could be photographed or painted. At least that's the way he saw her in his mind's eye. He hadn't actually seen her in years. He had known her, though, all her life, watched her grow up in the neighborhood as the brightest, loveliest, spunkiest kid around. She had followed him around, not worshipfully but as if he were the only person worth her attention.

And it was true. Even though she was nine years his junior, she seemed to understand and appreciate him best. That's why, wherever he was and wherever she was, he always kept track of her, why whenever he thought about one ideal woman to make a life with it was little Sharon projected into maturity as his imagination conceived of her.

According to his latest reports, Sharon now was free to be with him, ironically just when he had Lydia. Well, maybe he was getting ready for the one by experiencing the other, and he sure as hell was enjoying the experience.

Sharon had married a brilliant, charismatic, young cultural anthropologist at Cornell, but he knew that two other men had courted her both before and after the wedding. She had resisted both the urbane campaign of a famous Fielding scholar and the persistent attentions of a clinician known around the greater Ithaca area as the Great Jewish Seducer. But the marriage had not survived because Sharon couldn't go on subordinating herself to a macho husband. She tried, by drinking too much and then submitting herself to a twelve-step recovery program despite her intellectual abhorrence of its explicit spirituality. But she knew now it wasn't worth the struggle. She had to be herself, go her own way.

She hadn't told him any of this, but she had written him, even sending a current picture, and suggested a visit. He was working out the details. He had arranged for Lydia to get a job managing theaters in Ohio where *Deep Throat* was running. Thanks to that phony fight, she was happy to get as far away from him as she could, at least for a time. Time enough and just in time, he thought. He was confident that he could woo Lydia back, if he wished, especially if he mentioned marriage—in case things didn't work out with Sharon. But it was time to put the Sharon dream to the test.

Meanwhile, his surge of manic energy reached new peaks. There was instant money to be made, a myriad of big numbers to juggle, all over the world. They heard the Molinas laugh from Madras to Mazatlan. He described himself in that mocking way that was more brag than joke as an Edmund fucking Hillary of finance, scaling new Himalayan deals. And the higher he got, the more gleefully he looked down and thought that it was beneath him ever to have to pay any debts.

Chapter 27:
Safe House

T he Thunder Eagle Lodge, named from local Indian lore, is located on a 4,800-foot peak where the San Jacinto Mountains reach over into San Bernardino County. It was built in the 20s as one of the finest resort hotels in the world. Its opulence and magnificence were enhanced by a degree of graciousness and charm that made it unique in its day, in contrast with the other lavish monuments to big new money and manic ostentatiousness in the extended western domain of Beverly Hills. The grandest icon in the Thunder Eagle was the massive oak bar in the lounge, hailed as one of the seven wonders of the civilized world.

When the Lodge was sold and closed in the early 50s, it was said that the whole property, over 200 glorious acres, was going to be developed as an exclusive vacation community. But when the last guest moved out—a remarkable old woman who lived in her own suite while she continued to direct the fortunes of the small department-store chain founded by her late husband—no development took place. Rumor had it that the operation was in a holding pattern while the complicated details of interlocking holding companies were worked out. Meanwhile the Lodge was maintained by a new skeleton staff and opened periodically for "retreats" attended, apparently, by officers of those companies.

It was there, on an early summer day in 1975, that a small group of executives retreated from their overheated activities in Los Angeles, San Diego, and Las Vegas for a conference. They had come in, at their ease, at various times of the morning, some directly from their homes in Palm Springs, Rancho Mirage, Rancho La Costa, and La Jolla, though their original homes were likely to have been in New York, Detroit, Cleveland, or Chicago. They joked sometimes about being the first division of the old American League. Several had brought their wives, and three of the younger men had their children with them. The recreational facilities were maintained year round. A few days in the cool, old-fashioned luxury was a treat for all.

The main reason, however, for the selection of this location was its privacy. Almost all of these men had been mentioned in reports by the FBI or organized crime task forces. Some of them had taps on their phones or had otherwise been under electronic surveillance. The Thunder Eagle Lodge was a safe house. In fact, the CIA had on at least two occasions used it as a safe house, which was probably the best indication that the FBI didn't know about it.

They were a distinguished-looking group. Their cars were German and conservative, their hair styled carefully to enhance rather than disguise the gray, and their clothes were custom-tailored Savile Row. The main exception was the one they called Sidney, whose Ferrari bore Nevada plates and whose silks were of Italian cut.

As they gathered in the conference room, it was clear that there were five principals among them and that the other eight, who tended to be younger and who carried the briefcases, were subordinates. They all moved easily, their manner was low-key and cordial, and the distinctions and deferences among them were subtle, suggestive of a comfortable hierarchy. None of them smoked. They sat around the table and were joined by the director of the resident staff, who sat not at the table but to the left and behind the man who sat at the head, in the manner of a recording secretary, though he took no notes and no active part in the discussion while following every word with keen eyes.

His name was Jerome, he called himself Paul, but everyone knew him as Sonny. It was a traditional joke among them that Paul was "Sonny the Sony"—a human tape recorder. Trained in the mnemonic techniques of oral cultures, Paul was a living record of important business for people who did not commit to writing anything but what they wanted others to see, that is, the clever covers, the official fictions for the unwritten realities.

The man at the head began proceedings by clearing his throat, sticking out his lower jaw, and saying in a fake hoarse voice, "I've called the five families together..." It was another standing joke, greeted with warm smiles around the room, though no one laughed aloud. A number of matters were discussed and dealt with quickly, almost casually, but to apparent satisfaction. To each other they used only first names, but in a strikingly stilted way. Except for Sonny, there were no nicknames, no short forms. Where once you might have expected shortened versions of ethnic names, with perhaps a sobriquet added, like Big Chin for Vicenzo, Sando the Shrimp for Allesandro, or Fat Funzi for Alphonso, you now heard only Vincent or Alexander—and Alphonse had long since changed his name to Allen.

"Now, gentlemen," said the man called Peter, the apparent chairman, "some of you may want to settle other matters while we're here, but I believe there's nothing else that concerns us all except this problem we share. For reasons of historical interest and nostalgia, let's refer to this problem as Mr. X."

This time there was laughter in general, but Sidney, on the edge of his seat, began to talk right over it. "It's about time we got to this. It's why I'm here, and I want it done right." The appearance of flashy elegance in Sidney was undermined by his obvious agitation about the subject. He looked like he was ready to jump on the table. "And I don't think it's funny, what he's gotten away with."

"Hold on, Sidney." Peter smiled benignly. "Let's be orderly about this, and thorough as well. There have been too many careless, hasty mistakes made lately in the heat of emotion, and we have all been placed under unnecessary pressure. Let's exercise proper discipline and decorum, making sure we do the right thing without stirring up reprisals."

A murmur of assent accompanied Sidney's slump in his chair. But it wasn't relaxation. His mouth was twisted; he was biting his tongue, waiting his turn. Peter continued.

"I've gathered some background. Sonny," he said, nodding to his left, "please correct me if you know of any discrepancies here. The earliest connection we can trace is to the Genovese family. Apparently Tom Eboli knew X as a boy, took a liking to him."

"Excuse me, Peter." This was Vincent speaking, genuine amusement in his blue eyes accompanying his smile. In his tanned face, only when he smiled did the deep creases around the eyes and mouth give any clue to his age. "That was a million years ago, in the dark ages. Do we have to have ancient history here?"

Peter was about to reply but instead recognized Richard, one of the briefcase-carriers, whose mustache and longish sandy hair parted in the middle were only slightly incongruous in this conservatively-groomed company yet perhaps moved him to assert his presence.

"I think the point here is important. Too often lately we've been caught unawares by long-standing enmity, bad blood if you will. It can be useful just to acknowledge the historical situation, at least to see if it bears on the present."

"Exactly, Richard. At the risk of making Sidney squirm a little longer, let's touch all the relevant bases. Any credit X might have had with that family he exhausted when he was sent away in the '60s. He shortened his sentence by supplying solid information about two different situations. I'm sure you all remember that. Meanwhile, X had made problems for Chicago, Pittsburgh, and St. Louis, while he was still involved in what he went away for. And I think that's all the ancient history. The recent past is more complicated. Thomas?"

Perhaps the oldest man in the room, Thomas was also the heaviest. Even his custom tailoring couldn't disguise a lifetime of living high on the hog. He took pleasure in all his activities, including this conference.

"Yes. In the interest of thoroughness," he said, enjoying Sidney's impatience, "have you checked out a possible connection with Meyer?"

"Why should there be one? Just because they're co-religionists?" Though the laughter was general again, it seemed forced from three of the company.

"Well, this X was very close to one man in the Bronx, and this was a man who always did the right thing."

"Do we all understand that Thomas is talking about a gentleman once known as Joe Jalop?"

Nods all around.

"Well, he was part of that boxing thing that Frankie ran for Meyer, even though he walked away from it," Thomas said, no doubt enjoying the display of his knowledge.

"Meyer walked too, " Vincent snorted.

"We actually checked that out. Those connections were broken, with no obligations, long ago. And now we get close to home. Barely five years ago X comes into our country, and right away he's a big conspicuous consumer. Suppose we start with Sidney, now, since X's reputation as a gambler preceded him."

"Thanks, Peter." Sidney's mouth was twitching all during his recital, while his audience, with calm amusement at the performer, nevertheless attended to the details of the narration. "He no sooner gets to L.A. than he's booking action, all on his own, wherever he goes. And instead of using regular lay-offs, he's just betting through his own contacts whenever he doesn't like the balance of his action. Never a fucking word about doing the right thing."

"Any fixes?"

"No."

"Well, this is no more than a thousand other guys do. Until they go broke."

"This X doesn't go broke, but does he pay his losses? Forget about it. Anyway, he starts coming over to Vegas. First he's in and out of the sports books, especially Churchill Downs, betting every ballgame in sight, good-sized action, always flashing a big roll. Next thing you know he's at the Dunes, comped of course, and Artie Selman OKs a five thousand line of credit. He plays some blackjack and mostly hits the craps tables. Good-sized action again and well-mannered, you know, compared to a lot. And his reputation for big parties and all the broads? None of that. He's usually with a few men, maybe a broad or two, but all smiles, real cordial, no noise, no trouble.

"Next thing, he comes into the Tropicana. Now he's established, right? High roller, good credit. Naturally he's comped. Minny Cardello gives him a twenty-five thousand dollar line. He runs through twenty so fast it's hard to see how he's losing it all. And maybe he isn't. Because the dice get hot at his table and he walks away, they tell me, a fifty thousand winner, that's seventy thousand in chips that he cashed all over the strip that night.

"They go to his room in the morning for the twenty, and he acts real pissed off. Tells them he picked up a hooker in their lounge and took her to his room, and when he wakes up she's gone and so is all his money. Says they're responsible, figures they owe him fifty."

Sidney had been getting angrier and angrier during this recital and now was fairly sputtering with rage, unable for a minute to continue.

"Anything else?"

"Yes. When this story hits the street, they start getting bookies coming in with their own claims. The guy, this X, has been betting privately on all sports all over town. But he don't pay. Forgets making losing bets. Forgets! There's about another fifty thousand of bad paper around on this guy. If anyone ever deserved to get clipped, he's it. But I'd like to see some of our people get some of their money back first."

The last was spoken tiredly. Sidney slumped back in his seat, emotionally spent. The others, no longer smiling condescendingly at him, digested the report in a moment's silence, until Peter continued.

"Here's a bookmaker who does not pay his debts to other bookmakers. The same pattern appears in loan-sharking. He's shylocking for himself but doesn't pay the shylocks he borrows from. Alexander?"

"Richard here, our virtuoso of the computer terminals, has put this report together. I'll ask him to make it."

"X has an extraordinary ability to juggle money. He moves bank accounts so often and so quickly that the same hundred thousand can turn up in three different places within any given week. That way it looks like three hundred, and you can be sure that the account he draws big checks on is not the one that has the balance when they clear. We believe he also has a number of blind accounts under dummy names along with safety deposit boxes. He doesn't keep boxes at the banks that hold the legitimate accounts, but we have not been able to identify or confirm the others."

"FBI contacts help?"

"Blank. Until November it hadn't occurred to them to look closely at X, for reasons that escape me. The point is that he does the same thing on the street that he does with the banks. Any time he can get assurance of returns from a business, out of the gross of any cash-flow operation, he's quick to lend. And if he needs cash to make the loan he gets it from a shylock. Some of them have also booked his bets, though they've now stopped doing either. The total runs to about a hundred and fifty thousand. We don't believe there's any real hope for recovery. I personally wouldn't buy his paper for a nickel on the dollar.

"The main problem here is an overriding claim for a loan from New York, two hundred forty-seven thousand. The loan is rumored to be protected by the Profaci or Columbo family. Whether it is a prior claim is moot, the point being that it is a stronger claim, and we believe it should be honored if we begin to assign priorities."

"Excellent, Richard," said Peter. "In fact I have already given assurances that it will be so honored, with the understanding that our decision will be accepted if we determine that the highest priority of nothing is still nothing. Ironically, that isn't even the largest outstanding debt, as Vincent will explain."

Vincent began with a shrug, a sardonic expression on his face, and an attitude of smugness that tended to make some of the others narrow their eyes in slight winces of a discomfort they would rather not display. "We do the processing for all the porno. It's not a cash business because we know the producers and distributors can't come up with the money usually till after sales and screenings, so we have a graduated scale for payments according to the time lapse. As far as X is concerned, for the X-rated processing, he now owes us over a quarter of a million."

"Isn't he out of the business?"

"So he says. But we dealt with him. He made the deal. We figure it's his debt. But we can write it off because we can just take the movies back and sell them to someone else. We'd also like to write X off, period."

"Now," Peter said, "before we oversimplify the situation, let's study some of the complications. X seems to have some credit with the Gambino family for an obvious reason. You remember that Aniello Dellacroce was nearly hit by Carlo Lombardi, who ought to have been called a miss-man. Anyway, the two men, Musolino and Salanardi, who flew in from our country to take care of Lombardi were staying with X as his guests. Hold on a moment, Vincent. We have checked this out and there is no obligation outstanding." Vincent nodded, satisfied. "Now, so far as the Zaffarano connection is concerned, correct me if I'm wrong, Vincent, there's no outstanding obligation there either. Mickey settled your earlier dispute and was paid for it. If it is convenient for him, as he supervises his widespread film interests, to stay in the Hollywood Hills with X from time to time, that is not a mitigating factor in our matters. And that, too, has been confirmed.

"Finally, there's the matter of Tieri's problem, which does conflict with ours. A Genovese soldier, a small-time bookie, loan shark, and porn operator, took his own family's shylocks for a considerable amount and moved into our country."

"Ullo?"

"Correct. Joseph Spencer Ullo. Right away the man's doing business with our Mr. X, booking and shylocking back and forth. It's like a reunion of long-lost brothers. Where their account stands on any given day is anyone's guess. Tieri and Gigante want to send their own man out to recover what he can from Ullo and then bury him. But they have been persuaded to postpone that action in the hopes that we can satisfactorily deal with our problem, cut everyone's losses, and kill two birds with one stone as it were. What should have led to a satisfactory conclusion took place in November. I asked Thomas to assign Lucas here to that matter at the time. What can you tell us, Lucas?"

Probably the youngest man in the room, Lucas was also the most conservatively dressed, in gray flannel despite the season, with narrow lapels and skinny, striped tie despite the fashion. His black hair, cut unfashionably short, gave his close-set eyes an open, embarrassed look. Physically he resembled the older men in the room, though he might have been mistaken for an FBI agent, at least until he spoke. He spoke with the kind of drawl that sugarcoats a sneer, in the manner of Princeton and Virginia Law School, which in fact were where, after the Hill School, he had gotten the manner along with his degrees.

"Yes, well, we have here a somewhat unusual matter of contracts. Our X and his furrier partner had a contractual arrangement that, in return for his initial investment, allowed X to withdraw unilaterally from the partnership on prearranged terms. Subsequently the partners entered into a limited term contract with the Massachusetts Indemnity Company, insuring each other's life for half a million dollars. Pursuant to mounting losses, X exercised his option to withdraw from the partnership. The papers were duly drawn, processed, and delivered. Though no payments in settlement were actually made, the partnership was nevertheless legally terminated. The insurance contract, however, failed to stipulate a continuation of the partnership as a contingent term of the policy. Therefore, when the furrier was murdered sixteen days before the insurance contract was to be terminated, X was entitled to payment, which he duly received.

"Only in the event that X were held responsible for the furrier's death could payment have been withheld. X was substantially alibied for the entire period of the murder, and no evidence for conspiracy was brought forward. Any hesitance on the part of Massachusetts Indemnity would have been construed as accusation and resulted in a massive and crippling lawsuit. They paid promptly.

"The murder itself was a messy affair. Yet although vulnerable to accidental witnessing by its setting, it has proven invulnerable to investigation. There are no leads. The police are baffled. The FBI has been unable to help.

"A logical presumption is that X entered into a contract for the furrier's murder. But we haven't been able to adduce any solid evidence to support that presumption. It seems probable that X has reneged on any contract, which might be a convenient motivation for possible reprisals. In spite of that, or perhaps because of that, a claim of sorts has been made. A certain..." He paused here, glancing from Thomas to Peter. Both nodded encouragement or approval, and Lucas drawled on. "A certain Rizzi, a.k.a. Rizzitello, has been trying to establish himself in our country, with Fratianno, with Regace, with Bompensiero. Everyone but the Weasel seems to shy away from him. His background is service with Crazy Joe Gallo, nine years for armed robbery and kidnapping, lifetime parole. He is big enough to have beaten the furrier to death, but the question in point is this: would X, as Rizzi boasts, have paid him fifty thousand dollars for the job?

"We think not. Oliver will have more to say on this subject, but we think not because we cannot trace any such movement of money. Richard, for one, would have known of it. We believe that Rizzi, seeking advancement, has moved into a vacuum to take credit for a genuinely mysterious killing. The allegation that he killed for money should be counterproductive to his efforts in any case. Moreover, he has apparently attempted to extort payment from X, in the amount of five, not fifty, thousand. And X, it will surprise no one here, has stridently declined to honor the claim."

There was an almost tangible urge to applaud this report, but it was successfully repressed as Peter continued. "Half a million could have satisfied a good portion of his obligations here, but X has rejected our suggestions that he move accordingly. It's about six months since he collected, and he's paid nothing back on any account. The last question that remains before we make a final decision is whether there is significant hope for recovery. I've asked Oliver, whose expertise as you know extends beyond market research to behaviorism in general, for an opinion."

Oliver looked like the bright young man in the Xerox commercial, the gold-wire-framed glasses and understated demeanor failing to mask the intensity and zeal burning in and behind the eyes. Peter beamed on him as he spoke, while Alexander, Thomas, and Vincent exchanged looks of strained tolerance, bordering on exasperation when Oliver sounded most like a clinical psychologist.

"This is a curious case. The insurance money has not changed his behavior so much as it has triggered an intensification of existent patterns. His interests have broadened, his activities multiplied. He has traveled to India, to the Cayman Islands, and to Mexico to set deals up. Incidentally, he cleared things in San Diego with Bomp to move large volumes of fish imported from Mazatlan. He has jumped into a TV chain store operation, from Las Vegas to Omaha, and he looks at a dozen investment opportunities a day, from new inventions to old scams. All of this without letting up on his usual activities. He's gambling as much as ever and still playing basketball.

"In his present modality he seems unable to stop reaching out in terms of spending, traveling, and acquiring. He's ordered elaborate renovations in his house, and he doesn't even own it. He's ordered thousands of dollars' worth of household goods like a bride with no ceiling on a trousseau. And his borrowing from banks has grown with his new credit.

"In short, the behavior pattern is pathological. He is in an escalating manic phase and at the same time has become obsessive-compulsive about acquisitions. There is a self-destructive element at the heart of it all, so that we could never expect him to let loose of anything, to pay a debt, or to be brought down to a level of negotiating on a quid pro quo basis. His only satisfaction comes from spiraling higher and higher in his mania, and his ultimate serenity will be achieved in death, which he subconsciously intends to control by bringing it upon himself. X's syndrome is what I would call the Icarus complex."

Peter smiled broadly now. "Any questions? Then let's decide. Sidney?"

"It's a dead loss," he said, but there was as much whine as resignation in his voice. "Clip the deadbeat."

"Vincent?"

"Terminate."

"Thomas?"

"Terminate."

"Alexander?"

"Final solution."

"I agree. Unanimous for us. Any observations from the rest of you? Good, then here is what I propose. Let us all agree to surrender the honor of carrying out this decision. Let the contract be given to Joseph Spencer Ullo. Let him be told that in return he will be released from his New York obligations. In turn, in time, he will be justly, legally punished for the crime, but this will be very carefully arranged.

"New York has not only agreed but has provided us with a tool for the job. Gentlemen, we now have in our hands the prototype of a weapon developed especially for law enforcement agencies in the East. It is an ordinary .22 long to which has been attached a sophisticated but simple laser guidance system. It's as easy as aiming a flashlight. The bullet follows the beam directly to the target. It is precise, has excellent range, and is especially effective at night.

"Now our understanding with Ullo is to be explicit. The job will be done with our tool. The tool is to be returned. Anytime an execution is performed so inexpertly as to result in detection and apprehension, the executor will be held responsible for other jobs done with the same tool. This is an incentive for professionalism as well as an opportunity for any single amateurish job to wipe the slate clean on several professional ones. Further, we guarantee the life, inside or outside, of anyone who accepts the other conditions. In the case of Ullo, of course, he knows that he has no choice but to accept them. In fact, for the guarantee of his life, he'd do anything at this point.

"Vincent, you may move to recover X's X-rated movies at any time. Alexander, is it your intention to arrange for seizure of whatever stock of furs is available?"

"Yes, and there could be substantial recovery involved, properly handled."

"The right thing," Thomas observed, "would be to move any merchandise through New York, give them a chance to cut their losses as well."

"That's all been arranged, on a 60-40 basis in New York's favor." Alexander shrugged as he spoke. "Tieri and DiBello will decide between them on a proper split."

"Yes, I know," said Thomas, and whatever tension remained in the room dissolved in a common laugh.

"Thank you, gentlemen," said Peter. "Everything all right, Sonny? Then I hope you all enjoy your retreat."

"Wait a minute," said Thomas. "Before we go I gotta tell you the latest Sinatra story. This comes straight from a guy who used to handle a lot of productions at Columbia Records.

"Remember that great Cole Porter song, 'Just One of Those Things'? It was one of Frank's biggest hits, single and album. You always hear the record on the radio but he never sings the song in concert. Here's why.

"The guy tells me when they cut that record they had to do like a million takes. Because every time Frank starts to sing the lyric, he goes, "It was just one of them things."'

They left laughing, Thomas most of all.

PART VI:
Continuing Education

Chapter 28:
Life After
Molinas

So Molinas was a compulsive gambler after all. He played to lose in the biggest games of all. The only way to find out how far you can go is to go too far. No trickster can be a hero without seeking a definition of limits and then exceeding them. Trickster-heroes are the individuals who, by their excesses, test, prove, define, and refine our systems. They are compelled to live by their own rules, and we learn from them how the rest of us must live by ours. Molinas went too far in 1953 and lost his basketball career. He went too far in 1961 and lost his profession and his freedom. He went too far in 1975 and lost his life.

*　　*　　*　　*　　*

Junior Torchio survived Molinas by only three weeks. He was knocked down and killed by a moving vehicle on a Las Vegas street. The death was ruled an accident. The driver, 67, had no chance to stop when Torchio ran out in front of his car. Junior's carelessness and haste, by no means uncharacteristic, were occasioned by the approach of two pedestrians he did not wish to see, though witnesses were of the opinion that the two men wished to see him. Those two men were not among the witnesses who came forward, nor were they among those who attempted to aid the accident victim.

*   *   *   *   *

Sharon recovered quickly from a slight wound in her neck. The bullet that killed Molinas had passed through his head and struck her. But she was severely traumatized by his violent death. Apparently she never recovered from that shock. She died in 1978 of a drug overdose.

Lydia recovered quickly, too. She was angry about Sharon's role in Molinas's final scene so she indulged in a spectacular three nights of grieving, spent mostly at the Stardust Grille, a shit-kicking country music bar in Youngstown. She is a survivor.

*   *   *   *   *

Joseph Spencer Ullo was not the kind of man who would meticulously assemble a group of professional people for a specific mission, after the manner of the Mission Impossible Team or of Sam Jaffe as the Professor in *The Asphalt Jungle*. As a subcontractor he simply made use of his contacts from bookmaking and shylocking to put together a ragtag bunch of guys who needed some cash and didn't care what they did for it.

Eugene Connor ran a heating and air-conditioning shop in Van Nuys, but Ullo knew that he was specializing in stealing trucks. Connor got to use the chosen tool. Robert Zander, who once worked as a repairman for Connor, served as armed lookout for a two hundred dollar fee. His friend, Craig Petzold, was the driver.

The mission was accomplished rather smoothly, despite the crew. But Ullo failed to comply with one of the terms of the contract. He did not return the tool. That was enough of a pretext for Tieri and Gigante in New York to abrogate the arrangement, after several patient months, and once again seek collection of their due bill from Ullo. They assigned this portfolio to their man Gazut, Gaspare Vincent Calderazzo.

His embassy failed. One year and two weeks to the day after the Molinas murder, Gazut was lured into an ambush by Zander and Petzold in the guest house on Ullo's Northridge property. Ullo, who by then had established a jewelry store as a front, sandbagged Gazut with a gem of a crowbar. Connor helped beat him senseless. The triggerman was a new recruit, Johnny Kern, described in the press as a former Simi Valley nightclub owner. Zander and Petzold buried the body in the desert near Victorville, where it was found seven months later.

When Gazut disappeared, his bosses voted to kill Ullo, but the vendetta has not as yet been carried out. Ullo was convicted of extortion in December, 1977, for trying to enforce payment from a shylock client, and was on bail pending appeal of his five-year sentence when he was tried for the murders of Molinas and Calderazzo. Zander, Petzold, and Kern pleaded guilty as accessories to murder, testified for the prosecution, and had their murder and assault charges dropped. Connor was convicted of killing Molinas, but the jury acquitted him in the case of Calderazzo. The same jury acquitted Ullo in both cases, not because they believed him innocent—they said later they believed he murdered both men—but because they strictly applied the law against conviction based on unsupported accomplice testimony.

Meanwhile, the bosses who ordered Ullo's death have been indicted by a federal grand jury, another strike force has secured indictments against the L.A. gang that killed Bompensiero in 1977, Jimmy the Weasel Fratianno is testifying everywhere he can from the relative security of the Federal Witness Program, and business and life go on as usual.

The superprofessionals who ordered Molinas hit and set Ullo up for it recede safely into the protective foliage of respectability. And Ullo and his band of bumptious amateurs, except for Connor, are walking around big as life. Well, as Molinas used to say, you win some and you lose some, the idea being to collect your winnings and not pay your losses.

*   *   *   *   *

Red Benjamin lives on the island of Abaco in the Bahamas, where he retired in 1976. Everyone there calls him Saul, with respect, although his full beard has come in a rich golden red. He is in the best physical shape of his life, and he maintains it by running every day on the beach, sometimes with weights in his hands. Occasionally, for a token fee, he will agree to give some financial advice to a friend, running some numbers through his personal computer on programs of his own device.

He is no longer active in the market himself. He has enough to take very good care, for the rest of their lives, of himself, his wife (a Dutch girl he met on one of his early Caribbean trips in search of just the right bank and property for a secured future), and the imported Balearic hounds who share their house and their runs on the beach.

He remembers Jack Molinas with gratitude. It is to connections he made through Jack that he owes his happy existence. He made a number of friends by setting up some innovative programs for disguising holdings—what is vulgarly called laundering money. He never refused a friend of a friend a favor.

And when, in return, he was offered inside information that was sure to lead to spectacular profits in the market, he did not refuse that either. He took the ball and ran with it as far as he had to, to get where he wanted to be, and then he stopped. And he feels that it was his old friend Jack who somehow gave him that wisdom too.

*   *   *   *   *

At last report, Joe Hacken continues to ply his trade, quietly, with respect, in lower New York. He makes good his losses. He regrets very little about his life, but shakes his head once in a while when he thinks about Molinas.

His old friend Arnold Auerbach is retired now, no longer coach or general manager of the Boston Celtics, but still active in basketball, especially when he can get media attention. He has a stock answer whenever questioned about Hacken, Molinas, rumors of fixes, and the like: "I won't dignify that with an answer."

Vinny Richter, who insists he has heard a recording of wire-tapped conversation between Hacken and Auerbach, retired early from public law enforcement. He works in security in the private sector, but often on contract with official agencies. He says the going rate for an NBA game in the late '50s was twenty grand, but that it's very rare for anyone to be doing business in the league now. He admires Hacken, laughs at Auerbach, and names Molinas to his all-time slime team.

*   *   *   *   *

When Pat Flynn was fired from her network job she considered filing a sex-bias suit. But her attorney, who was also her lover at the time, cautiously counseled her that any trial would publicize the extent to which she'd used her own sex to bias a successful career.

She has returned, finally, to what she does best. She

writes punchy magazine and supplement features. She rarely appears on TV anymore, and no one ever calls her Patsy.

*   *   *   *   *

At 95, Maurice Podoloff was as sharp as ever. He lived in a nursing home in West Haven, Connecticut and entertained visitors like Jesse with his flair for language and the vivid accuracy of his reminiscences. Except for a five-year period during his eighties, which a selective amnesia had blocked out, he could name names and dates and places and numbers from any other time of his life.

The word that was triggered by the name of Jack Molinas was "greed." With absolute certainty he said he did the right thing in that case and quoted verbatim not only from that meeting in his office but also from the report that precipitated it.

Podoloff did have some regrets. He didn't like it that they changed the title of his original position: "In this country, we have a president. I was president of the league. Commissioner sounds too much like Commissar." And he was angry that Danny Biasone was not in the Basketball Hall of Fame: "He not only nurtured the Syracuse franchise when the league needed it, but he saved the whole operation when he came up with the idea of a 24-second clock for Clair Bee's committee." Maurice Podoloff died at 96. He did not live to observe the struggle of his former neighbor in New Haven, Bart Giamatti, over Pete Rose's gambling.

*   *   *   *   *

News of Molinas's killing was heard, by people who knew

him, with relief, satisfaction, vindication, spite, indifference, and resignation. And yet there was always a sense of surprise. They knew that anyone who flies too high has to have his wings burned eventually, but in each of them a small part clung to the belief that Molinas would yet achieve the artifice of escape.

No one who knew him mourned the man. Yet everyone of them—from Hacken and Benjamin to Torchio and Kraw, from Sharon to Lydia—could mourn the death of something in themselves, some loss of the play element magnified in him to dimensions of cosmic absurdity. He had made them laugh at life, and to laugh at him in death was, in a literal sense, to have a last laugh.

Had there been one, none of these people would have come to his funeral. Lydia would have wanted to be seen there, but she was furious about Sharon and enjoyed flaring out her fury and grief in Ohio. But the police investigation overrode religious scruples, and the family was glad for the excuse to have a burial in the total privacy of their shame. Mickey Zaffarano and his family and friends were also relieved, because otherwise they would have had a dilemma in satisfying their scruples about "doing the right thing."

Yet there were many others who didn't know him but only knew about him, or who were acquainted at a flattering distance, or who enjoyed afar the flashy melodrama of his life. And from their numbers came the only genuine mourning a Molinas can ever claim. It is a mourning with wonder but without understanding.

Their elegiac themes are "How are the mighty fallen" and "You can't win." That is why they perpetuate a symbolic Molinas and pay tribute to anti-virtues that can still be called heroic. There is some desperation in their tenacious clinging to that heroism, but a society needs such desperate tenacity when its values erode, when it makes heroes of athletic celebrities, when it endows objects of notoriety with qualities they do not have.

In their tributes, then, they are not eulogizing Molinas himself but their own heroic image of him. And that is what they cling to, instinctively, with a gut feeling they can never diagnose even as they bethink themselves or will themselves to let it go.

And what can their eulogy say about Jack Molinas in this larger context? That he belonged to the class of '53, a generation that was born in the depths of the Depression, raised on The War and its economic recovery, and graduated into Korean and Cold Wars. That they allowed no thought of the Rosenbergs' execution to intrude on their own commencement celebrations. That they laughed at the strident McCarthyism which seemed to have no connection with them. That as they aged they floundered about in a dismaying youth-and-celebrity culture and through a media explosion, without a sound value system of their own to help them cope. That to the extent that they adhered to older structures, they cynically embraced hypocrisy. And to the extent that they courted the new, the clever, and the trendy, they abandoned hope of independence and integrity.

*   *   *   *   *

Pursuing his story of Jack Molinas, Jesse Miller came to some peace in his own life as single custodial parent. He and Susannah talked a lot and he realized that it is no bad thing to share a life, fleeting but precious for its very transience, with a teen-age daughter. He could even greet with some serenity the threats that if he told the story he might be killed, either by the Molinas family (because no one is more aggressively fanatical than Sephardim and the shame this story brings to them arouses monstrous feelings) or by the families here identified as his killers (no monstrous feelings—just a matter of principle, of business; a lesson). Jesse rationalized his decision to proceed on the shaky grounds of his doing it as fiction. Can one be killed for his fantasies, even if there is a compelling plausibility of truth in them? It has happened. But would people kill to draw attention to the plotted guesswork of fiction? His educated guess was that they would not.

Such thinking, however, reminded Jesse of Molinas's fatal mistake. Either he believed he'd never get caught, could get away with everything, could outplay the world at all its games; or he persisted in overstepping limitations, hoping to be caught and punished. Feeling unworthy of all he was and all he got, he craved comeuppance. No, Jesse concluded that his own foolishness was of an entirely different kind.

At first, when Rachel left, he felt, even knowing the worst about her, that if she didn't come back he wanted to die. And then he had to develop the peaceful acknowledgment that he wanted her back but it was all right if it never happened: a meaningful breakthrough in therapy. The next step could be called the result of Susannah's therapy-at-home: the realization that wanting Rachel back was an emotional luxury he could afford only because he knew it would never happen.

"I'm a hopeless romantic, incorrigible. That's my heritage and conditioning."

"Not hopeless, Dad. You're still learning. And you already know how much better off you are, how awful you two were together and always would be. I mean, impossible."

"Well, we must have done something right. Look at you and your brothers." It was the only good thing he could say to her about her mother.

*   *   *   *   *

The Molinas project went slowly. Jesse was teaching and parenting full-time, and he sometimes pursued tangential subjects for occasional pieces in magazines and newspapers. One of his better ideas was to interview Gifford about Exley and Exley about Gifford. He knew that after *A Fan's Notes* came out they had struck up an acquaintance and he wanted to hear what they had to say about each other now and about the issue of fame, the problems of a celebrity society, and the like. He was looking for some insights into what anthropologist John Caughey calls "artificial social relationships," the kind of thing Exley describes in the book about his fixation on Gifford, the kind of thing that led to the shootings of Ed Waitkus, John Lennon, and Ronald Reagan, the kind of thing that provides a plausible premise for thriller movies like *Eye Witness* and *Misery*.

Frank Gifford was accessible and gracious. They chatted comfortably in the press box at Memorial Stadium before the Colts upset the Redskins on Monday Night Football. Jesse found him to be as direct, open, straightforward, unassuming, and uncondescendingly pleasant as the image he projects on camera. He struck Jesse as a real mensch who can handle personal tragedy without becoming a public object of attention, without essentially wavering from the natural self that is the public personage.

Gifford talked easily about Exley, describing their meetings over the years, the phone calls (e.g., collect from London), the requests for football tickets. And he talked easily about fame, about how sports trigger celebrity if not hero-worship, about how TV cannibalizes that celebrity and magnifies it. He seemed comfortable with the society implied by such phenomena, comfortable with his own role in that society. He's a culture-hero who stands easily at the

heart of his culture, Jesse thought, neither above nor outside it. The only thing that bothered him about Exley was,
"I hate to see anyone spill his guts out like that."

Exley was far more difficult to track down. He triangu-
lates his life among the Florida Keys, Alexandria Bay in
upstate New York, and Hawaii. To Jesse, he was one of the
most gifted writers of their generation, though probably better known as a prodigious drinker. Through helpful interme-
diaries Jesse was granted a Florida phone number and a
date and time to call it. He got no answer then and none for
weeks at that time of day, finally trying other times until he
caught up with him at ten one morning. Gifford had
described the personality change that takes place in Exley
after a couple of drinks, and the voice on the phone matched
that description. He didn't want to talk then, but suggested
Jesse write out some questions and send them to Alexandria
Bay where he was going in a few days. Then he'd answer
them into a tape recorder, to give the semblance of a spontaneous answer, and send Jesse a transcription of the tape.

That sounded perfect to Jesse, and he sent his questions.
A week went by, weeks, two months. A friendly intercessor
gave him a number to call in Alexandria Bay. A bemused
voice there gave him another. An amused voice gave him
the number of a bar. A friendly voice, female, said he'd gone
on to another bar. An unamused voice, male, said he'd just
left for a third. And that's where Jesse reached him.

After identification, "Did you ever get my questions?"

"Yeah, I gottem."

"But you never answered them?"

"Nah, sounded too mush like a fuckin essay exam."

Jesse's laugh was a hearty acknowledgment that, of course,
he was right. It was an inauspicious preamble to an interview, but he managed to sustain Exley's attention long
enough to get some answers to those questions anyway,

just in time because he was leaving for Hawaii within the day. He corroborated Gifford's account of their acquaintance and, surprisingly, echoed Gifford's acceptance of the fame/celebrity elements in this society, the obvious difference being that he sees himself outside if not above the mainstream of the culture. He disdained the topic of his own fame, perhaps because his revised notions had appeared in *Pages from a Cold Island*, while *Last Notes from Home* was still years away.

Before he got away, Jesse told him what Gifford had said about spilling his guts. "Yeah," he said, "tha's jis wha' Frank would say."

Jesse marveled at the rightness of that tag line. His own admiration for Gifford the person, inseparable from Gifford the personage, might be excessive, but even saying that much he had begun to spill his guts. Gifford, he saw, is a man who puts his cards on the table. There's nothing up his sleeve, but his heart isn't on it either. And without that wearing of emotional colors there can be no writing, no art.

The lesson of his own little newspaper piece might have been lost on Jesse except that he later found it articulated in *Sophie's Choice*. The injunction comes to Stingo (Styron) from a character named Farrell, a writer manqué: "Son, *write your guts out*." The young Styron took that lesson to heart; it made him an important writer. And in *Sophie's Choice*, still writing his guts out but now able to describe both the gut-practice of writing and the gut-practice of living and loving, he produced what Jesse regarded as a masterpiece.

*   *   *   *   *

Jesse learned even more about himself than about Molinas—and in good part by negative example. He recognized the hollowness of his own hunger for fame and that its achievement would be equally hollow. He would never say, as Exley did of Gifford, either in resignation or exultation, that Molinas was his fame. Intimate knowledge thus gave way to distanced understanding, and he could bury his own Jack Molinas with a private eulogy:

He went his own way. He was outside all that the rest of us were or did or knew or believed. He flouted every institution and structure and rule. He not only played with it all, he flaunted his playing.

They kicked him out of professions and held him upside down out of windows. They tried him, jailed him, and executed him. But he was right when he said they could never touch him. They never dented his self.

But that was an evil self anyway—uncaring, hurtful, amoral, vicious—wasn't it?

Well, was he a rogue hero or what? What do you expect a rogue hero to be—trustworthy, loyal, courteous, and kind?

How can that be evil which inspires affection and adulation in so many? The same way that that can be good which inspires war and persecution?

In the manner of eulogies one may say that such contradictions are in the nature of things.

He got high only on the myriad games he played and the kick of juggling the meaningless abstractions of numbers around so giddily that they took on meaning the way energy clusters move so fast they solidify as matter.

He believed in nothing but himself, having seen everything proved false except the one cliché he lived by, that what goes around comes around.

He forgot even that and then died proving it.

*   *   *   *   *

The complex phenomena that were Jack Molinas and his

life were most succinctly explained for Jesse by one of their many contemporaries he had tracked down: "He delighted himself and others, and he hurt himself and others, by playing games with the enormous gifts he was born with. But he was also born bent."